LORI COPELAND

MEN *of the* SADDLE

the Peacemaker

Tyndale House Publishers, Inc.
WHEATON, ILLINOIS

Visit Tyndale's exciting Web site at www.tyndale.com

Edited by Kathryn S. Olson

Designed by Catherine Bergstrom

Scripture quotations are taken from the *Holy Bible*, King James Version.

The Scripture in the epigraph is taken from *THE MESSAGE*. Copyright © by Eugene H. Peterson, 1993, 1994, 1995, 1996. Used by permission of NavPress Publishing Group.

Published in association with the literary agency of Alive Communications, Inc., 7680 Goddard Street, Suite 200, Colorado Springs, CO 80920.

Library of Congress Cataloging-in-Publication Data

Copeland, Lori.
  The peacemaker / Lori Copeland.
    p. cm. – (Men of the saddle ; #1)
  ISBN 0-8423-6930-9 (sc)
  I. Title.
  PS3553.O6336P43 2004
  813'.54–dc22   2004017202

Printed in the United States of America

10 09 08 07 06 05 04
 9   8   7   6   5   4   3   2   1

To the faithful followers of Brides of the West:
I hope you find joy and renewed commitment in this new series
of men and their quest to find everlasting love.

At that point
Peter got up the nerve to ask,
"Master, how many times
do I forgive a brother
or sister who hurts me?
Seven?"

Jesus replied,
"Seven! Hardly.
Try seventy times seven."

Matthew 18:21-2

(The Message)

Cole Claxton reined up and sat for a moment looking out over the soggy landscape. New Orleans lay before him, the place where he and the other riders planned to split up, each man going his own way. The men had fought for their own states, but the weeks following the war had thrown them together and forged a bond.

The war was over. Cole had begun to think this day would never come. Since he'd left his home in the Ozarks four years earlier, the days had merged into weeks, and then into years, blurring into an endless repetition of fighting and regrouping, killing and dying.

Trey McAllister—tall, handsome, with curly red hair—voiced the thoughts of all the men. "Well, boys, it's finally over and we came out alive."

The dark half-breed, Dallas Ewing, said little, but his friends knew he was a man of few words. Dallas would be heading home to Oklahoma.

Bill Trotter, short, blond, and a lot thinner than he had been when he joined up, spat a stream of tobacco juice. "I'm heading back to Ohio. Gonna put my boots 'neath the welcome table."

The others laughed, throwing friendly gibes in jovial Bill's direction.

"Me?" Elmer Cox put in. "I'm heading straight for Fort Knox, Kentucky, brothers. Gonna get me a kiss and batch of fried chicken—in that order."

"Amen, brother. Me too." This came from Elmer's brother, George.

"Home sounds mighty good," Cole agreed, looking at his brother, Beau. He'd miss these men. But it was time to go home. He held out his hand. "Fellows?"

One by one the men shook hands and turned their horses in the various directions they called home.

As Cole and Beau moved away from the others, Bill Trotter called over his shoulder. "If you ever need anything . . ." He didn't need to finish the thought. *If any one man ever needed anything . . .*

Cole reined up to watch the men ride off, disappearing into the mist and fog. Then with a word to his horse, he hurried on to where his brother waited. Together they would make the final leg of the journey home. *Home.*

CHAPTER 1

July 1865

Wynne Elliot coughed and daintily lifted a handkerchief
to her nose as clouds of choking dust swept through the open
stagecoach window. She flashed a weak smile for what seemed
like the hundredth time at the gentlemen who sat across from
her and fervently wished the tiresome trip were over. She'd
never dreamed it would take so long to travel from Georgia to
Missouri.

Turning back to the scenery, she compared the harsh countryside to her own beloved Georgia. July, a time when flowers
were blooming, when breezes were moist and balmy and moss
draped through the trees like a bride's spidery veil.

Here the ground was hard, the grass dry from lack of moisture. While there was little evidence of the death and destruction
her dear South had endured, there were still visible scars. Burned
homesteads. Barren fields. The war had taken its toll here too, but
not with the terrible devastation she had witnessed farther south.

The farther the coach traveled the more rugged the contour of the land. Ozark mountain country, she'd been told, was a place where people either survived or didn't, and given the landscape, she could well imagine why.

Low mountains with virtually untouched forests dotted the landscape, and the road they traveled twisted and snaked through gaps and valleys with endless walls of shale and limestone. On at least two occasions the coach had stopped and the driver and guard had removed fallen rocks from the way. Wynne had taken to watching the hillsides looking for rolling boulders, although if she saw any moving in their direction, it would already be too late to avoid impact.

She feared that at any turn in the road a band of outlaws would gallop from behind those massive boulders to waylay the coach. During the last rest stop, she'd heard mention of Alf Bolin and his men, an unsavory faction that waylaid unsuspecting travelers. And there was talk about Ozark vigilantes meting out their own bloody brand of justice. The men's casual conversation had given Wynne the willies.

It wasn't the first time she'd heard such shocking tales. Stage hands at the way stations delighted in relating such stories to shock and distress lady passengers.

But she had to admit that nothing she had been told had prepared her for Missouri's rugged beauty. And the land was beautiful. Great oaks and maples. By the size of the trees alone she guessed them to be hundreds of years old. Colonies of ferns spread a lacy carpet across the forest floor. Branches as big around as her waist reached out to form a canopy over the trail. Sturdy tree trunks sank deep roots into soil that was alternately black loam and rich red clay, but so stony that no plant could hope to survive. Still, natives of the area appeared to eke out an adequate living, and apparently in Springfield—a regular metropolis, she'd heard—businesses were thriving. Just yesterday she'd overheard that the railroad and more stores and hotels would locate there soon. If this was true, then Missouri would come out of the Great Conflict in better shape than her own beloved Georgia.

She sighed as the stagecoach tossed its passengers about. How much farther to River Run? Traveling by coach had not been easy—the jostling about, the dust, and the insufferable heat. How she longed for a bath—a long, hot bath with scented soap and shampoo. She sighed longingly. Revenge could indeed be tedious at times.

Absently, she rubbed the smooth, odd-colored stone she'd carried for over a year. He had given the token to her. Strange that she hadn't rid herself of this last painful reminder of him. She didn't need anything to remind her of Cass Claxton. His image was burned into her mind.

That *man*.

The worthless trinket worn smooth by the continual wash of river water had become her worry stone. Her thumb fit perfectly in the tiny hollow, which looked as though it could have been formed for such a purpose—but then, Wynne knew worrying was not of God. Nor was revenge, for that matter. She couldn't expect the Almighty to look with approval on the purpose of her journey, but her blood ran too hot, her anger too deep, to forgive and forget.

Her fingers endlessly smoothed the rock in silent litany: *I'll get him. . . . I'll get him if it's the last thing I do. . . . I'll get that man.*

The journey to Missouri had been long and tiresome, and it

wasn't over yet. She tried to bolster her wilting spirits by reminding herself that it wouldn't be much longer. As soon as she caught that deceiver . . . she would go home. Home to baths and warm food, a comfortable bed and people who loved her. Home to Moss Oak, the plantation where she had been born and raised. The only home she'd ever known.

Wynne wiped ineffectually at the small trickle of perspiration that escaped from beneath her hairline, and then adjusted her hat. It was hard to stay presentable, but she wanted to look her best. When she finally ran Cass to the ground, she wanted him to see what he had walked away from.

Her attention settled on the flamboyant young woman dressed in red sitting next to her. Now here was a fascinating example of womanhood. One that she had never expected to find in her circle of acquaintances.

Miss Penelope Pettibone was on her way to a new job at Hattie's Place. According to Penelope, Hattie's Place was a drinking establishment where a man could go for a hand of cards and "other gentlemanly pursuits." At the mention of "other gentlemanly pursuits," Wynne's eyes had widened knowingly, and she had felt her cheeks burn. She had never met one of "those" women before, and she found she had a certain adverse fascination with Miss Pettibone. Penelope smiled and winked at the man sitting opposite her, and Wynne fanned herself quickly and turned back to the Missouri countryside. A lady never winked, or if she did, she should have something in her eye.

Only that scoundrel, that disgraceful, deplorable, unforgivable Cass Claxton, occupied her thoughts now. The mere thought of that rogue left her breathless with anger. Not only had he left her standing at the altar in complete disgrace, but he'd also managed to walk away with every penny she had except the small pittance she kept in a tin box under her mattress for extreme emergencies.

True, she'd been foolish to fall in love with a man she knew so little about, and even more imprudent to offer financial assistance to a business venture he was about to embark upon, but she had always been one to put her whole heart into everything—especially in matters of love. Of course, she'd not had all that much experience with matters of love, but after studying at Miss Marelda Fielding's Finishing School for Young Ladies, she considered herself a sophisticated woman of the world. That's why it hurt so much that she had let Cass Claxton take advantage of her.

If it hadn't been for the war and her suspicion that Cass had enlisted the day they were meant to marry, she would have tracked him down like a rabid skunk and put a hunk of lead straight through his thieving heart for sullying her trust— not to mention her character. But surely it would have been considered treason to shoot a Confederate soldier, a defender of the homeland, no matter how much he had it coming. However, the fighting had ended, and now she felt free to wreak her vengeance on the lout who had taken advantage of her in such a shameful way.

Her temper still boiled when she thought how gullible she'd been. Well, she was no longer gullible. Quite by chance she'd been told by a close acquaintance of Cass that he had indeed enlisted, survived, and had been seen in Kansas City a few weeks ago. The friend had said Cass was en route to his home in River Run and should arrive any day now. She intended to be there to meet him.

Wynne clenched her fan in her hand; her eyes narrowed pensively. It had been a long time coming, but Mr. Cass Claxton would soon pay for his sins. She smiled in satisfaction. Very soon Cass would rue the day he'd ever heard of Wynne Elliot.

She'd learned a valuable lesson: *no* man could be trusted. She wasn't necessarily permanently soured on men—Papa had been a man of sterling reputation, but Papa had been an exception. She would never allow herself to be fooled by a man again. Not even one as good-looking as Cass Claxton.

The coach lurched along. Wynne studied the two male passengers dozing in the seat across from her. Undoubtedly they were scoundrels, she speculated. After all, they were *men*. She could rest her case. Argument closed.

She had to admit she liked to watch the way stuffy Mr. Rutcliff's fat little jowls jiggled every time the stage hit a rut in the road, but when it came to females, she'd bet he was just as fickle as all men, even if he was nearly seventy years old. She guessed age didn't make much difference where men were concerned.

Covering her mouth with her handkerchief, she'd managed to keep from laughing out loud a couple of times when a bump had nearly unseated the small man. He'd snorted himself awake and angrily glanced around as if to ask *who* the culprit had been that had dared interrupt his napping. After a moment his eyes had closed, and soon he could be heard snoring again. Fat little jowls a-jiggle.

Henry McPherson, the second gentleman traveler, was younger than Mr. Rutcliff and boringly polite. He constantly tipped his hat and said, "Yes, ma'am" and "No, ma'am" in response to any comment either she or Penelope ventured.

Wynne had the impression the two men had been scared to death of Penelope since they'd overheard her discussing her destination with Wynne. She doubted if they'd be dropping into Hattie's Place for any "gentlemanly pursuits." But then, who could tell? They were, after all, men, and therefore could not be trusted. Miss Marelda had definitely been correct on that score.

Miss Marelda had never married, claiming the natural cupidity of men as the reason, but Wynne wondered if maybe the biggest reason was that she'd never been asked. Wynne's conscience smote her. She needed to ask God to forgive her for such unkind thoughts, although to tell the truth, since she'd set out to bring Cass Claxton to justice, she hadn't been on comfortable terms with God. How could she ask Him to bless her plans when she knew He would want no part of them?

The coach picked up speed, and Wynne glanced out the window at the scenery now rushing by. "Does it seem to you we're going faster?" she asked of no one in particular. A frown creased her forehead. Surely such excessive speed on this rough road couldn't be safe.

"We can't go fast enough for me," Penelope said with an exasperated sigh. "I can't wait for this trip to be over." She made a useless effort to knock the layer of dust off her dress and grimaced in distaste when it only settled back on the light material. "I really expected the journey to be more genteel." She flashed a glance from under her eyelids at Mr. McPherson, who blushed and looked away.

Puzzled by the increasing momentum of the coach, Wynne peered out the window. Her mouth dropped open and she immediately jerked her head back in. "My stars! I think we're about to be robbed!" she blurted in disbelief.

Both men's eyes flew open. Mr. Rutcliff craned his neck out the window to verify her statement. "Oh, my! I do believe you're right!"

Penelope sent up an instant wail, fluttering her fan and looking like she was about to break out in tears. "I knew it! I knew it! We'll all be killed!"

Wynne shot the young woman an impatient glance. Over the past few days she'd noticed that optimism did not seem to be the girl's strong point. "Penelope, really! I'm sure we are well protected." The guard, the driver, and two male passengers: there was no cause for immediate alarm. The team could probably outrun the outlaws without the slightest problem. At least she hoped her assessment of the situation was accurate.

A few minutes later her optimism sagged. Her heart beat wildly as gunshots filled the air. Another glance out the window showed the riders drawing steadily closer.

Wynne cast a worried glance at the gentlemen seated across from her, noticing that neither man looked overly confident. She doubted if either one would be much help in case of a holdup. They didn't even appear to be armed.

"Shouldn't we do something?" she asked, clutching the worry stone in her fist. The two men peered out the coach window apprehensively. Neither one seemed to be inclined to action. Penelope looked like she might faint at any moment. Wynne dismissed them all as useless in the present situation.

"There's nothing to do but pray," Mr. Rutcliff murmured in a barely audible voice.

Pray? Wynne blinked back hot tears. When was the last time she'd prayed—asked God for anything other than bodily harm toward Cass? What was the use of continuing to try to fool herself? She couldn't ask God for anything except forgiveness for what she had planned, and in order to do that, she'd have to change those plans. She wasn't ready to consider doing that. But she sure hoped God would be patient enough with her to spare them injury or worse at the hands of these outlaws. She'd heard Missouri was filled with violent men who weren't afraid to break the law. Apparently those rumors were correct. She dropped to the floor when the masked riders slowly but surely gained ground on the wildly swaying coach.

Wynne tried to pray, but the words stuck in her throat. She couldn't even think clearly. It looked like she was on her own this time.

The noonday sun bore down on the two dusty riders like a flat-iron on a hot stove. Cole and Beau Claxton rested their horses on a small rise overlooking a field of withered corn. A faint, teasing wisp of a breeze grazed the horses' manes. The heat was so intense it was hard to catch a deep breath. July in the Ozarks. You could stand still and sweat.

"Look at it, Beau. Home." Cole, the older of the two brothers, spoke first, his deep baritone husky with emotion. He'd dreamed about this view: thought of it at night around the campfires and on waking in the morning. Nothing he'd seen in the time he'd been gone could rival the Ozarks for pure natural beauty. It was God's country, and he was so glad to be back he could shout for the pure pleasure of hearing the surrounding hills throw back an echo.

He sat leaning forward, resting his elbow on the saddle horn and looking out over the rolling hills of their southwest Missouri home, just savoring the moment, which had been a long time coming. "Looks good, doesn't it?" Cole asked.

"It sure does," Beau answered.

Cole let his reins go slack as he slumped wearily in the saddle, his eyes hungrily drinking in the familiar sight spread before him. There had been times he hadn't expected to see it again. A lot of good men wouldn't be coming home from the war. He had much to be thankful for.

The gently sloping terrain was no longer the lush, fertile green that would have met their eyes if it had been spring. The blazing summer sun had taken its toll on the land and crops, burning them to dry cinder. But it was still a long-awaited, welcome sight to one who had seen nothing but death and destruction for the last few years.

Four years. Four years of not knowing if he would ever see home again. Four years of watching men die by the thousands and wondering if he would be next, living with the unspeakable horrors of war day after day after day. Through it all, he'd grown closer to God. War had that effect on a man. Every day you didn't die was like a personal gift. He didn't know why he and Beau had been spared when so many others hadn't. Seemed like God might have had a purpose for letting them live, but he didn't know what it could be—unless it was Ma's and Willa's prayers. Whatever the reason, he was grateful. Mighty grateful.

Home. The word held a new and more sacred meaning. He

breathed silent thanks to his Maker for bringing him intact through the carnage and destruction.

"There were times when I thought I'd never see this again," Beau confessed.

"I had those times too."

Beau echoed his thoughts. "We were lucky, you know. There are so many who won't come home—"

"Hope Ma and Willa have some of that chicken 'n' dumplings waiting for us," Cole interrupted. He'd had enough dying and sorrow to last him a lifetime. He wanted to forget the past four years, not relive them. Wanted to shuck them off like worn dirty clothes, like this uniform, and get back to being a civilian with nothing more to worry about except getting in a crop and looking into that marshal's job.

He thought about his ma and their Indian housekeeper's cooking. Willa had been with the family since he was a baby and had been as much of a mother to the three Claxton boys as their own ma had been. When the family had moved from Georgia to Missouri back in the late forties, they'd established a homestead and built a new life. Samuel Claxton died five years into the adventure, leaving behind a wife with three young sons to rear. No one could argue that Willa had been nothing short of a godsend to Lilly Claxton.

"I can eat six pans of corn bread and three dozen fried-apple pies before I even hit the front door," Beau said. "Makes my mouth fairly water to think of it."

"If I were you, I'd eat that pie and corn bread even before I went over to see Betsy." Cole teased him with a knowing wink.

"You're right," Beau said solemnly. "Only sensible thing to do."

The brothers broke out in laughter. Cole knew the first

place Beau would head would be old man Collins's place. Beau and Betsy had been about to be married when the war intervened. Now the wedding would take place as soon as possible.

"Who wants ol' Betsy when they can have Willa's cooking?" Beau grinned mischievously, his eyes twinkling. "You know, now that the war's over, you ought to think about settling down too, Cole."

Cole chuckled softly, letting his gaze return to the valley below them. "Betsy's the prettiest girl in the county, and you're claiming her. Who would I marry?"

"Aw, come on," Beau chided. "You know you wouldn't marry Betsy if you could. I'm beginning to worry about you, Cole!"

Cole laughed. "Well, don't. When the right woman comes along, I might give marrying some serious thought."

"It'll never happen," Beau said. "You're never going to find a woman who'll suit you because you're too everlasting picky."

"I'll run across her someday. Happen to favor a woman with a little spirit." Cole's gaze drank in the familiar surroundings. This was a familiar argument, one his whole family had utilized. Cole's mother and Willa were fond of questioning when he, the eldest, was going to marry and produce offspring.

"Spirit, huh? What about Priscilla, Betsy's sister? There's a fine figure of a woman if I ever saw one." Beau grinned. "Strong as a bull moose, healthy as a horse, and sturdy as an oak fence post. Why, I've seen her and her father cut a rick of wood in a couple of hours and never raise a sweat. She'd make some man a fine wife. Got a *lot* of spirit too," he added. "Saw her hand wrestle an Indian brave once, and she didn't do badly."

Cole's mouth curved with an indulgent smile. "She didn't win, did she?"

"She didn't win, but she didn't do all that bad," Beau insisted.

Cole chuckled at the younger man's sincerity. "Somehow, little brother, the thought of a woman hand wrestling a brave, cutting a rick of wood in a couple of hours, and never raising a sweat doesn't appeal to me."

"Well, what *does?* I've seen you go through more women than I can count, and not one of them suits you. You're just too picky!"

Cole shifted in his saddle. His bones ached, and he was dead tired. "Don't start with me, Beau." Little brother could nag as long and hard as any granny when he set his mind to it, and Cole was in no mood for a lecture on women. "When I find a woman who can wrestle the Indian brave and *win,* then turn around and be soft as cotton and smell as pretty as a lilac bush in May, that's the day you'll see me heading for the altar."

Beau shook his head. "I've never known a woman to wrestle an Indian brave and then smell like a lilac bush in May," he complained.

Cole took off his hat and wiped away rolling sweat. His eyes scanned the valley below, then narrowed and lingered on the cloud of dust being kicked up in the far distance.

"Stage coming in," he noted.

Beau leaned forward in his saddle, his eyes centered on the road below. "Driver's sure got the horses whipped up—will you look at that!"

Leather creaked as Cole's horse shifted restlessly beneath his weight. His eyes followed the path of the coach barreling along the dusty road. The driver whipped the horses to greater speed. The coach careered crazily as the team tried to outrun the small band of riders galloping after it.

Beau whistled under his breath. "Looks like trouble."

Cole set his hat back on his head and took up his reins, his eyes focused on the frantic race. "Better see what we can do to help."

The brothers spurred their mounts, and the powerful steeds sprang forward, covering the ground with lightning speed, steadily gaining on the swaying coach.

Six masked riders had brought the stage to a halt and the passengers were filing out with their hands held high above their heads. Penelope sobbed quietly, while Wynne tried to master her fear. She wasn't about to let these ruffians see her true emotions.

The leader of the grizzly pack vaulted out of his saddle. While he held a gun on the driver and guard, others began pulling luggage off the top of the coach.

"Don't anybody make a move and you won't get hurt," the second rider warned in a gravelly voice. "Driver! You and Shotgun throw down your guns and the gold box."

The driver and guard looked at each other. *Don't do it,* Wynne thought, and wondered if she had spoken the words out loud. The driver reached for his pistol as the guard lifted his rifle. Before they could bring them into firing position, two shots rang out. The driver and the man who rode shotgun sagged against the seat, weapons falling from their limp hands. Penelope screamed and covered her eyes as the bodies tumbled from their high perch. Even as inexperienced as she was, Wynne realized that the men were dead by the time they hit the ground. She closed her eyes, feeling sick to her stomach. Those men never had a chance. They had been gunned down in cold blood.

Three of the bandits returned to dragging valises off the top of the coach, ripping through the contents in search of valuables.

The passengers stood by in dismay, watching as their personal items were strewn about in the frenzied search. Wynne stood in shock. Her undergarments were being handled by rough, dirty hands, the lace pieces thrown into the dust with no regard to the fragility of the material.

In a vain attempt to stop the robbery, Penelope edged forward and batted her eyes coyly at the leader. Wynne watched, fascinated. So this was the way a woman like that charmed the men. "Really, sir, we have nothing of any value," Penelope said. "Won't you please let us pass—?"

The man angrily pushed her aside. "Out of my way, woman." His hand caught the large emerald brooch pinned to the front of her dress and ripped it free of the fabric. Penelope stumbled and almost fell.

Wynne gasped at the outlaw's audacity. For a moment she forgot her own paralyzing fear and marched to stand protectively in front of the sobbing girl. "Why don't you pick on someone your own size, you inconsiderate brute!"

Her heart beat like a tom-tom when the robber's eyes narrowed in rage. He reached out with a huge hand and caught the front of her dress. Her heart nearly stopped beating altogether when the bandit jerked her up close to him and made a thorough search of her body with his beady eyes. He held her that way for a moment before releasing her. She pressed her lips together, staring back at him. He grabbed her fist and quickly relieved her of the pearl ring on her left hand, scraping her knuckle painfully in the process. Before she could stop him, he jerked her purse from her arm and rummaged around in it, removing all the cash. He focused his attention on her. "This all you got, lady?"

Her eyes met his in what she hoped was a cold stare. "I am not a fool. Of course, you have it all . . . and please get out of my face." She tilted her head to avoid his offensive odor. Thank goodness he had a mask over his face to dull the stench of his odious breath.

"Ah, am I offending Her Majesty?" He chuckled and jerked her closer, lifting his mask above his mouth. The sight of yellow, tobacco-stained teeth made her stomach lurch.

Slowly his greedy gaze lowered to the décolletage of her emerald-colored dress, lingering there. "What's the matter, honey? Ain't I pleasing 'nough for you?" He laughed when she continued to avert her nose from his rancid smell. "Yore a pretty little filly." He breathed against her ear. "How's about giving ol' Jake a little kiss?"

"See here! Rob us if you will, but I must insist on your treating the ladies with respect!" Henry McPherson stepped forward in Wynne's defense. One of the masked men lifted a gun butt and promptly knocked the young man unconscious.

His body slumped to the ground and the assailant waved his pistol in a menacing manner. "Don't anyone else try anything foolish if you don't want to get hurt."

"Come on, Jake! Quit fooling around and get on with it!" Another bandit shot an apprehensive glance at two riders fast approaching from the west. "We got company coming."

Jake laughed once more and shoved Wynne aside. "Sorry, honey. We'll have to take this up another time."

"In a pig's eye we will." Wynne retained enough sense about her to speak under her breath.

The bandit paused, and his evil eyes narrowed angrily. "What'd you say?"

She grinned weakly. "I said, yes . . . some other time . . . surely."

"Come on, Jake! Would you quit socializing and come on?"

After another degrading sweep of her body with cold, dark eyes, Jake brutally ripped the fragile gold chain from around Wynne's neck.

"You give that back!" she screeched, snatching for the keepsake. He stuffed the necklace into the bag he was carrying.

"Sorry, Red, but I just got a sudden hankering for little gold chains." He chuckled again and strode in a rolling gait to his waiting horse.

"That necklace isn't worth anything," she protested angrily, "except for sentimental value to me! My father gave that to me minutes before he died—"

Her words fell on deaf ears. The man tipped his hat in a mocking salute. Then the six riders spun their mounts and galloped off.

"Well, all right then! Take the necklace, but I won't forget this!" Wynne shouted into the cloud of dust their horses kicked up. She grabbed her tilting hat and stared at the robbers' retreating backs. Seconds later the other two riders neared and quickly took off in hot pursuit of the culprits.

The dazed passengers just stood around looking stunned. Wynne rushed to kneel beside the injured Henry, who was beginning to come around. He moaned and opened his eyes to look about in bewilderment. "What happened?"

"Lie still, Mr. McPherson." Wynne reached for one of the pieces of scattered clothing to place under his head. "You were knocked out by one of the ruffians, but they're gone now." Glancing around, she saw the others hadn't moved.

Mr. Rutcliff snapped out of his stupor and immediately knelt between the driver and shotgun rider. Shaking his head, he glanced back to meet Wynne's questioning gaze. "Dead as a doornail. Shot 'em both clean through the heart."

Penelope collapsed in tears. Wynne got to her feet and absently reached over and patted the young woman's shoulder. "It's all right. They're gone now. Why don't you go sit under that tree until you get yourself under control?"

"But we all could have been *killed*," Penelope wailed. "I tried to stop them, but you saw what happened—"

"But we weren't killed," Wynne said, asking the good Lord to give her patience. "Mr. Rutcliff, are you all right?"

The elderly man looked pale and mopped at the perspiration trickling down inside his collar. "Why, yes, I believe so. Quite a disturbing chain of events, wouldn't you say?"

"Yes, I would say that." Wynne blew a wisp of hair out of her face. "Quite disturbing." He called that right enough. If only she'd had sense enough to carry a gun. After all, she was out on a mission of vengeance. She should have had enough forethought to provide herself with a weapon.

Cole and Beau pushed their horses to the limit, but the gang of robbers was already disappearing into the distance. As Cole watched the outlaws fade from view, he realized they were long gone. About all he and Beau were accomplishing was eating their dust. He'd suspected from the beginning they couldn't do anything about the robbery, but a man couldn't stand by and watch when others were in a bind. He pulled his mount to a halt.

"What do you think?" Beau shouted as he reined up beside Cole, his shirt flapping in the stiff breeze.

"They're too far gone. We'll only wind the horses more."

Beau's eyes followed the cloud of dust. "You're right—but I'd like to have caught them. Let's go see what we can do to help the passengers."

Cole shook his head. Beau never gave up. That good-hearted streak of his was going to get them both in trouble one of these days. It evidently didn't bother him that they had been outnumbered six to two and this wasn't their fight.

He pulled his mare around and followed his brother back to the stage.

When the two riders came into view, Wynne paused in picking up her scattered clothing. She watched warily as they approached.

One of the guns was still lying on the ground, and she lunged for it, leveling the muzzle at the approaching pair. One robbery a day was all she was going to put up with, thank you. If these two ruffians had come for the same purpose, she would take care of this personally.

Penelope, huddled under a nearby tree, crying and fanning herself, was useless in a situation like this. Mr. Rutcliff was trying in vain to comfort the injured Henry McPherson. That left only Wynne to defend what was left of their meager possessions. She shot a disgusted glance in their direction. A lot of help they were. Leaving a woman to protect them.

The two men cautiously reined in their horses, wearing incredulous expressions as they looked down the barrels of the twelve-gauge shotgun Wynne pointed at them.

"Throw your guns down, gentlemen," she commanded in a firm voice.

"Now, ma'am," the younger one said, "we don't make a habit of parting with our guns—"

"Now!" She hefted the shotgun an inch higher on her shoulder. As if she cared about their habits. She had a few more important things to worry about.

Both men slowly unbuckled their gun belts and let them drop to the ground.

"Now your rifles."

"Ma'am . . . ," the young one protested. "I'm not about to let my Springfield be taken away by anyone." He looked like he wanted to laugh.

Wynne knew she probably didn't look very frightening with her torn collar and dust smudges on her face. And this hat! Whatever had possessed her to purchase the wide-brimmed straw hat topped by a bird in a nest? The silly thing kept tipping forward, so she had to keep nudging it back, causing the gun to sway with in a most disconcerting manner.

The young man smiled. "Judging from your charming Southern drawl, I'd guess you're from Georgia. I've heard that speech pattern before."

I'll just bet you have, she thought. *Yankees*. They'd overrun her beloved state. She'd heard *their* nasal twang before too. Way too many times.

"Never you mind where I'm from. I said throw down your rifles." She waved the gun in their general direction.

Moving slowly, the man carefully slid his rifle to the ground. Only then did she lower her weapon a fraction. "Now, if you don't have anything more to say, I think you two best be moving on."

The young man swung his hat off and flashed what he evidently hoped was a winning smile. She'd seen better.

"The name's Beau, and me and my brother, Cole, was wondering if everyone was all right here. We thought we might be of service. Looks like you had a run-in with a gang of thieves."

In Wynne's opinion, this newest set of strangers didn't look a whole lot better than the last one. The men were rumpled and dirty, both in need of a shave and a haircut and wearing the wrong kind of uniform. The only difference she could discern between these two and the band of unsavory hoodlums who had fled was that they didn't smell as bad—at least not from this distance.

She studied the two carefully. Both men were large in stature and impressively muscular, if one liked that sort of man. But they were the exact opposites in coloring. Beau, the one who had been doing all the talking, had hair streaked whitish blond by the sun and dancing blue eyes. He sat in his saddle with a rakish air. Cole, the second one, was older, his skin toasted to a deep nut-brown, his hair jet-black with a trace of unruly curls softening his rugged features.

They were wearing the ragged blue uniforms of the North. She prayed that on top of everything else this rotten day had brought her she hadn't had the misfortune to meet up with a pair of renegade Union men. She'd heard what their sort was capable of.

Wynne swallowed hard and steadied her hold on the shotgun. My stars, the thing was unbelievably heavy! "Don't come any closer," she warned as the men's horses shifted.

"Ma'am, why don't you put the gun down?" Beau coaxed. "Someone might get hurt."

Wynne took a firm step forward to show them she was not in the least intimidated by their presence. She focused the length of the gun barrel on Beau, figuring he was trying to wheedle her into relaxing her guard. "It's quite possible someone might—namely, you. I'm warning you, mister, you'd better not rile me. You'd best state your business and move on, or I'll have to use this."

"I don't think that'll be necessary." Beau turned slightly in his saddle to face the other man. Wynne let her eyes follow his. She had a hunch he would be the most dangerous. Right now he was keeping a fixed eye on her trigger finger.

Beau shifted. "I'd better state our business, Cole."

He started to dismount and stopped short as Wynne's voice rang out. "Stop right there!" she demanded.

Deciding she'd better let them know in no uncertain terms

who had the upper hand, she marched forward, determined to settle this once and for all. Unfortunately she stumbled over a discarded valise in her path, giving her shin a painful crack and pitching her forward. Still clutching the gun, she twisted to the side, falling to one knee.

Cole and Beau ducked as the gun went off, spraying buckshot over their heads. Confusion reigned. Wynne fought to regain control of the gun and her destroyed composure. She grabbed her hat when it tilted over her face, blocking her view. Beau and Cole rolled out of their saddles onto their knees, still hanging on to their horses, which were prancing and shying away.

Wynne staggered to her feet, kicking the valise aside, the gun firmly back on her targets. "Gentlemen, don't be misled," she cautioned. "I assure you, I *do* know how to use this gun and shall not hesitate to do so if the need arises. I suggest you move on. My fellow passengers and I have nothing left but the clothes scattered in the road, so you're wasting your time if you've come to rob us."

Wynne glanced uneasily at the dark-complexioned rider slowly getting to his feet. His face was grim, and his eyes narrowed. She didn't like the set of his mouth. In fact, she didn't like anything about him. Probably a ruthless desperado preying on innocent victims.

She knew she looked like an utter fool, but then she had the gun and he didn't.

Cole's electrifying blue eyes centered directly on her. He studied the scene before he remounted his horse. His face looked like it had been carved from a slab of oak, hard and unyielding. The glance he shot her was contemptuous enough to shrivel a weaker woman. Wynne tilted her chin. Who did he think he was, looking at her like that? She was merely defending what was hers along with protecting her fellow passengers.

"Ma'am," Beau protested with a weak grin, "I think you've got the wrong idea. We're here to help, not rob you."

"Oh, really?" Wynne's eyebrows lifted with skepticism. He did have a point, though. They had chased the gang off, but it could have very well been for their own evil purposes. After all, she had decided not to trust *any* men, and these two were quite definitely men. Rather attractive ones too, under all of that travel dust.

"Honest," Beau declared. "We're sorry we weren't in time to prevent this unfortunate mishap." He swept his hat off and bowed gallantly. She was once more the recipient of a most charming smile.

"That may be so, but you're still a *Yankee!*" She spit the words out as if they left a vile taste in her mouth. "And I wouldn't believe a thing a *Yankee* said!"

"Ma'am, the war's over. Can't we let bygones be bygones?"

She took aim at his heart. "Easy for you to say. *You* won. Now you listen to me. I'm in no mood for argument. I'm sweating like a mule, I'm hungry, and this has been the worst day of my life."

Sweating like a mule. Miss Marelda would frown on that choice of words, but truth was truth.

Beau shrugged. "I had help with the war."

Wynne shot him a dirty look. He wasn't taking the situation seriously.

He slowly eased his way over to her. "Why don't you calm down and let me and my brother take you and the other passengers into town?"

Wynne glanced at the lifeless bodies of the driver and guard and realized she was at this man's mercy even though she was holding the gun. It was obvious that neither she nor Penelope could drive the stage, and the two male passengers were in no condition to attempt such a feat.

"Well . . . maybe that would be a good idea, but bear in mind, I'll have this gun pointed at you all the way in case you try something underhanded." She shot the other brother a warning look. "And that goes double for you."

Cole kept silent. Wynne tilted her chin and stared back at him. His expression seemed to say that if it had been up to *him*, he'd have taken the gun away from her ten minutes ago and turned her across his knee. She'd like to see him try.

"What's the matter with him? Can't the pompous fool talk?" Wynne whispered crossly, motioning to Cole. All the man had done since he arrived was stare at her as if she were a raving maniac!

Beau glanced over his shoulder. "Who, Cole? Sure he talks, when he wants to." His gaze switched back to her, studying the hat, which was tilting again. "You don't have to be afraid of us. Do we look like the type of men who would take advantage of a lady?"

Wynne studied him for a moment before her gaze drifted involuntarily to Cole. His posture remained aloof as she looked up and met his direct gaze.

Beau didn't seem the type to take advantage of a woman, but his brother certainly looked questionable. Wynne gave a fleeting thought to what it would be like to have a man like him take advantage . . . She pulled her wandering thoughts back into line. What had come over her? Miss Marelda Fielding would be horrified to think of one of her students being so . . . so unseemly. Wynne had best be attending to business.

"Nevertheless, you've been warned," she stated, then turned toward the stage. Somehow she got her feet tangled in one of Penelope's stray petticoats lying on the ground. In the scuffle to retain her balance, her own skirt wrapped itself around her legs, pitching her forward. She threw out her hands to keep from falling, and the gun spun out of her grip to land in the dirt at Beau's feet. Dust puffed up around her, filling her nostrils as she hit the ground. She sneezed and barely halted the automatic move to wipe her nose. How had she ended up flat on her back staring up at the sky? She looked up directly into the brilliant blue eyes of silent brother Cole, who was watching her as if she were the main attraction in a sideshow. She flushed with embarrassment, realizing she wasn't coming off too well in this encounter.

Beau reached down a hand and helped Wynne to her feet. She dusted off her seat, twitching her skirt into more orderly folds. He handed the gun back to her with a courtly bow and a polite smile. "Allow me, ma'am."

"Thank you . . . sir." She felt her cheeks flame. She snatched the gun back and reached up to straighten her hat, which as usual had gone askew in the turmoil. "I'll get the passengers in the stage," she announced.

"That would be fine, ma'am." Beau grinned.

He made his way to where Cole sat on his horse watching the fiasco. Wynne strained to hear the men's brief exchange while trying to look as if she wasn't paying attention. But she heard—oh, she heard, all right.

"What do you think you're doing?" Cole asked calmly.

"Getting ready to escort the stage back to town," Beau answered.

"Why did you give that gun back to her?"

"Oh, that." He adjusted his hat. "She's not going to shoot anyone. She's just scared."

"I *know* she's not going to shoot anyone intentionally," Cole said, "but I think we're in serious danger of getting our heads blown off by her stupidity."

Wynne fumed. She'd like to show Mr. High-and-Mighty how well she could handle a gun. She'd teach him a lesson that would wipe that smirk right off his face. Call her stupid, would he?

"Come on, Cole. Look at them. They're helpless as a turtle on its back." Beau's gaze shifted to the shaken passengers, filing slowly back into the coach. "Let her think she's running the show. It's not going to hurt anything."

Wynne stiffened. Let her *think*? Of all the arrogant . . . If she didn't need them so badly she'd send them packing. Just who had the gun here? She *was* running this show, and he'd better not forget it.

Cole looked in her direction. "In my opinion, everything is under control, and one of the men can take the stage on into town."

She waited, holding her breath.

Beau shook his head. "They need help, Cole."

"You're a born sucker when it comes to a pretty face."

Beau reached for his reins. "Might be, but it's our duty to get them into town safely."

Cole sighed. "We made it all the way through a war without an injury, and I'll be blamed if I'm about to have some snip of a woman ruin my perfect record less than ten miles from home.

There's no reason for us to get mixed up in this. We can send Tal out to help them when we ride through town."

"I don't want to do that," Beau argued. "We can't just ride off and leave the ladies out here unprotected. It won't take fifteen minutes to escort them to town, and then we'll be on our way."

Cole's unshaven jaw firmed. "I say we stay out of it."

"If you don't want to help, then I'll do it myself."

"You've got a cross-eyed mule beat when it comes to stubborn. All right, all right, I'll help. But I'm warning you, she's going to be trouble."

"Don't have to like her," Beau grumbled. "All you got to do is help. Wouldn't be right leaving them alone." The last passenger clambered aboard the coach. "You drive the stage; I'll load the driver and guard onto our horses and be right behind you."

Cole, still grumbling, dismounted and strode over to the coach, leaving Beau to take care of the dead bodies.

Wynne breathed easier. They may look like outlaws, but apparently they were going to escort the stage back to town. She had no illusions as to what a mess they'd be in if left to their own devices. An injured man and one who might as well be hurt, no more help than he'd been so far, and a flighty woman who wasn't any better. They'd be sitting pigeons for the next band of outlaws who might happen along.

Cole had planted his foot on the wheel of the stage and started to climb aboard when Wynne tapped the barrel of the gun on his shoulder. He slowly turned around to meet her calculating eyes.

"Don't forget. I'll be watching you, mister."

He bit out his words impatiently. "Ma'am, I'm quivering in

my boots." His drawl was a mixture of Georgia softness and Missouri twang.

Wynne narrowed her eyes. There was something vaguely familiar about this man, though she was certain she had never met him before. Something about his eyes . . .

In spite of herself, she found herself admiring Cole's very even and white teeth, and though he had obviously been riding for some time, he was not nearly as dirty and offensive as the bandits had been. The humidity had curled his dark hair around his tanned face, and his eyes—well, she'd seen blue eyes in her time, but she'd never seen that particular shade before.

For a brief moment she tried to imagine what he would look like with a shave, a haircut, and clean clothes. The image was disturbing. She shook the thought away. There wasn't the chance of a snowball in July she'd ever see him again, yet as she turned away, she couldn't shake the feeling that he reminded her of someone.

Wynne primly tucked herself and the gun into the coach and slammed the door. "Like I said, I'm watching you. Drive directly into town. No detours, no unnecessary stops."

Beau rode up, and Wynne saw Cole shoot his brother a dirty look. "I don't know why I let you talk me into these things!" he snapped.

Beau was still grinning when Cole, with an impatient whistle, slapped the reins. The team bolted, and with the barrel of a shotgun pointed straight at his head, Cole headed for town.

CHAPTER 2

The stage rolled into River Run, Missouri, to the sound of jangling harnesses and a cloud of boiling dust. The townspeople came running, clearly surprised to see Cole sitting in the driver's seat. Cole could have told them he was a bit surprised himself. If Beau hadn't been such a stubborn, muleheaded so-and-so they could have been home by now instead of playing Good Samaritans.

"Cole, boy!" Tal Franklin, county sheriff, climbed aboard the coach and slapped him soundly on the back. "Good to see you, son!"

Cole could have sworn Tal's eyes misted before he dragged out a large handkerchief and hurriedly wiped his nose. The crowd pressed closer, and Cole grinned. Looked like the whole town had turned out to meet them, and it was a heartwarming sight.

"Good to see you, Tal." Cole grinned, clasping the sheriff's calloused hand. Mere words were inadequate for the emotions that blocked his throat when he looked at the face he'd known for most of his thirty years. It was good to be home!

"Looks like you come through the war without a scratch." Tal beamed; then his smile faded. "Have you seen either of your brothers?" The sheriff looked like he hated to even ask the question, probably dreading the answer he'd heard too often in the past few months. Cole understood. A lot of boys who went away wouldn't be coming back, and too many of the ones who did make it home were destroyed by their experiences. And like him, they were bone-weary and disillusioned.

"One of them is right behind me." Cole set the brake. "I ran into Beau a couple hundred miles back, and we rode home together."

"Aw, your ma's going to be beside herself! Two of her boys home the same day!" Tal slapped him on the back again. "What in the world are you doing driving the stage?"

Beau rounded the corner by the saloon, leading Cole's horse with the bodies of the stage driver and shotgun guard draped across the saddle. The town gave him a wide berth. Sheriff Franklin turned to look over his shoulder. "What's going on here?"

"Stage was robbed about five miles back." Cole waved at several friendly voices that called out to him, and his heart felt like it was about to burst with gladness. Home. He was finally home.

There was old Nathan at the blacksmith shop, grinning at him with his gold tooth shining in the afternoon sunlight. Nute Brower leaning on his broom on the front porch of his general store, watching all the commotion taking place. The way everyone was acting, it was almost like a holiday celebration.

Mary Beth Parker, town spinster, sat in the post office window and waved her hanky at him. He remembered Miss Parker's smile from when he was a small boy and his ma would send him into town to pick up the mail each month. Mary Beth had been the postmistress of River Run over fifty years, and it wouldn't seem right to come home and see anyone else sitting in her place.

Cole threw the reins to Jim Parker and climbed down off the high seat. The townspeople made room for him as he walked back to the coach and opened the door. Finis Rutcliff barreled out. Penelope Pettibone was next, stepping lightly into Cole's waiting arms. He swung her small frame down easily and then quickly doffed his hat. "Ma'am, I hope the ride wasn't too uncomfortable for you."

Penelope's sultry gaze slid over his shoulders and chest as she removed her arms ever so slowly from around his neck. She batted her long, black eyelashes at him. "Why, thank you, sir. I surely do appreciate your being such a gentleman. I'm feeling much better now, thank you." Her soft Southern accent drifted as lightly as jasmine on the hot, sultry air.

Cole felt his smile widening to a silly grin, and he mentally caught his emotion. How long had it been since he'd seen such a sweet-smelling, pretty-looking woman? Too long.

His grin spread over his face as he reluctantly set Penelope aside and turned to the next passenger. Instead of warm flesh, his hand came in contact with cold metal. His grin died a sudden death. He'd forgotten that fool woman and her gun. It was a wonder she hadn't blown his head off yet. It looked like his guardian angel was still on the job.

Wynne Elliot forced the burdensome shotgun ahead of her and tried to work her billowing skirts and the hatbox she was carrying out the narrow doorway. The brim of her hat scraped the doorframe, tilting over her eyes.

Cole didn't make any move to help her. He knew he'd probably overdone the courteous treatment with Miss Pettibone, and
he felt guilty about not helping Miss Elliot in the same considerate manner, but if he offered his hand, she'd probably take a
shot at him. Most cantankerous woman he'd ever met.

Miss Elliot didn't seem to notice as she stubbornly worked
her purse, the hatbox, and the gun out the narrow door. A dog
barked somewhere close by. She jerked as though the sound
startled her, and her foot slid off the bottom step. The hatbox
was crushed against the doorframe, and the gun barrel reared
upward as she slid feetfirst out the door.

Cole ducked quickly to one side and automatically flinched
against the anticipated blast. The gun didn't go off. He straightened in time to see Miss Elliot sit down in the dust, flat on her
backside, the gun and hatbox beside her. That silly hat was
tilted down covering her eyes, and the bird looked like it was
giving serious thought to flying south. Her feet stuck straight
out in front of her, revealing trim ankles. She shoved the hat
back and shot a frustrated look in his direction. Her face flamed
a bright red when she saw the smirk he couldn't conceal.

Cole bit his lip to control the laugh he knew was ready to
explode. The tough, gun-toting Southern belle couldn't keep
from tripping over her own feet. They were just lucky she hadn't
shot anyone by accident. She sat there looking like she didn't
know what to do next. The humiliation in her eyes got to him.

Drawing a resigned breath, he picked up his hat, dusted it
off on his uniform, and jammed it back on his head. Against his
better judgment, he walked over to Miss Elliot and leaned down
until his face was level with hers. With an expression as serious
as gallstones, he spoke in as polite a manner as he could manage

without bursting into a guffaw. "Miss, allow me to assist you with your hatbox."

Something akin to a growl escaped her tightly compressed lips. She struggled to her feet, steadfastly refusing to look at the gawking crowd. The smothered chuckles from the bystanders brought blood rushing to her face again. He had a hunch she felt like this was the last straw. Poor kid. She'd had a tough day, but she hadn't lost her spunk.

She glared up at him, green eyes blazing. "Thank you . . . *sir*, but I believe I can manage by myself."

He felt a twinge of remorse. She had a right to be angry with him, but he wasn't going to say so. He'd helped Miss Porcelain out of the stage like a high-priced doll and then let *her* fall out on her backside. Ma would have been ashamed of him.

Miss Elliot shook the dust from her skirt and reached for the hatbox. Cole's hand snaked out to snatch the gun away. When she would have protested, he said—with a smile—"Please, I insist on being of service. At least let me carry your weapon."

With an obvious effort, she gathered the shredded remnants of her composure, squared her shoulders, and lifted her small chin. "Yes . . . well, thank you. That would be most helpful." Her nose tilted a fraction higher. She lifted the hem of her skirt and brushed past him.

He followed, grinning. The townsfolk's welcome made him feel so good he couldn't be angry at this little Southern spitfire. Even if she was a royal pain in the neck.

Tal Franklin was talking to Beau, discussing the details of the robbery as Wynne approached. "I'm certainly glad to see you, Sheriff." She dropped the hatbox onto the ground beside him, ignoring Cole, who had followed her, still carrying the gun.

"You will find the culprits today?" She peered up at Tal while adjusting her hat and tucking up stray strands of hair, which now dangled like wet noodles around her dirty, perspiration-dampened face.

Cole watched as Tal regained his composure. He had witnessed Wynne's unseemly stage exit, and you could bet those shrewd eyes of his had noticed the obvious animosity between the two of them. Tal noticed everything. That was why he was the best sheriff west of the Mississippi. Right now he had a stunned expression on his face as he eyed Wynne's hat. Eastern fashions were slow to get to the Midwest, and generally the ladies were interested in seeing the new styles, but Cole would bet his last dollar not a woman in town would be caught dead wearing that thing.

"I'll sure try my best, ma'am," Tal said, "but the gang got a pretty good head start on me. One of my men's rounding up a posse right now and we'll be on our way soon as they get here."

Wynne's shoulders slumped. "I'd hoped you'd know who they were."

"From the description Rutcliff gave me, sounds like it's the Beasons. They've been giving us a peck of trouble lately. If it's them, they'll head straight for the hills, and it'll be nigh onto impossible to find them." Tal's tone of voice didn't offer much encouragement.

Wynne kicked dust. "But you will find them? They stole every cent I have plus the locket Papa gave me. I haven't anything left except my clothes!"

"Sure sorry, ma'am. We'll do everything we can. You'll excuse me now? I've got things to see about." Tal tipped his hat to her and hurried over to help one of the men lift the lifeless body of the guard off Cole's horse. The driver already lay stretched out on the ground.

Cole trailed after him, pausing to talk to his brother.

"What about the women?" Beau asked.

"Penelope told me she's here to work at Hattie's," Cole said. "She didn't say, but I assume that's where the crazy one's headed too. So you can stop playing mother hen."

Beau's gaze studied Wynne's small, wilted form, and he looked disappointed as Cole's words registered. "Oh? I wouldn't have thought she'd be one of . . . those kinds of women."

"Well, apparently she is, so let's just play it smart and move on." Cole resettled his hat and turned toward his horse. "If you want to spend time socializing with the lovely Miss Pettibone in the future, you can always ride back to town."

"Like thunder I can," Beau said, but Cole thought he sounded tempted. Cole knew, like him, it had been a long time since Beau had enjoyed a female's company, and Penelope was a very pretty young woman. "Betsy would wring my neck like a Sunday chicken."

Wynne sank down to sit on her hatbox as she tried to think what to do next. The sun hammered through her hat, making her feel faint, and the air was thick with dust. Her cotton dress stuck to her moist skin. She fanned her heat-flushed face with her handkerchief. How could Missouri be so hot?

She sighed, plucking absently at the drawstrings of her

purse. She was indeed in a pickle and needed advice. Sound advice. She was penniless without the slightest idea of what to do next. She'd been carrying every last cent she had left, but at best she would only have had enough to see her through a few months.

By then she'd planned to have her revenge on Cass Claxton and be on her way back to Georgia to try to sell the only asset she had left in this world: the land her family home had been built on. Now she was stranded in a strange town, impoverished, and without a vague notion of where to turn. Since Papa's death the only family she could claim was a distant aunt in Arizona, who she didn't think would even remember her name, let alone wire money.

She could get a job, but she wasn't trained for anything other than being a lady. Five years at Miss Marelda Fielding's Finishing School for Young Ladies in Philadelphia had given her genteel manners and behavior befitting a proper lady, but Miss Marelda had hardly prepared her students to be sitting in the middle of the street on their hatboxes, alone and flat broke.

Wynne fanned herself harder and forced back a hysterical giggle. Miss Prim-and-Proper Marelda Fielding would positively *swoon* if she could see the fine muddle she'd gotten herself into this time.

Cole and Beau talked in low undertones. She watched them, thinking they seemed to be arguing. The younger one, Beau, was all right, but that Cole was the most arrogant, irritating male she had ever met. She caught them casting an occasional glance in her direction. Somehow she had the feeling they were discussing her situation, and it unnerved her.

The sheriff motioned to Cole, and Beau strolled back to

where Wynne sat and knelt down beside her. "I think we're through here. Sheriff Franklin will notify the families. Are you going to be all right?"

"To be honest, Mr. . . ." She paused, searching for a name. She'd given her name earlier, as well as the other passengers, but the two strangers had not reciprocated.

Beau swept off his hat. "Beau, ma'am."

"Yes, Beau." Didn't the man have a last name? "And you may call me Wynne."

"Wynne. That's a right pretty name."

"Thank you . . . Beau . . . but as I was saying, I'm afraid this robbery has left me in quite a quandary." She drew a deep breath, shooting him a timid smile.

"Oh?" Beau frowned. "Well, I know you must have been real scared, but you're safe now."

"I'm not concerned for my safety," Wynne confessed. "It's . . . well, they took all my money, and now I'm not quite sure what I'm going to do." She fought the tears hovering precariously close to the surface. She couldn't sit here in the street forever, but she had no idea where to go or what to do.

Beau dropped his gaze from hers, looking decidedly embarrassed. "Why, I don't imagine you'll have to worry about your keep," he said weakly. "I've heard—though I have no firsthand knowledge—that Hattie takes right good care of her . . . girls."

Wynne stared back at him vacantly. "Hattie?"

"Yeah . . . you know, Hattie Mason . . . she runs the local saloon and . . . well, you know, the lady who owns Hattie's Place—"

Wynne felt the blood drain from her face. "Hattie's Place!" She sprang to her feet, and Beau's head snapped back.

He rose more slowly. "Well, yeah . . . Cole said he thought you and Miss Pettibone were headed for the same . . ." His voice trailed off as she drew herself up as far as her small stature allowed.

"Oh, he did, did he?" She shot a scathing glance in the direction of the gossipy, ill-mannered lout. "Well, you can tell *him* he'd better get his facts straight before he starts maligning my good character!"

"Now, ma'am," Beau soothed, "my brother doesn't mean any harm. He just sort of assumed since you and Miss Pettibone were traveling together . . . you know, you two being such pretty women and all—"

Wynne stamped her foot and glared up at him. "Well, he assumed wrong!"

"Yes, ma'am. I'll tell him," Beau agreed.

Wynne snorted and shot visual daggers at Cole, who was still immersed in deep conversation with the sheriff. "Hattie's Place. How dare he!"

Cole glanced in Wynne's direction at the sound of her upraised voice, and she sent him a scathing glare that could rightly singe pinfeathers.

Beau changed the subject. "Now, don't you be fretting yourself any. Cole and I will be happy to take you to your folks, and hopefully, in a few days, the sheriff will arrest the Beasons and return your money."

Wynne barely heard his optimistic predictions. Her angry gaze bore into the tall, dark-haired man who had finished his conversation with the sheriff and was now making idle conversation with Penelope in front of the saloon. She seriously doubted if Cole would be thrilled about Beau's generosity.

Her temper simmered when she noted the respectful way Cole treated Penelope. She couldn't help comparing his chivalrous manner toward the petite blonde with his egotistical behavior toward her a few moments earlier. His gentility had taken wing when he had let her fall out of the coach and make a complete fool of herself for the second time today!

"You don't understand." She interrupted Beau's attempt to soothe her ruffled feathers. "I don't have any family."

Surprise flickered briefly in his eyes. "None?"

"None," Wynne confirmed.

"You're not from around here?"

"Savannah is my home . . . or was until Papa died last winter."

"Georgia." Beau seemed surprised. "What's a young lady like you doing traveling to Missouri alone?"

Her eyes narrowed to viperous slits as she reminded herself why she was here. That no-account Cass Claxton! It was his fault she was in this mess. Another score she had to settle with him. "I'm looking for someone."

Relief crossed Beau's features. "Good, at least there's someone. A lady friend?"

Wynne shrugged lamely. "A man. I heard his home was in River Run. Even though I know he's been off fighting the war, I understand he's coming back now that the fighting's over."

"A man." A devilish gleam lit Beau's eyes. "A beau, huh? Well, take heart, Miss Elliot. Me and Cole have lived in these parts all our lives, so we know about everyone in the area. If your friend lives around here, we can help you find him."

Wynne's face lit with expectation, her concerns suddenly

lighter. It would save a lot of time if they could direct her to where Cass lived. Wouldn't the varmint be surprised when she showed up. She'd teach him a lesson he wouldn't forget. She smiled up at Beau. "You'd do that for me?"

"I certainly would!" Beau affirmed. "And about your lost money . . . don't worry about that. We'll take you home with us. Ma always has room for one more, and she'd be ashamed of us if she found out you was in trouble and we hadn't done our Christian duty."

"Oh, no. Really, I couldn't impose on you like that," Wynne protested.

"Impose!" Beau appeared to warm to the idea. "We'd be right proud to have you come along with us. Soon as me and Cole get settled in, we'll start looking for your man." His face creased in a disarming grin as he offered Wynne his arm. "No more arguments. You're coming home with us."

She placed her hand in the crook of his elbow, and he picked up the hatbox and escorted her to his horse, assuring her all the while that everything would work out. "You ride with me," he said. "I'll get Cole to take your bags."

Wynne wasn't sure she was doing the right thing; she knew going home with two perfect strangers was highly improper, but she suddenly found herself being lifted up and set firmly on the back of Beau's horse.

She leaned over to catch his arm. "Don't you think you should check with your brother before you invite me to your home?" She could imagine what *his* reaction was going to be to this latest piece of news.

Beau swung his large frame up behind her and grinned. "Not to worry, Miss Elliot. He won't care. He's been gone four years; all he wants to do is get home. He doesn't care who goes with him."

She cast a dubious glance toward the man in question. "I still don't think he'll be too happy about all this."

"He won't care," Beau insisted.

Beau nudged the horse's flanks gently and set the animal into motion. Seconds later they ambled up beside Cole and Penelope. Cole glanced up, and Wynne bit back a smirk when surprise flickered across his face. Seeing her mounted in front of Beau had to unnerve him. In spite of Beau's assurances to the contrary, she realized Cole would definitely mind her going home with them.

"You about ready to leave?" Beau inquired pleasantly. "Wynne's coming home with us."

Wynne bit her lip hard when Mr. Smarty-Pants's jaw dropped like a rock, but he recovered quickly. "I thought she was headed for Hattie's."

"It so happens you thought wrong," Wynne said. She proceeded to bestow on him one of her loveliest—albeit snooti-est—smiles, one Miss Marelda Fielding would have been proud to witness. "Your brother has kindly offered the hospitality of your home until I can regain my financial losses." Her voice dripped honey. "Beau said you wouldn't mind one little bit carrying my valises." She crossed her hands over her chest in mock admira-tion. "My, your chivalry simply leaves me without words!"

Cole glanced sharply at Beau, then back at Wynne. He had a grim set to his mouth. "My mind cannot comprehend someone as fair as you without words, Miss Elliot." He bent his head respectfully. "Ladies—Miss Elliot, if you would excuse us for a moment I'd like to have a word with my brother."

Beau slid down off the horse and handed the reins to Wynne with a knowing wink. "I shall return."

Wynne stiffened. The cad. She'd caught that thinly disguised salutation. *Ladies,* meaning Penelope.

"Pompous idiot." She hadn't meant to speak out loud, but a quick check satisfied her that no one except Penelope was close enough to hear her caustic observation. Not that she would mind all that much if that ill-mannered lout had heard her. Someone needed to take him down a peg.

The two brothers disappeared around the corner of the building while Wynne said her good-byes to Penelope.

The minute they were out of sight of the women, Cole grabbed Beau's arm and demanded, "What are you doing this time?"

"Hey, calm down." Beau glanced back over his shoulder. "I knew you wouldn't be too happy about the arrangement, but the poor girl's up a creek, Cole."

"I fail to see where she's our responsibility." Cole's jaw set in a grim line. "She's Hattie's problem."

"She told you. She wasn't coming to work for Hattie. Penelope is the only one planning to work there," Beau explained.

Beau sounded so reasonable, Cole wanted to box some sense into him. Crazy kid. Hadn't he learned anything from being in the war? You didn't just pick up strange females and take them home with you. "Then what is Miss Elliot doing tramping all over the country in that silly hat and falling out of stagecoaches? Crazy fool woman." Just his luck to run into her. Look how they'd already been delayed by her shenanigans. If Beau hadn't insisted on getting them involved in this mess, he would have been sitting down to supper right now.

"She's looking for a man."

Cole snorted. "I bet she is—let's hope, for his sake, she doesn't find him."

Beau sighed. "What have you got against her? She hasn't said ten words to you and you act like she's done something wrong. Besides, you're the one who is always carping about wanting a woman to have a little spirit. Well, she's spirited enough."

"I don't want a spirited, addlebrained female." Any man who took her on could count on a short, frustrated life. If she didn't shoot him by accident, she would drive him to shoot himself.

"So she doesn't know how to handle a gun. Is that what you've got against her? Lots of women don't. Betsy and Priscilla don't—"

"I don't want to hear any more about Priscilla! Okay?" Cole felt he had just about reached his limit. He didn't want a woman. All he wanted was to get home, see Ma, eat some home cooking, and start getting his life back to the way it used to be before the war had changed everything.

"Okay, okay. But you can't hold not being able to handle a gun against Wynne," Beau pointed out. "For the life of me, I can't understand why you're so dead set against helping her. You're usually a little more gentlemanly when it comes to women. Ma would be ashamed of you."

Cole took a step back and crossed his arms. He raised his eyebrows. "Now it's 'Wynne'?"

"She said I could call her by her first name."

"You're asking for trouble," Cole said. "I say we turn her over to Tal and be on our way."

"I can't do that."

"You can't *do* that," Cole repeated in exasperation. "Why *can't* you do that? She means nothing to us one way or the other. We stumbled on a robbery! We didn't take her to raise!" And he sure didn't want to take her home with him. He didn't want strangers spoiling his homecoming.

"I know, but somehow I sort of feel responsible for her, Cole. Look at her. Does she look like she can take care of herself? Don't ask me why, but I think the Lord's put her right here with us, and I'm going to take her home to Ma for now, and then I'm going to help her find the man she's looking for." Beau crossed his arms. "All I'm asking you to do is carry her valises. Is that asking too much?"

"You're a fool." Cole pulled off his hat and swiped a forearm sleeve across his forehead. He'd helped raise this boy; why hadn't he taught him some plain common sense?

Beau's lips firmed. "So be it, but that's the way I'm going to do it. Now, are you going to carry her bags, or am I going to have to make another trip back into town to get them?"

Cole raked his fingers through his dark hair. "I don't know why I let you talk me into these things," he muttered. "She's only going to be trouble for us. Remember that when she turns into more headache than she's worth."

"I'll remember—as long as you're carrying her bags." Beau grinned and slapped him good-naturedly on the back as they walked around the corner. "I'll tell Tal she'll be out at our place if he needs her. I'll only be a minute."

Cole grunted and went over to pick up the two bags sitting on the ground in front of the stage. After hefting them up onto his shoulders, he walked back to his horse and started tying them on.

He watched as Wynne fanned herself energetically, swatting at the flies buzzing around her head. Aggravating female. Seemed like if there was any way she could be a problem she would find it. He yanked hard on the leather strap he used to bind the bags behind his saddle. And Beau was just as bad. Couldn't do a thing with either one of them.

Now she slid off the horse and walked toward him. Should have known she couldn't sit still and stay out of the way. Maybe if he ignored her she would leave, but he knew he couldn't be that lucky.

She stopped some three feet away and cleared her throat. "Excuse me."

Cole glanced up. Even with a dirty face and her hair straggling in her eyes she was still pretty. Too bad she didn't have a lick of common logic to go along with her looks. He went back to fastening her bags on his horse. His horse. This poor animal was as tired as he was, and now thanks to his scatterbrained brother, it was being used as a packhorse too. Sometimes he wondered about Beau. Well, he might have to take Miss Elliot home with him, but he didn't have to like it.

"Sir?"

This time he stared at her, and she smiled back timidly.

"Are you speaking to me?" he asked.

Her smile faded. "Well, of course I'm talking to you. Who do you think I'm talking to? The horse?"

"Wouldn't surprise me." He went about his work, dismissing

the strained conversation. There wasn't anything that said he had to talk to her either. He should have known it wouldn't be that easy. She wasn't the kind to give up.

She cleared her throat again. "Since we'll be in each other's company for the next few days, we should properly introduce ourselves."

He grunted.

"I'm Wynne Elliot." She extended her hand.

"And I'm Pompous Idiot," he replied evenly, cinching the rope around her bags. He ignored her hand.

A flush rose up the column of her neck as her gaze slid away in embarrassment. "Oh, dear. You heard that."

"I'm pompous. Not deaf."

"Well, I must apologize—is it Cole?"

He shot her another prickly look and continued his task. Why didn't she do something about that hat?

"I suppose this whole ordeal has unnerved me, and I have completely forgotten my manners." Once again she extended her hand in a friendly gesture. "My name is Wynne Elliot, but you may call me *Miss* Elliot." Apparently she was willing to give only so much in the name of peace. That was all right with him. He didn't feel much like going the extra mile himself. Turning the other cheek was all very well, unless the person slapping you down just kept on slapping. He'd about had enough of *Miss* Wynne Elliot.

Cole stared at her hand, dirty from her recent fall. He hesitated, not wanting to accept it, but Ma's teaching ran too deep to be ignored. He took the grubby little paw in his own. "*Miss* Elliot—" he bowed mockingly— "I wish I could say it was an honor to make your acquaintance."

Her lips tightened, but she made an obvious effort to ignore his deliberate attempt to rile her. "I'm sorry I called you a pompous idiot."

"And I'm sorry I called you what I did."

She frowned. "What did you call me?"

"Addlebrained. Careless. That's two that come to mind right off," he confessed. He grinned, knowing he was irritating her all the more.

Her frown deepened. "Addlebrained? You called me addlebrained?" She jerked her hand free. "I suppose you think I'm addlebrained because I dropped the gun and tripped over it?"

"That was part of it, and then you fell out of the stage," he confessed. "That's where the *careless* came in."

The corners of his eyes crinkled with amusement when she shook her head in anger and the hat slipped over her nose. She shoved it back on her head, and the bird rocked in its nest. He grinned, thinking if there were eggs in that nest they must be scrambled by now.

"Well, I can assure you I am *not* careless or addlebrained," Wynne said. "You happened to catch me at a bad moment."

"You can think that if it pleases you, Miss Elliot." Cole picked up the reins of his horse and swung into the saddle. "Seems to me you're just being yourself."

Beau came out of the sheriff's office and approached them, looking ready to go.

"I'll follow you," Cole said. "Let's try to make it home for supper." He hoped they didn't come across any more stagecoaches being held up or any more damsels in distress. One addlebrained female was one more than any sane man could be expected to put up with.

"Sounds good to me!" Beau agreed as he helped Wynne up onto the horse and then mounted behind her. He gathered up the reins and gave a loud rebel yell as he kicked his horse into action. Wynne shot a cross look in Cole's direction as they rode out of town in a cloud of dust.

He grinned when he heard her mutter, "Addlebrained indeed!"

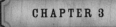

CHAPTER 3

This was the hour Cole had lived for the past four years. In his mind he'd walked the old paths, climbed the hills, slept in his own bed. Nothing he'd seen in the East or South could compare with the sights, the smells around him now.

July was too late to see the wild roses in bloom, but the golden flowers of the black-eyed Susan lined the roadway. The blue stars of chicory mingled with the white of Queen Anne's lace. Ma would probably have a big bouquet of wildflowers in the old ironstone pitcher sitting on the library table in the front room.

Life felt pretty good. Cole had been afraid of what he would find here. Even though he'd been a long way from home, he'd heard about the fierce border war between Missouri and Kansas. Guerrilla bands had fought back and forth, the Missouri men called Bushwhackers and the Kansas ones called Jayhawkers or Redlegs. He supposed it didn't matter what you called a man; there wasn't much difference in war.

Quantrill's band of Bushwackers had fought here, and from

what he'd heard, Frank and Jesse James had ridden with him. The James boys, like a lot of young men, had been forced into this war to protect what they saw as theirs. And what they believed. Frank and Jesse had been Southern sympathizers. Cole had fought for the Union.

The war had turned neighbor against neighbor, brother against brother. As for him, he'd never felt like he had a choice. He'd never been able to think that anyone Almighty God had created should be held in slavery because they looked different or belonged to a different race. Didn't seem right somehow.

He focused on Wynne Elliot, riding in front of Beau. One hundred pounds of trouble on the hoof. Ma would probably take her in all right. She'd take in a stray dog, had lots of times, but they'd be lucky if this stray didn't shoot someone or set fire to the house. Miss Wynne Elliot was an accident waiting to happen.

Life was unpredictable. Wynne clung to the saddle horn and thought how odd it was that she was here, in Missouri, trusting her very life to strangers. Not all that long ago the only thing she'd had to worry about was the color of her next ball gown.

Life had been grand back home in Georgia—before both Mama and Papa passed away. She'd been an only child, raised in an affluent home by doting parents. Moss Oak had been one of the biggest cotton plantations in the South before the fighting broke out.

Then the war had come, and Papa had sent her away to the East to learn the fine art of being a lady, which he thought she sorely needed. Real ladies weren't supposed to know the basics of farming. She wondered what he would say if he could see her now, riding astride a horse in front of a man she had met for the first time today. Papa definitely wouldn't have approved.

Beau was taking her to see his mother. Well, she'd had a mother too before she'd been taken ill with a strange sickness. Papa had brought Wynne home from school to be of comfort, but nothing had been the same since.

She clung tighter when Beau urged his horse to a canter, remembering the feeling of helplessness as she and her father stood by and watched Rose Elliot struggle to overcome the sickness that ravaged her. There was nothing doctors could to do to still the nausea and the swift weight loss that beset her frail body. Then came the terrible pain. Wynne was still tormented sometimes by the memory of her mother's soft sobbing in the night and her father's agonized voice trying to ease her torment and contain his own. Weeks had seemed like years back then.

Tears stung her eyes. Why was she thinking of that now? Was it because Beau and Cole seemed so anxious to get home and see their mother again? Well, she could identify with that. She'd spent hours praying that the good Lord would relieve the suffering and take away the agony they all were experiencing.

She guessed God had His own way of looking at things. He hadn't saved her mother, and He had done nothing to stop the war. All that killing and dying, and for what? Nothing she could see. Surely the problem of slavery could have been solved another way.

At least she could be grateful her mother hadn't lived to see the destruction of the plantation she loved so dearly. When the end came, Rose Elliot simply went to sleep and never woke up.

Wynne watched the unfamiliar scenery rushing by. She was used to cleared fields and stately houses. The trees here grew so close together it was like riding through a green tunnel. The few houses they passed looked neglected, like no one cared about them. Papa had taken good care of their home. Or he had before her mother's death had ripped the heart out of him.

Her mother's sickness had been heartbreaking enough, but the pain was nothing compared to her father's grieving his life away after her mother's death. He'd roamed the halls at night in search of something that Wynne had never quite understood. Once she'd passed his study late in the evening and heard the tortured weeping of a man who had suffered an unspeakable loss, one with which he could not cope.

The horse stumbled and Wynne caught her breath. If this fool horse fell, he'd kill them both the way Beau kept urging the animal to a faster gallop. She knew he was in a hurry to get home, but as long as they'd been away, surely a few minutes couldn't matter. Not enough to take a chance on having a fatal accident. She turned slightly, observing Cole. Now there was a man who'd take a lot of taming—far more than she could fathom.

She turned back, tightening her lips, suddenly flushed with anger. Men. It was just after Mama's death that Cass had come into her life. He'd been a gentle, loving man who had helped her through the agony of loss with his sunny disposition, quick wit, and remarkable charm.

She'd met him through a mutual friend at a Christmas ball. When she questioned why he hadn't enlisted in the Southern cause, he'd explained that he had family obligations, and he had paid someone to take his place. The idea that any man could pay his way out of service to his country bothered her. For five hundred dollars, another man would fight on his behalf. She even knew it was customary practice for men of means to do so, but the thought still disturbed her.

Undoubtedly Cass came from an affluent and prosperous family, which should make it easier to find him. From what she'd seen of River Run there couldn't be too many families around here that met the criteria. You had only to look at Cass to know he came from good stock. He had been in Savannah visiting kin—prominent, wealthy pillars of the community. She had been so totally captivated by Cass's impeccable manners and his chivalrous ways that all else seemed secondary in her mind.

She supposed there was some excuse for the way she fell for him. After all, it had been such a rare treat for the belles of Georgia to have a fascinating, eligible young man in their midst. She had simply forgotten about the war and let her heart be won by those pretty words that had dripped off his tongue like rich, warm honey—lying, deceitful words that she still hated to admit she had actually been gullible enough to believe!

He'd caught her at a vulnerable time, of course.

A scant six weeks after her mother's death, she'd heard a shot ring out in the night. Papa had chosen to leave his daughter behind. By his own hand he had gone on to be with the woman he had loved so much he no longer wanted to live without her. For months she had heard the reverberation over and over again.

She'd been left alone and more frightened than she had ever been in her life. And then the Yankees came through and burned Moss Oak and the surrounding buildings. Mercifully they had left the main house standing, but they had ransacked and carried off the furnishings while she and the servants stood by and watched the pillaging in stunned silence.

"Are you comfortable?" Beau's voice broke into her painful thoughts and drew her quickly back to the present.

Immersed in her sad memories, Wynne had forgotten her uncomfortable perch in a saddle too large for her and the closeness of the man riding behind her. She plucked at the material of her dress, attempting to allow some air to circulate against her skin. The sun was a ball of fire in the sky, making her nearly limp with heat. She was anything but comfortable, but considering how kind Beau had been, she decided it would be ungrateful to complain.

"I'm fine, thank you." She shifted slightly, increasingly aware of the pressure of Beau's arms around her as he held the reins. Surely it couldn't be much farther. "Are we almost there?"

"Another three miles or so. We can stop and let you rest a spell if you'd like."

"That won't be necessary. I'll be fine."

She was most appreciative of what he was doing for her. Not all men would have taken her under their wing the way Beau had.

She turned her head slightly, her eyes fastening on the rider trailing a safe distance behind them. *He* certainly would have left her for the buzzards to pick clean.

For a reason she couldn't understand, that train of thought made her think of Cass, handsome rogue that he was, which set her to seething all over again.

The only good thing Cass Claxton had done was to be there

for her to lean on during the most tragic time of her life. And in all honesty, he had never failed her once during those dark days. He'd helped her face reality, always there when she swore she couldn't bear the sorrow, wiping away her tears and confidently assuring her that through God she could bear all things. For a young man of twenty-two, he readily admitted he didn't have all of life's answers, but together they would find them.

Then one day he'd been offered an opportunity to go into business with one of his cousins. They wanted to buy a plant that manufactured gunpowder. Wynne had been ecstatic. The business venture meant Cass would be staying in Savannah. She suspected now that she had been happier about the business prospect than he was. Had she pushed him into accepting the offer? She'd wanted to keep him close. Even began dropping marriage hints, viewing Cass as a most pleasant avenue to salvage her broken life.

As further enticement she'd offered the money from her inheritance for the business prospect. It wasn't long before she persuaded Cass to accept her generosity. Now that she'd had time to think about it, seemed like she'd done an awful lot of persuading, and maybe she'd brought some pressure to bear on the marrying part too. The night before they were to be married, she handed over all her money—with the exception of the meager amount she kept in that small tin box under her mattress—assuming his business endeavor would be concluded early the following morning.

Looking back, she wondered if Cass ever really loved her or if he had asked for her hand in marriage simply to appease a heartbroken girl for whom nothing in life had gone well lately. Certainly his family could have lent him the money to go into business, but instead, Cass had asked her to marry him. So surely he'd cared about her, but if so, why had he left her literally standing in front of the church?

Her cheeks felt hot when she recalled her "wedding day." The morning had dawned cold and gray with the promise of rain in the air. Tilly, her mammy since childhood, had lovingly dressed her for the ceremony, fretting over her like a mother hen.

Even now, she could remember smiling and gazing at herself in the large looking glass in her parents' bedroom, the soft, delicate folds of her mother's ivory wedding gown billowing out around her and sweeping to the floor. She had stared back at the reflection that could have been Rose nineteen years earlier, her eyes misty with grief.

"Do you think Mama and Papa would approve of what I'm doing, Tilly?" she'd asked softly.

Tilly had heaved a big sigh and patted her shoulder reassuringly. "A body's got to do what they think best, sweet baby." The large, rawboned servant gently tucked a lock of red hair behind Wynne's ear. "I'm sure your man will be real good to you."

Wynne shrugged. She supposed Tilly had been right. Cass would have been good to her—had he made it to the wedding.

The pain and humiliation she'd felt standing in front of the church, anxiously awaiting her bridegroom's arrival still hurt. She and the guests had waited at the church for Cass to arrive that afternoon. And waited and waited and waited . . . She could never forgive Cass Claxton for that. She could almost overlook the money, though that was bad enough, but nothing could ever make her forget the way she had felt, standing there in the growing twilight, witnessing the pity in the eyes of friends and neighbors she had known all her life.

That was why Mr. Cass Claxton was going to pay for what he had done.

Wynne ignored the tremor of discomfort—as if God might be reminding her about forgiveness. And she'd forgive Cass. Indeed she would, the moment she'd made him sorry he'd ever been such a lying, thieving, two-timing polecat.

Why else would she be here, enduring heat and holdups and Cole—a man who she'd bet could best Cass in the ornery-man department.

She'd left the morning after the unfinished wedding to return to Marelda Fielding's Finishing School, a feeble effort on her part to put her life back together.

The death of her parents, the war, and Cass's humiliating rejection—all had taken their toll. It had seemed to her she just had to take some sort of revenge.

Slowly a plan—a very simple plan to avenge her pride and uphold the Elliot name—began to take root. She would find Cass Claxton and kill him for what he had done to her. Put a lead slug right through his double-dealing heart. Not only had he stolen her blind, but he had made her the laughingstock of Savannah in the process! Surely such action could not go unpunished.

Cass Claxton had not seen the last of her. She would find him if it was the last thing she did, and before she killed him, she would demand an explanation for his despicable behavior. She shut her mind to the nagging voice that kept whispering, "Vengeance is mine, saith the Lord."

This time the Lord was going to have a little help. Surely He wouldn't begrudge her this one slightly irregular take on the eye-for-an-eye suggestion.

Squinting against the glaring sun, she turned to look over her shoulder. The man riding behind seemed intent on his destination, his dusty features hidden beneath a thick, dark beard. It was either her vivid imagination, or else *he* even *looked* like Cass. No, that couldn't be. She turned to look straight ahead. The two men only looked alike because she had been thinking about her former fiancé. Other than being uncommonly handsome, they bore no similarities.

But her imagination wasn't playing tricks on her. It suddenly dawned on her why she thought she'd met Cole before. Cass had the same brash but completely charming way of addressing a female. Of course, Cole hadn't been all that charming to her, but he'd oozed with appeal when he was talking to Penelope. She leaned back in the saddle, peering more closely at the brother trailing behind. Even the remembered set of Cass's chin suggested the same stubborn streak she now suspected might be in Cole's, hidden beneath that thick beard. It wasn't so much that they looked alike, but the personality similarities were unmistakable. Both were self-assured, arrogant, not to be trusted. Her eyes skimmed the rider's tanned features and paused at the opening of his shirt. A mat of thick, dark hair shadowed the neckline.

Wynne's pulse quickened.

Powerful and ruggedly virile, Cole sat in his saddle with the same aura of authority that Cass possessed, and for a moment Wynne found her heart thumping at the remembrance of being held tightly against the broad expanse of a chest.

She wasn't certain why her gaze lifted suddenly, but it did, and she found herself staring into a set of mocking blue eyes that held ill-concealed amusement at her disgraceful observation of him. She felt color flood her face, and she hurriedly looked away, but she could feel his arrogant eyes boring into the back of her head. She refused to give him the satisfaction of looking back.

She was sure her face was bright as a sunrise!

"Did you say something?" Beau called above the clatter of horse's hooves.

"Nothing!" At least she hoped she hadn't voiced her thoughts out loud. For the remainder of the ride she carefully kept her eyes fixed on the scenery and her mind blank. When the two riders finally turned into a winding lane and let their horses have their head, Wynne breathed a sigh of relief.

The horses thundered down the road. Cole and Beau grinned mischievously at each other and apparently reverted to their childhood, each trying to outrace the other home. Wynne held tightly to the saddle horn, fearing both men had taken leave of their senses.

Flanking the mare's side, Cole shot around Beau and galloped the remaining half mile to the farmyard. With a whoop of joy, he sprang from his saddle before the horse stopped and enfolded in his arms the woman who had burst out the door, waving her apron. Lifting her high above his head, he swung Lilly Claxton around and around, his face a wreath of smiles. "I'm home, Ma!"

"Cole!" Tears filled Lilly's eyes and her laughter joined his. "Oh, Cole, you're home. Thank God."

His mother's eyes searched his face, and Cole saw the worry wrinkles that hadn't been there when he left. He knew she'd have spent hours on her knees interceding for the sons who were so far away and in danger. He watched her blink away her tears, and he waited while her searching fingertips examined every contour of his face, looking for signs of the boy who had ridden off to war. He knew those signs weren't there. He'd seen too much, heard too much, fought too many battles. You didn't have much innocence left after four years of hell.

"Beau? Have you heard from Beau?" she questioned.

Before he could answer, Beau and Wynne rode into the barnyard.

A second round of joyous praise and laughter erupted. Beau tumbled off the horse and caught his mother up in his arms. He laughed as he tossed her up into the air and caught her safely back in his arms. He gently set her back on her feet, smiling down at her.

"Beau and Cole! Back home on the same day. Praise the Lord!" Tears spilled over and she reached to clasp her arms around both men's necks, hugging them tightly, as if she would never let them go.

"It's good to be home, Ma," Cole said.

"And your brother . . . have you seen or heard from him?" Her eyes mutely pleaded for the right answer.

Cole met her question with surprise. "Isn't he here with you?"

"No—no, I got a letter a few months ago. Said he had joined up—"

"I thought he was staying here to help out." Beau took off his hat.

Lilly wiped the corners of her eyes with her faded apron as she tried to defend her youngest son. "I know, but . . . well . . . he always had a wandering streak in him . . . just like your pa."

"Don't worry, Ma. Now that the war's over, he'll be riding in any day." Cole tried to console her, but his heart was heavy. Why in tarnation couldn't that boy have stayed home and taken care of Ma the way he was supposed to? That's why they'd paid five hundred dollars to keep him out of the war in the first place—so she wouldn't be here alone.

Lilly flung her arms back around her boys' shoulders, hugging them simultaneously. "Well, I thank the Lord you're here. I can't believe you're both home at the same time! When we heard the war was over, we started looking for you to come, but since we hadn't heard anything from either one of you in so long, we didn't know what to expect."

"I would have written, Ma," Beau apologized, "but I figured I'd probably get here before the letter did."

"And what's your excuse?" Lilly put her hands on her hips and turned on Cole with accusing eyes that only a mother can manage. He'd never realized how *much* he'd missed her until he got back home. Now he grinned and let his shoulders rise in a lame shrug.

"Ah, Ma . . . you know me. I never was good at writing letters."

For the first time since all the excitement had broken out, Lilly glanced up at Wynne and smiled. "Land sakes! All this ruckus and we plumb forgot our manners! Who have you brought home with you?"

"Ma, this is Wynne Elliot." Beau walked over and lifted Wynne off his horse and set her down on the ground. "She was on the stage to River Run when it was robbed. The Beason gang stole all her money, and since she don't have any kin around here, we brought her home to stay with us for a few days."

"Robbed! Why, that must have been real frightening." Lilly reached out and pumped Wynne's hand warmly. "I'm glad Beau brought you home. You're welcome to stay as long as you like."

Cole looked on cynically. Like he figured, Ma would take her in and feed her. To tell the truth, he'd forgotten about her in the excitement of being home. Well, they'd gotten her here, and he could wash his hands of her. What she did now didn't concern him and he was going to make sure it stayed that way.

"Thank you," Wynne murmured gratefully. "I should be able to move on in a few days. The sheriff is looking for the bandits right now."

Cole leaned against the porch and watched Miss Elliot try to talk her way into Ma's good graces. What was a woman like her doing out here by herself? Looking for some man, Beau said. Well, if that man was smart, he'd keep running while he had the chance. He narrowed his eyes thoughtfully. Something about Miss Wynne Elliot didn't quite ring true. He'd survived the last four years by recognizing a lie when he heard it, and while he wouldn't go so far as to say that Miss Elliot had lied, he wasn't so sure she had told them the whole truth.

"Well, don't you fret, honey. Tal will find those thieves if anyone can. He's a good man. Now, come along." Lilly wrapped her arms around her sons' waists and gave them another motherly squeeze. "It just so happens Willa and I have a big pot of those chicken and dumplings you're so fond of simmering on the stove. 'Course, you're not either one going to sit at my table till you shave and wash some of that road grime off you." She tugged affectionately at Cole's beard.

Beau's face lit with expectancy. "No kidding, Ma? You really have chicken and dumplings? I was just telling Cole this morning how I hoped you would. Now that's real luck."

"Luck!" Lilly scoffed. "We've had a pot of them chicken and dumplings on the stove since we heard the war was over. Almost wiped out the flock, and I've eaten so many dumplings I'm sick of the sight of them. We've been praying and waiting for you two to come home and eat them for months!"

As suddenly as it appeared, the laughter drained out of her voice and her eyes misted. "I guess I'm going to have to stay down on my knees an extra long time tonight and thank the good Lord He seen fit to send you back to me." She reached up and pinched Cole's cheek. "It's good to have you back, son."

Cole grinned. "Thanks, Ma. It's good to be home."

CHAPTER 4

Man alive, it was hot! Bertram G. Mallory mopped his forehead with a lank handkerchief and studied the scene before him. A merciless, blazing afternoon sun beat down, sending a shimmer of heat haze across the landscape.

There it was: Springfield, Missouri. He was close now.

He reached up and took another swipe at the sweat rolling from his hatband and looked up for some sign of relief, but the endless blue of a summer sky met his gaze. His weary horse plodded along, its hooves raising little of the dust from the dry road. It had been more than three months since it had rained in these parts, he'd heard. Too long. Brown, scorched grass—dry streambeds. Hotter than an oven on baking day. His patience was wearing thin. Not only with the weather, but also with Wynne Elliot.

Every time he got near that stubborn filly she somehow managed to slip through his fingers. But she wouldn't do it again. He ran a long, lean hand over his prickly beard. No sir, he'd make sure he had her this time.

He reined in the horse and with a low, painful groan slid out of the saddle. His hand automatically went to shield his still-tender left side. The result of the untimely accident he'd encountered a few weeks ago was sensitive to the touch, not to mention the thought. His eyes narrowed when he recalled the harrowing incident that had left him with three busted ribs and a splitting headache for days.

When he'd heard that Miss Elliot was reportedly attending a finishing school for ladies back East, he'd set out to capture the little spitfire. But when he'd arrived in Philadelphia at Miss Marelda Fielding's Finishing School for Young Ladies, Miss Fielding had told him that Wynne wasn't there. Apparently the Elliot woman had decided to pay a visit to Missouri. River Run, Miss Fielding had said. Well, he knew right then that meant a peck of trouble unless he could get to her before she got there.

At the time, it had seemed like a good idea to hop the train. River Run, by stage, was a good several weeks' travel from Philadelphia. Since he had very little time to catch up with her, he'd decided to catch the first train going west and hope it would take him to within a reasonable riding distance of River Run.

It was a good plan and ought to have worked.

He'd sold his horse and pocketed the money, figuring that when he arrived in Missouri by train several days ahead of Miss Elliot, relaxed and completely rested, he would buy another horse. No need to waste his money on a ticket. He'd wait until the train passed under a big bluff and then jump on top of the car and stay there until the conductor collected the fares. Then he would casually blend himself in with the other passengers and enjoy the ride.

He flinched when a sharp, excruciating pain rippled through his side. The plan would have worked too, if his timing hadn't been a fraction off, and if the train had run as far as Missouri.

He'd jumped off the bluff as planned and hit the top of the railcar with the speed of a bullet. His calculation had been a mite off. The train had been traveling faster than he'd figured— not much, but enough to throw off his rapid descent.

He landed wide-eyed in spread-eagle position flat against the top of the fast-moving boxcar. He'd frantically grasped for something to hold on to while the train shot around a bend in the track. Even now he could remember the terror he had felt when his fingers began to slip and he'd realized he and the train would soon be parting company.

He'd tried to dig his toes in for support, but there wasn't anything to get a toehold on, so to speak. He'd lost his grip on the deepest bend. The train's speed catapulted him off the side of the car and his life had flashed before his eyes when he hurtled through the air. His body had been flung like a rag doll to the ground, where he rolled for what must have been fifteen minutes down a deep, briar-blanketed ravine. When he came to it was night and he was certain every bone in his body had been shattered. An old prospector was bending over him.

Probably hadn't helped much to be ridden into town slung over the back of the old man's donkey. The prospector had left him with the doctor and, after refusing payment, which had been right neighborly of him, had waved off Bertram's gratitude and disappeared out the front door.

Bertram straightened and caught the small of his back. He was still amazed that he was alive. The harrowing brush with death had left him with three cracked ribs, a bad back, and a busted skull. The accident had been enough to lay him up at the local hotel for several weeks.

Then he'd found out that all the pain and inconvenience had been for nothing. The track had ended twenty miles down the road.

How was he to know that?

Merchants throughout the country had a hard time getting goods delivered overland by wagon, not to mention the toll it took on animals. Terrible road conditions in most states brought about railroad fever. Tracks were springing up all over the country, and the people were crying for rail service. He'd been certain he could get to Missouri with no problem.

When he healed, he'd worked long enough to buy another horse, and then once more he set off in pursuit of the elusive Miss Elliot.

Bertram shook his head. He was just too reliable, that's what. Too loyal. Any other man would have given up by now, but not him. He'd been forced to go back to Miss Marelda Fielding's Finishing School for Young Ladies, hoping that by now Wynne might have returned. He could still remember the sinking knot in the pit of his stomach when Miss Fielding told him she assumed Wynne was still visiting in Missouri.

But he had given his word. Bertram G. Mallory was a man to whom a promise meant something. A man's word was his honor. He would go to great lengths to fulfill an obligation, and his responsibility was to find Wynne Elliot, no matter how long it took.

Now his mission was finally nearing an end. And none too soon. He winced, bringing his hand up to shield his ribs. River

Run was just a half day's ride from Springfield. By late tomorrow afternoon, he hoped to meet Miss Elliot face-to-face.

Tonight he'd rest a spell. He longed for a clean bed, a bath, a shave, and a hot meal, but he knew that was foolish thinking. He didn't have funds for that sort of luxury. Instead, he'd settle for a campfire and a bedroll on the outskirts of this fair metropolis.

His eyes skimmed the town ahead. He was surprised to see so much activity on the streets at this hour. Pulling a watch fob from a side pocket, he noted it was nearing six. He'd figured most folks would be home taking supper about now. He rewound the timepiece before carefully placing it back in his pocket and refocusing on Springfield. Big towns had a faster way of life, he decided.

Even from this distance, he spotted a group of bedraggled-looking women standing next to the livery. It wasn't unusual to encounter hundreds of female Confederate refugees swarming about the towns, looking for food and shelter. That worried Bertram. The females were a destitute, heart-wrenching sight, and he didn't like to think about a woman being alone. Women should be taken care of, pampered, and held gently. It always saddened him to see those women. After what he'd experienced during the war, he'd have thought he would have become accustomed to the poverty and degradation the conflict had brought upon the people, but he hadn't and he guessed he never would. He had fought for only a few days when he suffered a wound that had sent him back to Savannah. But he'd seen all the killing he cared to.

Picking up the reins of his horse, he rode the short distance into town and threaded his way along the fringes of the crowd milling about, conversing in low tones. They all seemed to be waiting for something. He wondered if one of those medicine shows might be coming to town.

Suddenly the hushed murmurs stilled. Everyone stood quietly waiting. Bertram's puzzled gaze studied the small crowds gathered in the doorways and alleys surrounding the square, and his brow furrowed with curiosity.

As far as he could tell, there was nothing unusual happening, yet the crowd seemed apprehensive and watchful. He threw the reins over the nearest hitching post and stepped onto the porch of the general store, where he spoke to one of the old-timers leaning back in a chair, whittling on a piece of wood.

"Howdy."

The man's knife paused, and he glanced up at the new-comer, giving him a friendly grin. A battered hat sat on his head, and his snow white beard was spotted with tobacco juice. The man didn't have a single tooth left in his head.

"Howdy," the old-timer said, leaning over the rail to spit a long stream of brown liquid into the dust.

Bertram stepped out of the line of fire, then pushed his hat back on his head before he hunched down beside the man's chair. "Hot, isn't it?"

"Shorely is."

"Could use some rain."

"Yep." The old-timer leaned over the rail and spat. "It'll rain soon, though. Saw a black snake in a tree this morning." He spat again and wiped at his mouth on the cuff of his sleeve. "Hit's a sure sign rain's on the way."

"Yeah. So I've heard." A black snake in a tree was about as accurate a prediction of rain as Bertram could think of, with the

exception of birds flying low or walking on the ground. They
always meant rain, and he was grateful for any small sign the
drought would soon be over.

"You're a stranger to these parts, ain't you, boy?"

"Just passing through."

"Humph." The old man leaned over and spat on the porch.

Bertram surveyed the milling crowd. "What's going on?"

"Gonna be a shooting," the old man said. His gnarled hands
gently rubbed the carving he was working on.

Bertram wasn't sure he'd heard right. "A shooting?"

"Yep."

Bertram's wary gaze sought the restless crowd. "Who's going
to be doing it?"

The old-timer looked up, and a toothless grin spread across
his weather-beaten face. "You ever heard of Wild Bill Hickok?"

Bertram blinked in surprise. "Hasn't everyone?" It was a
well-known fact that Wild Bill's reputation and skill with a gun
had made him the constable of Monticello, Kansas, when he was
still a teenager. Rumor had it that young Bill had worked as a
Union sharpshooter and scout during the past few years.
Bertram had even heard speculation that Wild Bill had been a
spy for the Union, posing as a Confederate throughout southern
Missouri and Arkansas.

"Well, Wild Bill's gonna get his watch back today," the
old-timer announced, chuckling.

Bertram frowned. "Someone took his watch?" He whistled
under his breath. That sounded mighty daring to him. Most men
gave Wild Bill a wide berth. He couldn't imagine anyone being
foolish enough to steal the man's watch.

"Guess you could say that. Him and Tutt ain't exactly the

bosom buddies, if you know what I mean. They've had some real hard feelings over Susannah Moore, a woman they both had a hankering for, but that's not what they're fighting about."

"Oh?"

"Nope, they ain't fighting over her this time. They were playing cards the other day, and after Hickok had won most of Dave's money, Dave reminded him of the thirty-five dollars Bill still owed him from another time they had played. Well, Wild Bill said he owed him only twenty-five dollars, and he laid it on the table in front of Tutt."

The old man appeared to warm to the subject, his fingers fondling the carving as he ran the sharp knife blade over the soft wood. "Tutt took his money all right, but he also took Wild Bill's gold watch that was a-laying there, saying he figured that would about make up for the other ten Bill owed him."

Bertram would have sworn that Tutt would have been a dead man before he could have gotten the watch in his pocket. "Wild Bill let him have the watch?"

"Oh, wouldn't say that exactly. Bill jumped up and told Tutt to put the watch back down on the table. But Dave ignored him and left with the watch anyway. The air's been real thick betwixt the two ever since."

"And that's what the shooting's about?"

"Yep. Wild Bill warned Tutt not to wear the watch in public, but he paid Bill no heed. Went right ahead and wore it anyway. We knowed something was bound to happen, and sure enough, it has."

A stream of tobacco flew across the porch and raised dust beside the walk. "Some of Tutt's men sent word to Bill that Dave would be crossing the square around six o'clock tonight if he wanted to try and get his watch back. Hickok sent word back that Dave wouldn't be carrying his watch across the square unless dead men had started walking." The old man cackled.

Bertram fumbled in his pocket and hastily withdrew his watch, noting with dismay that the appointed hour was upon them. "It's six o'clock now. Dave Tutt's a fool for taunting Hickok like that. Hickok will kill him for sure."

The old man leaned closer. "Maybe, maybe not. Dave Tutt ain't exactly shabby with a gun himself. But there's one thing for certain. Trouble like you ain't never seen is gonna break loose in a minute."

If there was one thing Bertram had no desire for, it was to become remotely entangled in a shoot-out on a public street with two known gunslingers. Even watching the spectacle held no interest for him. "Well, I think I'll just mosey on—" He turned when a breathless hush fell over the crowd.

Up the street to one side a bearded man stepped into view. About the same time another man with shoulder-length dark hair and a long brush of a mustache appeared on the opposite side of the square. The flat-crowned hat, black coat, and tucked shirt identified the second man as Wild Bill Hickok.

"You'd better stay on that side of the square if you want to live, Tutt," Hickok warned. His words echoed down the now-deserted town square.

Spellbound, Bertram watched the exchange.

Tutt made no effort to reply. But neither did he dally. He merely stepped out into the street, drawing his gun as he walked.

In a flash, Hickok drew, and both men fired at the same time. The bullet from Hickok's gun went straight through Tutt's heart, and he fell dead in a crumpled heap in the dusty street.

Hickok quickly whirled and pointed his gun in the direction of Tutt's friends, who by now had drawn their own weapons. "Holster those guns or there'll be more than one man dead here today."

Bertram had seen enough. He spun and started for cover. But as luck would have it, his foot caught on a loose board. It was like a hand had come out of the sidewalk and grabbed his ankle, jerking him to a sudden stop. He reeled off the porch onto the street, landing with a thud beneath the watering trough. His ankle throbbed with excruciating pain.

The old-timer jumped up from his chair and peered over the trough. On the square, Tutt's men slowly holstered their weapons and melted into the crowd.

With one final glance around him, Wild Bill calmly walked over to Tutt's body and recovered his gold Waltham watch and chain, then turned and sauntered to the courthouse to surrender his pistols to the sheriff.

"Here, boy. Let me help ya. Are you bad hurt?" The old man rolled Bertram over onto his back.

Bertram groaned and held on tightly to his rapidly swelling ankle. If he didn't get the boot off soon, he knew he'd have to cut it off, and he couldn't afford another pair.

"I think I busted my ankle." He gritted the words out. The pain was white-hot and searing. He was having trouble breathing, let alone talking.

The old man squatted beside him and gingerly rotated the injured foot.

"Aaagh!" Bertram screamed.

"Yore right," the old-timer said. He motioned for some of his cronies still sitting on the porch whittling to lend a helping hand. "We'll have to get you over to Doc Pierson's and let him have a look-see."

A busted ankle! If his foot didn't hurt so bad Bertram would have kicked something. That was all he needed now to lay him up again for another who knew how many weeks!

He groaned when four elderly men hovered above him. They seemed hardly strong enough to support their own weight, let alone carry him, but each man dutifully scooped up an arm or a leg. Bertram bit down, clenching his teeth, when they unceremoniously hauled him across the street to the doctor's office, like a wilted sack of flour, and folded him onto the doc's operating table.

"Take care of my horse," Bertram shouted as the old men melted back out the doorway.

"Shore will. He'll be at the livery," the old-timer assured him.

Bertram groaned. Now a livery bill! What else?

The doctor leaned over him. "All right, son, let's see what's happened here."

A firm hand clasped Bertram's boot, and he clamped his eyes shut when pain shot through his leg. He prayed to pass out.

CHAPTER 5

"The war's over, but there's still men out there in the bushes who don't know that yet." Cole glanced up and smiled at his mother, who had just cut him another thick slice of gooseberry pie. "Careful there, Ma; you're going to have me so big I can't get back on my horse," he complained, but Wynne noticed he had no trouble polishing off the second serving of dessert.

Now that Cole was freshly bathed and cleanly shaved, she had to admit he was even more handsome. Only his despicable disposition spoiled everything.

"You're skinny as a shitepoke," Lilly said, quickly slipping another piece of pie on Wynne's plate before she could stop her.

"Thank you, Lilly, but I really couldn't eat another bite," she protested. For two days she had sat at the dinner table and nearly burst. Willa's meals were large and plentiful. She was surprised at such an abundance of food on the table each day, especially when every other homestead she had passed while riding the stage seemed to be in a depressing state of shortage of even the barest essentials.

She had been surprised by the house too. True, whitewash and repairs were needed, but the home reflected an affluent life-style she'd not expected to find. The house was quite large, with the parlor and family rooms on the main floor. The five upstairs bedrooms, each furnished with a double bed, a clothespress, a nightstand, and a full-length mirror, were much like her room back home at Moss Oak.

There was also almost a Southern flavor to their lifestyle. Meals were at set times, and manners were observed religiously. The best china, glass, and silver had been used on the night of Cole and Beau's return, and in this house they thanked God for their food before every meal. All of this was comforting to Wynne, although it brought a faint sadness along with memories of the home she used to have that was now gone forever. The house was still there, of course, but what good was a house without the presence of the people who had made it a home?

Lilly's voice broke through her thoughts. "It wouldn't hurt for you to have a little more meat on your bones," she told Wynne as she busied herself refilling their cups with the dark chicory coffee that Wynne had come to despise. The brew was tangy and bitter, and she would just as soon do without than have to drink it.

"Praise the Lord the garden's doing well," Lilly murmured, almost as if she had read Wynne's mind. "And Elmo Ferguson's been seeing that we have fresh meat on the table at least twice a week."

"I'll have to stop by and thank Elmo for looking out for you," Cole said with a roguish twinkle in his eye. "I'll bet he's been invited in for a piece of sweet-potato pie every now and again."

"Oh, occasionally I've had one cooling on the windowsill,"

Lilly said. "So, you're a captain now. I'm real proud of you, son. Now you can settle down and see to the farm."

Wynne noted she had quickly changed the subject. She suspected Lilly didn't like to be teased about Elmo, and Cole knew it. It would be just like him to latch onto something a person didn't want to talk about and drag it into the conversation. He had to be one of the most contrary men ever to draw breath.

"Thanks, Ma—I'll help around here, but I'm going to look into that U.S. marshal job."

She frowned. "Oh, Cole, I wish you'd reconsider. Seems you love to put yourself in harm's way—a true man of the saddle."

He leaned over and pinched her cheek. "That's me, Ma, and law's my life. When the good Lord says it's my time to go, then I'll be leaving this old earth whether I'm hunting down a wanted man or sitting here eating fried chicken. Of course, I'd prefer the latter, but I'm not afraid of the former."

Wynne felt his eyes on her as she quietly pushed the second piece of pie aside. She didn't want to offend Lilly, who had immediately taken her in and treated her as part of the family, but she was stuffed as tight as a tick. "If you don't mind, I think I'll save this for a little later on," she murmured as she looked up and saw Cole watching her.

A set of cool, distant blue eyes locked obstinately with hers for a moment before he looked back down at his plate. "A lot of people would be glad to get that pie, Miss Elliot," he said curtly.

Wynne resented his attitude. For two long days Cole had purposely gone out of his way to ignore her, speaking to her only when forced to and, in general, treating her as if she were something he had picked up on his boot in the barnyard instead of a houseguest. She had tried to overcome the impression she had made at the stagecoach, but evidently Cole wasn't one to forgive and forget. Too bad *he* couldn't have spent some time at Miss Marelda Fielding's Finishing School. Miss Marelda would have taught him some manners.

Because Cole was beginning to fascinate her, she had taken the opportunity to observe him and his relationship with his mother. With Lilly, he was kind and thoughtful, even nice. Cole and Beau treated their mother with the utmost respect. There was genuine, honest warmth among them, evidenced daily by the continual bantering that volleyed back and forth in the household.

After being around Lilly for a couple of days, it wasn't hard to see where Beau had gotten his soft heart and sense of humor. Wynne only wished some of that goodwill had rubbed off on Cole. The tension between the two of them seemed to grow with each passing day, even though Wynne had gone out of her way to be pleasant to him. Well, if not out of her way, then she had at least made a conscious effort to be polite to him, far more than he had done for her.

"I'm aware there are people going to bed hungry tonight," she replied, daring him to look her in the eye, but when he complied, his eyes were so stern her hand reached feebly back for her fork. "Well . . . maybe a few more bites."

Cole polished off his pie and drank the chicory substitute for coffee. Now that he'd had time to observe Wynne Elliot, he realized she was pretty, about as pretty a woman as he'd ever seen, but she had the disposition of a bad-tempered sitting hen. Get too close to her private space and she could turn and flog a man until he ran for cover.

She was eating her pie now, and he felt a sneaky satisfaction that her capitulation had something to do with him. It was good to win one, even if it was over a piece of pie. He'd not won too many battles with Miss Elliot, which brought up an interesting question: what was she hiding? He didn't really care, but after spending four years fighting to survive he had developed certain instincts, and they were all on alert where this woman was concerned.

"That's all right, dear. I'll put the pie in the warming oven, and it will be there when you get hungry again." Lilly took her place at the end of the table and reached for her cup. "I wish Beau and Betsy would hurry and get back."

"They'll be here soon enough," Cole said. "You can't expect them to hurry. They'll have a lot to talk about. Four years is a long time."

"Too long." Lilly sighed. "I don't know how those two have endured the separation. They're so crazy about each other."

The sadness in his mother's voice made Cole realize those four years had taken a toll on the women left behind. Take Betsy for instance. There wasn't a school close to town anymore, so she had accepted a teaching job in a small community about twelve miles from River Run. She was there today, cleaning her schoolroom for the fall session. Beau had gone to help her and visit with her family for a few days. Seeing Beau and Betsy together again was good. The war had disrupted and destroyed too many lives. He was glad to see some sort of normalcy returning to his family. Beau and Betsy had a wedding to plan, and he intended to be there to kiss the bride.

This war had affected everybody. A state of martial law had existed in many areas during the past several years. Schools had closed, and churches had been disbanded. But the small community of Red Springs, where Betsy taught, had not been directly affected by the fighting. Although the community could barely afford to provide a roof over the new teacher's head and three meals a day, the board wanted its children's education to go on uninterrupted, and Betsy had answered the call.

She was a woman to be proud of, and Beau was a lucky man. For a minute Cole wished he could find a woman who would suit him as well. He cast a sour glance at the female sitting across from him. If he ever found one, she'd be as different from Wynne Elliot as possible.

He pushed away from the table. "That was some meal, Ma. I wish you and Willa had gone along to cook for us. Army cooks have a lot to learn."

No, he didn't really wish that. He never wanted the women in his family to see what he had seen. He wasn't sorry he'd gone to war, but he sure hoped he never had to fight in another one. Seemed like war brought out the worst in a man.

Outside, the sound of hoofbeats interrupted the early twilight. Several riders rode up to the house and reined to a halt.

"Now who could that be?" Lilly frowned. "It's nigh onto dark, and I can't think of a neighbor who would come calling at this hour."

She hurried over to pull the curtain aside to peek out, and Cole reached for his gun belt hanging on a peg next to the back door.

"Why, it's the sheriff," Lilly announced, her face breaking into a friendly smile. She pulled the door open and hurried outside onto the porch, leaving Cole and Wynne to follow.

No one could argue that at fifty-two the sheriff of Laxton County wasn't still a fine figure of a man. His six-foot-three frame sat in the saddle with an air of undisputed authority. The hint of gray in his sideburns was the only concession to getting older; his dark, hazel eyes were as clear and sharp as they had been thirty years ago. His body was honed as hard as steel, and the elements had tanned his skin to a deep bronze. Cole wondered if the ladies of River Run still blushed when he turned his smile in their direction.

"Evening, Lilly." Tal tipped his hat politely, his eyes warm and his smile extra friendly. Lilly smiled and blushed, fussing with her hair as Tal slid out of his saddle and handed the reins to one of his deputies.

Cole half turned as Wynne came up to stand beside him. He was suddenly conscious of her in a way he didn't like. She smelled pretty—and she looked . . . complete. Sort of put together in a way that didn't have much to do with her physical build. She fit somehow. He sniffed. What was that scent? Lemon? Ma must have loaned her some of her special shampoo. That meant his mother liked the Elliot woman, which might prove to be a problem if he found out what she was really up to. When his mother gave her approval to someone, she pretty well stuck with it.

Wynne's voice broke into his thoughts. "Are the sheriff and your mother . . . attracted to each other?" she whispered.

Cole glared at her. What did she mean by that? No better woman ever lived than Ma, and she wasn't the kind to be "attracted" to men. She was a decent, God-fearing woman who had raised her children right and had never looked for any man to replace Pa.

He stared at her coldly. "I wouldn't know."

"Oh, they both are," she said. "Can't you see the way they're looking at each other?"

The outrageous notion took Cole by surprise. He'd never considered his mother looking at another man that way—at least no one other than Elmo. Elmo was harmless.

"No, they're not," he said curtly.

Lilly's and Tal's heads snapped up at the sound of his annoyed tone. "Did you say something, dear?" Lilly called.

"No." Cole lowered his voice. "You have an overactive imagination, Miss Elliot. And remember, that's my mother you're talking about."

Wynne glanced at him, looking surprised. "I know she's your mother. I wasn't casting any aspersions on her. *You* obviously don't have a romantic bone in your entire body. I was making a simple observation."

"Well, stop making observations. Ma's got a full life here." What else could he expect from some soft Southern lady? Wynne Elliot probably never did a day's work in her life. She wouldn't have any ideas about real life. Probably couldn't imagine a woman being capable of handling her business without a man's help. He couldn't imagine her raising three small children on a hill-land farm with only Willa to help, the way Ma had done. It took grit and common sense to do that. While he had to admit Wynne Elliot had plenty of grit, such as it was, she was definitely lacking in the common-sense department. Still, her remarks bothered him.

He turned back to stare at his mother and Tal. *Ma and the sheriff?* The two were about the same age, and now that he thought about it, they were both reasonably good-looking people. He studied his mother in a new light. She still had a youthful, trim figure, laughing blue eyes, and pretty dark blonde hair with only a few threads of gray running through it. He realized she was beautiful. From the look on Tal's face, he was of the same opinion. But Cole knew his mother. She wasn't looking for another man. Last thing on her mind.

He growled in Wynne's ear, "Pa died in a hunting accident after my youngest brother was born, and Ma has never looked at another man except old Elmo, and that's purely in a friendly fashion—nothing more."

Wynne smiled at him sweetly. "It isn't my fault you can't see what's right under your nose."

He snorted. "That bird on your hat must have pecked a hole in your head."

She made a face at him and he itched to walk off, but she'd probably follow him, and besides, Ma would be upset if he acted rude in front of Tal.

"Won't you and your men come in and have some supper with us?" Lilly asked as the sheriff reached for a small leather pouch tied to his saddle horn.

"Can't, Lilly. The men want to get on home before dark. I stopped by to bring Miss Elliot something." He held the bag in his right hand, but Cole noticed Tal's attention was still centered solely on his mother. He wished the Elliot woman had kept quiet about her suspicions. He didn't need her putting foolish thoughts in his head. And he sure wasn't going to mention it to Ma. No use getting her to start thinking about things she had no business thinking about. She had enough on her plate without taking on a man.

Wynne approached the posse. "You have something for me, Sheriff?"

Tal colored slightly and diverted his attention from Lilly, obviously trying to get his mind back on the business at hand. Cole glowered at him. If the subject ever came up so it was convenient, he'd let Tal know there was no need to be getting notional about Ma. She wouldn't welcome the attention.

"Uh, yes, Miss Elliot, ma'am." Tal held the small pouch out to her. "We brought your ring back."

Wynne smiled and hurried down the porch steps to accept the bag. Cole watched as she loosened the drawstring and dumped the pearl ring out into the palm of her hand. The iridescent pearl centered on the gold band gleamed softly in the dim light. "Oh, this is marvelous! Where did you find it?"

"Down the road apiece from where the stage was held up. Must have dropped out of the bag when the Beasons was trying to make their getaway."

Cole had stepped off the porch to come stand beside Wynne, thinking it was time he got Ma off the hook. The way she blushed, she was probably embarrassed at Tal's attention— or if she wasn't she should have been.

The sheriff nodded at him. "Evening, Cole."

"Evening, Tal." Cole glanced at the ring in Wynne's hand. It didn't look like much to him, but he knew womenfolk, and the little circlet of gold and pearl probably had sentimental value to her. "This all you were able to find?"

"Afraid so," the sheriff admitted. "The gang seems to have

gotten clean away this time, but as soon as me and my men rest up we're going out again."

Tal didn't have to say he had his doubts about his manhunt turning out to be anything but useless. Cole knew these hills, and he knew how easy it would be for a few men to disappear into some lonely hollow and never be seen again. He'd heard the Beasons had a cave hideout somewhere. Could be anywhere. These hills were riddled with underground caverns known to only a few people.

Wynne's shoulders drooped, and for a moment Cole felt sorry for her. "Do you think you can recover the rest of my belongings?"

The sheriff shook his head. "It's been two days since the robbery. Those men are no doubt long gone by now. Like I said, we'll try, but I can't make any promises."

"Thank you anyway, Sheriff." Wynne sighed. "I'm thankful that you were able to recover my ring."

"We'll try to pick up the Beasons' trail in the morning," he promised her.

"You sure you won't come in and at least have a cup of coffee with us?" Lilly invited again, but the sheriff swung into his saddle.

Wynne looked over at Cole and grinned smugly. He shot her a censuring look. If she said one word to make it look like Ma was inviting the sheriff in for any reason except in a purely neighborly fashion, he'd straighten her out in a hurry. It was bad enough he had to have the Elliot woman in his home without her going out of her way to stir up trouble.

The sheriff shook his head. "I'd love to, Lilly, but we need to be getting along. Some other time, I promise."

"Thanks for your trouble, Tal." Cole reached out and shook the older man's hand. Tal hadn't needed to come by tonight to bring that piddling little pearl ring. It had been nice of him to do so, but Cole would be foolish to let an addlebrained Southern belle get him all het up over a so-called attraction between his mother and the sheriff. Trust Wynne to get all stirred up over some imagined romantic nonsense.

"No trouble," Tal said. "Just wish I could have gotten the rest of the little lady's things back for her." He tipped his hat politely at Wynne and Lilly. "Evening, ladies."

Cole nodded as the posse rode away. Just as he thought. A friendly gesture on the sheriff's part. No call to think otherwise.

Wynne watched with a heavy heart as the small group of riders left the yard in a cloud of dust.

Cole and Lilly had already started back to the house when her gaze dropped to her tightly clasped hand. She opened it slowly, feeling a mist of tears rise unexpectedly in her eyes as she stared at the ring cradled in her palm. One pearl ring. Not much to show for her life, but that was all she had left of the personal possessions she had brought with her. All her money was gone, her other jewelry, which would have been worth much more than the ring, lost. Of course, there was still Moss Oak, but that was of no value at all right now. Home was merely an empty house and a piece of land with charred fields and no owner to oversee its use. Even sadder was the thought that she didn't have anyone to care, much less to help her with her plight.

Lord, I never expected things to get this bad. It's just been one blow after another. These people have been good to me, taking me in like this, but I can't stay here forever. With both Papa and Mama gone, I don't have anyone except You to hold on to.

A memory of her plans popped into her head. Was her current run of bad luck because God wasn't happy with her plans for revenge?

She sighed. Well, right or wrong, here she was, and it looked like she had burned about every bridge behind her.

CHAPTER 6

Late Saturday afternoon, Beau returned from Red Springs with Betsy. Wynne watched while he lifted his fiancée down from the buckboard as carefully as if his hands held a precious jewel. He stole a brief but thorough kiss before he set her lightly on her feet.

The young woman turned a pretty pink, but her eyes shone with a radiant love. She primly straightened her hat and tried to pretend displeasure with Beau's rowdy ways, but it was plain to see she enjoyed his teasing.

Wynne felt a stab of jealousy. If Cass Claxton hadn't been such a muleheaded deceiver, she would be a married woman with a husband to love and protect her instead of being alone on this wild frontier. Of course, if she had Cass here right now she'd shoot him, which wouldn't help her situation a whole lot.

Beau grinned at Wynne. "I see you're still here."

"I'll be leaving soon. The sheriff came by and said he hadn't been able to recover my money—but he did find my ring." Wynne held out her hand to show him the recovered pearl ring.

He leaned closer, clearly impressed. "Well, that's more than I thought he would find." He introduced her to Betsy, and Wynne liked the young woman at first glance. Betsy had an air of innocence about her that was refreshing. Judging from his air of pride, you could bet Beau wouldn't leave her waiting at the altar.

"Beau told me all about the robbery," Betsy said. "I know it must have been terrible for you. What about your family? Will they be worried?"

"I don't have anyone," Wynne confessed. Seeing Beau and Betsy together had brought home to her how alone she really was. She did have Tilly, the black servant who had taken care of her most of her life, but that was all. She wasn't even sure Tilly was still there. Wynne hadn't told her old friend where she was going when she left. What would she do after she found Cass and meted out the punishment he had coming? She could go home to Savannah, and probably would someday, but not right now. At the moment she had unfinished business in River Run.

"You find that man you were looking for?" Beau asked.

"Are you looking for someone?" Lilly asked, looking interested. "Who might that be?"

Wynne blushed. "Just an acquaintance."

"Friend?"

She smiled. "Acquaintance."

"Well, that's good news," Lilly said. "When you find your gentlemen you'll have someone to take care of you. A woman doesn't have any business traveling alone these days. It's too dangerous."

Wynne kept quiet, feeling anything she had to say about her so-called acquaintance would fail to ease Lilly's fears. She wished Beau hadn't brought it up. She couldn't tell Lilly what she had in mind. Lilly was a lady. Well, so was she. A graduate of Miss Fielding's school. But she had a mission, and while Lilly might sympathize with her, she couldn't expect anyone else to understand the anger and humiliation that drove her to follow a man across several states with the intention of killing him. She wasn't sure she understood it herself.

Beau left to see about the horses, and the three women were alone. Lilly made a big fuss over Betsy, telling her how much she had missed seeing her in church on Sunday mornings, while Betsy smiled and nodded. Wynne felt left out. Lilly looped her arm through her future daughter-in-law's and walked her around to the side of the house to show her how well her flower bed was doing this year.

Wynne trailed behind, listening to the two women chatter about flowers and remembering the lovely gardens that had surrounded her home in Savannah. Her mother had loved flowers too, but the gardens had gone to ruin long ago. Trampled under soldiers' feet. The Yankees hadn't cared what they were doing to people's lives or property. They had come to destroy. Beau and Cole had worn those blue uniforms too, but somehow she couldn't imagine them taking part in the wanton destruction of the sort that had taken place at Moss Oak.

"I have to water every evening," Lilly confessed. "If it doesn't rain soon, I'll have to stop. I can't have the well going dry, and the vegetable garden's going to need watering more than these flowers do."

She leaned down to touch a delicate lavender petal. "They sure are pretty, though. The world's seen too little beauty since the war began. Too little beauty, too little happiness, too many tears. But thank God it's over now."

"They're truly lovely," Betsy said.

Wynne bent down to smell a big pink zinnia. Yes, the war was over, but putting her life back together would take a long time. A lot of people had lost everything, though. She at least had a house, and Lilly's home had been spared. They had a lot to be thankful for.

Beau rejoined them. "I've taken care of the horse and buckboard, and my stomach is reminding me I haven't eaten since early this morning. I hope we haven't missed supper."

Lilly laughed. "No, Willa's frying chicken, and I was just getting ready to put the biscuits in the oven."

Beau sniffed the air appreciatively. The aroma of meat sizzling in hot fat filled the late afternoon. "I hope she's fixed plenty."

"There'll be enough, Son." Lilly had a sad expression as she patted his arm. Wynne knew she was remembering that this child of hers had gone with bare rations and little or no meat while he was fighting. Maybe that accounted for the large quantity of food Willa put on the table every day. Trying to make up for all the hardships Lilly's sons had endured. War was hard on everyone—the ones who went and fought and the ones who were left behind.

They started for the house, catching up on the news as they walked. "Cole rode into town this morning to see what kind of supplies he could buy," Lilly said. "He should be back anytime now."

"It will be so good to see him again." Betsy smiled. "Beau says he's fine."

"He looks real good." Lilly beamed. "Thin, like this one here, but I'll have them both filled out in no time at all."

Wynne had liked Betsy from the start. They became friends almost immediately. She missed her friends back home and at the school. Betsy was the first person her own age she felt at ease with since coming to Missouri. There was Penelope, of course, but she had an entirely different way of looking at life. No, she didn't have much in common with Penelope. Betsy was different.

Lilly went to the kitchen to help Willa, and Wynne followed Betsy upstairs and waited while she washed and changed her travel-stained dress before supper. She sat on the side of the bed and listened attentively as Betsy chattered on about how she had known all of Beau's family since she was born, and how she had been in love with Beau for as long as she could remember. Wynne sighed. Would she ever have someone she could love, who would love her in return the way Betsy and Beau loved each other? She tried not to be jealous, but she couldn't help remembering her own disastrous venture into romance.

Cole rode into the courtyard as they were starting back down the stairway.

"Now that's another man who's going to make some lucky woman a fine husband one of these days," Betsy confided in hushed secrecy. "Isn't he about the most handsome thing you've ever seen? I mean, next to my Beau, of course."

Wynne hesitated to dash Betsy's high opinion of Cole by admitting that she wasn't impressed with Beau's older brother in the least. Oh, he looked well enough if you didn't mind his arrogant, overbearing manner. But *lucky* wasn't the word she'd apply to the woman unfortunate enough to hitch up with brother Cole.

"I suppose he would appeal to some women," Wynne replied evasively.

"Some women? Are you serious?" Betsy laughed, a delightful tinkling sound, like the wind chimes that had hung in the garden back home. "My older sister, Priscilla June? Why, she would absolutely swoon if Cole would ask her the time of day."

"Really?" Wynne forced her tone to remain agreeable. "What's the matter? Can't Cole tell time?"

Betsy looked blank for a moment then broke out in a fit of giggles. "Oh, Wynne, you're so funny!" Her cornflower blue eyes widened expectantly. "Listen, are you spoken for? Or is the gentleman you're looking for your fiancé?"

"No." Wynne smiled. "The man I'm looking for is not my fiancé." *Or a gentleman,* she longed to add but didn't. Maybe when she got to know Betsy a little better, she would confide in her about Cass. It would be nice to have someone to talk to, and somehow she sensed Betsy would understand and sympathize if she just knew the facts. But that had to wait until they knew each other better.

"Then you're not spoken for?" Betsy's grin widened. Her expression had matchmaker written all over it.

"I don't care to be," Wynne added quickly. "I've decided to be a spinster." She had even given serious thought to entering a convent as soon as she found Cass and took her revenge. By then she would have a whole list of grievances to be considered. The thought gave her sudden pause. Maybe she wouldn't be good enough to join a convent. They must have requirements. Killing a man probably wasn't one of them.

Betsy's face wilted with disappointment. "Oh, my, what a shame. . . ."

"Yes, isn't it," Wynne agreed serenely. "Some women just aren't meant for marriage, and I fear I'm one of them." She led the way down the last few steps, hoping her expression would convince Betsy the subject was closed.

Willa was setting heaping platters of fried chicken on the table when they entered the dining room and sat down at the long, well-appointed table.

Beau smiled at Betsy when she picked up her napkin and placed it in her lap. Cole started to pass a bowl of potatoes and completely ignored Wynne as she took the chair opposite him. She twitched impatiently. The man had the manners of a goat. How could a son raised by a lady like Lilly behave in such an obnoxious manner?

"We'll have prayer first," Lilly admonished, and Cole promptly set the potatoes down as they all bowed their heads.

"Lord, we thank You for the bounty we are about to receive, and for giving us another beautiful day of life," Lilly said softly. "We thank You that you've seen fit to put a stop to this terrible war, and I want to tell You again how much I appreciate You looking over Cole and Beau, and sending them home to me, safe and sound. I'm mighty beholden to You, Lord.

"If it wouldn't be too much bother, I'd ask that You send my baby home real soon, because I'm worrying about him something powerful too. But I know You have a lot of things on Your mind right now, and I want You to know I'm not demanding anything, just wanted to remind You about my baby in case You might have forgotten. If You have time, Lord, we could sure use some rain. Garden's getting awful dry, and the well's threatening to do the same.

"Well, guess I'll close now. Supper's getting cold. Wanted

You to know we love You, and ask that You'll forgive us for anything we might have done today that You wouldn't be right proud of. We didn't mean You any harm, Lord. You've been mighty good to us, and we won't be forgetting that. Amen."

"Amen," Cole and Beau echoed.

"Now—" Lilly looked up and smiled—"you may pass the potatoes, Cole."

"You know, Wynne, I've been doing some thinking about that robbery," Beau said while he spooned a mound of pole beans onto his plate. "You think you could recognize those men if you ever saw them again?"

Wynne glanced up, surprised at the question. "I don't know; they wore masks, but one of them did pull his off momentarily. I might recognize him." She suppressed a shudder at the memory of the outlaw's yellowed teeth and rancid breath.

"Well, I was wondering . . ." Beau hesitated. "Cole, you don't think that Frank and Jesse had anything to do with it, do you?"

"Frank and Jesse?" Lilly answered before Cole could. "Why, those James boys wouldn't do anything like that!"

Cole spared his mother an indulgent look. "Ma, Frank and Jesse have been riding with Quantrill's Raiders, and they certainly haven't been holding Sunday school picnics."

"And since when have I gone addlebrained? Their pa was a preacher, if you recall. And those boys were good boys; at least they were until the Jayhawkers took it in their heads to persecute them."

Wynne's mind was not solely on the conversation but rather on how she was going to get through another meal without popping the buttons on her dress. Now she looked up, caught by the unfamiliar word. "What is a Jayhawker?"

"Missouri is mostly Southern sympathizers," Beau explained. "Some of the men would up and march right over the border and kill all the Kansans they could find. Of course, the Kansans didn't take right friendly to that sort of thing, so they up and marched right back and knocked a few Missourians' heads together. Missouri men were called Bushwhackers; the Kansans were called Jayhawkers or sometimes Redlegs."

Cole glanced up, a steaming biscuit in his hand. "Or sometimes something not all that complimentary."

"Who are Frank and Jesse?" Wynne asked, passing the bowl of potatoes to the left.

"Frank and Jesse James." Beau repeated the names as if they should mean something to her.

"You sound as if you know them personally," Wynne said.

Cole shrugged. "Our paths have crossed a few times."

"Frank and Jesse floated in and out of Missouri during the war," Beau told her. "There's not a better place to hide than in these hills and hollers. We've got some of the roughest country you'll ever see. A man could get lost a hundred feet from his cabin in a few of those valleys, and down around the White River country is about the best place to start. There's where you'll find Frank and Jesse, if you're looking for them."

"Well, I'm not," Wynne said. "And I hope I never have the occasion to meet them." She had her own particular men problems. So Missouri was mostly Southern, but Beau and Cole had worn blue. She met Cole's eyes, and apparently he saw and recognized the question in hers.

His chin firmed. "I never felt comfortable with owning another human being, Miss Elliot. You got a problem with that?"

Wynne shook her head. "Certainly not." She wasn't about to

refight the War Between the States sitting at Lilly's dining-room table. That would be right unmannerly. Not that it would bother Cole in the least. He didn't have any manners to speak of anyway.

Lilly shook her head. "Next thing you know, those boys will be robbing banks."

Beau gave Betsy another moonstruck grin and picked up the bowl of poke greens and handed it to her. She shook her head, and he smiled with the most besotted expression Wynne had ever witnessed. Betsy didn't know how blessed she was.

"Have you and Betsy thought about a date for your wedding?" Lilly inquired.

"Thinking about maybe the last Sunday in October." Beau grinned. "It'll be cooling off by then."

Betsy's face flamed scarlet. She hurriedly groped for her water glass to avoid choking on the bite of chicken she had in her mouth.

"I mean . . . well, what I meant is . . . I thought . . . ," Beau stammered, his face turning as red as his fiancée's.

"I think we know what you meant, Beau," Cole said dryly.

"Well . . . no . . . you see, what I meant was—"

"What he meant was he and Betsy want to wait until early fall to get married so that Cass will be back home," Lilly intervened mercifully. "There'll be no marriage in the Claxton family unless the whole clan's present to wish Beau and Betsy well."

Wynne's fork clattered off the side of her plate, and four pairs of eyes switched in her direction all at once.

Cass Claxton.

Had she heard wrong? She fervently prayed she had.

"Are you all right, dear?" Lilly's fork paused in midair, and she peered anxiously at her guest.

Wynne realized that her face had suddenly gone white. She had actually felt the blood drain all the way to her toes. "No . . . I . . ." Her mind churned with confusion. Had she actually heard Lilly say Cass Claxton was her son? No—it wasn't possible, yet Lilly had clearly said *Cass* would be home and the *Claxton* family would be together. Well, wouldn't this rock your boat? She'd been dropped right into the viper's own nest this time! *Well, Lord, what do I do now?* If there was a way out of this mess she couldn't see it. How could she kill Cass in front of his mother? Particularly since Lilly and Beau had been so kind to her.

"Wynne?" Betsy's concerned voice slowly seeped through her paralyzed stupor. "Are you ill?"

Even Cole had stopped eating. She could feel his eyes on her when she removed her napkin from her lap and rose carefully on shaky limbs. She had to get out of this room before she fainted. "If you'll excuse me," she blurted, "I think I need a bit of fresh air."

She turned and bolted out of the room, knowing the others at the table were staring at one another in bewilderment. How could she ever explain her behavior?

Cole pursed his lips, thinking about Wynne's hurried escape from the table. What had set her off like that? He had been suspicious of her from the start, and he had a feeling he was close to finding out what the woman was up to. She looked like she'd had a sudden jolt.

"My word, what do you suppose happened?" Lilly asked.

"I can't imagine!" Betsy exclaimed.

"Maybe all that talk of war and Frank and Jesse upset her," Beau said.

Betsy rose from her chair. "I'd better go see about her—"

"Let her be, Betsy." Cole let his voice slice through the air.

Betsy whirled and faced him. "But, Cole, she might be ill. . . ."

"Finish your supper," he snapped. "If she was sick, she would have said so." If anyone checked on Miss Wynne Elliot it would be him. He had some questions to ask her, and it was time he got some answers.

Betsy glanced expectantly at Lilly.

"He's right, dear. Maybe the past few days have finally caught up with her and she needs time alone," Lilly said. "Why don't we give her a few minutes to herself, and then one of us will go check on her?"

Betsy obediently sank back in her chair. "Well . . . maybe just a few minutes, but then I'm going to see about her."

They finished the meal in strained silence. Betsy looked upset, and Lilly didn't have her usual composure, but with Cole's eyes on them, they stayed at the table. When Willa brought coffee and dessert, Cole stood up and excused himself and left the room.

He looked over his shoulder and noticed more than a few relieved looks being exchanged.

CHAPTER 7

Wynne stood on the front porch, arms gripping her waist so tightly she could hardly draw breath. *Where do I go from here? Oh, why, Lord?* Why did it have to be Cass's brothers who had befriended her? Hadn't she been hurt enough by the Claxton men?

She swiped angrily at the tears that suddenly threatened her composure. The Claxton family was probably wondering why she had left the room so quickly. How could she face them again? Right now she couldn't think of a convincing explanation for her behavior.

She stepped off the porch and looked up at the sun, sinking in a big, fiery orange ball behind the grove of cherry trees on the west side of the house. She headed in that direction. The hot air, so still and heavy, made breathing difficult. A furnace-blast wind burned her flushed cheeks, and she wondered when, if ever, she'd felt so betrayed, so emotionally wronged.

Where are You, God? Why don't You do something to help with all of these problems that keep coming, one after another, until I'm so overwhelmed I don't know what to do next?

When she was a small child, she'd healed disappointments and cried out her frustrations in the arms of a gnarled tree at Moss Oak. Somehow she'd drawn strength and security from that old tree. The cherry grove here seemed to beckon as though the trees would offer refuge for her inward turmoil, a haven for the chaos that had again come so unexpectedly.

Once she'd reached the shelter of the grove, she sank down in a thick carpet of grass. Above her, fruit was sparsely scattered about the branches. The aroma of sunbaked earth, sweet cherries, and the sultry end of a summer day teased her senses. Overcome with sadness and defeat, she dropped her face into her hands and let the tears flow.

After a few minutes she managed to regain control of her emotions. Betsy might come looking for her, and she didn't dare be caught crying. She had enough to explain as it was. She rubbed the backs of both hands across her cheeks and sniffed like an injured child.

The leaves on the cherry trees rustled in the evening breeze like gossipy women. The grass beneath her was soft and already turning brown. High, puffy clouds that held no promise of moisture burned in the afterglow of the sun's rays. Lilly was right, she thought dismally. If it didn't rain soon, everything was going to dry up and blow away. She hiccuped. Maybe, if she was lucky, the wind would take her right along with it.

She tilted her head, staring up at the sky through the tree branches. *Fool! Fool! You've done it again! Made a complete fool of yourself by stumbling right into the arms of Cass's family.* She buried her face in her hands again, wanting to hide from the world. The irony of the situation struck her, and she chuckled mirthlessly. Lowering her hands to her lap, she stared at a distant line of trees. What was she supposed to do now?

Her restless fingers found a loose thread hanging from the waist of her dress. Yielding to irritation, she twitched the fine string off and tossed it away. *Literally thousands of people between here and Savannah, but who did Almighty God send to rescue me?* She laughed out loud, a bitter sound in the evening quiet of the orchard. *Cass Claxton's brothers! That's who.* Even sent his dear saint of a mother to feed and shelter her. If it hadn't been so ironically funny, she would have bawled. She angrily brushed away ready tears.

Lord, I don't understand. Why, out of all the people in this world, would You let me stumble into this nest of vipers?

That wasn't fair, of course. Lilly and Beau were nice. So was Willa, and Betsy was a darling. Only Cole and Cass were snakes.

She leaned back against a tree, resting her head against its thick trunk. A hopeless sigh escaped her as she pondered the disturbing similarities in Cass and his family. Not his whole family, of course, but that rotten Cole was just like his brother— cold, calculating, and totally heartless. He'd never done anything spontaneous in his life, she'd bet. And he thought her the most foolish thing in the world—and he just might be right.

She was always reacting without thinking, but she'd thought out well what she'd do to Cass Claxton. She had a plan and she was going to work that plan and nothing would stop her.

It didn't matter that his family had taken her in when she had no place else to go. Nothing could change the enormity of what Cass had done to her. He couldn't toy with her feelings and steal her money without paying for it! And now that she was in the confines of his family she could no longer delay putting her plan into effect.

For days she'd lingered, praying that Sheriff Franklin would be able to recover her money, but now that she knew she was staying with Cass's family, she would have to move on. Oh, granted, she could just sit right here and wait for the rat to return to his nest. That would be the easiest way to handle the situation. Lilly had no idea who she was or her intentions—nor for that matter did Cole or Beau. Cass would undoubtedly return home one day soon, and she could shoot him and then be on her way.

Her hand absently toyed with her worry stone. But she had to face facts. If she stayed around until Cass returned, it was possible she would let slip what she was about to do, and then Cole would thwart her plan. She shot a dirty look toward the house. He'd love to get the best of her.

Her conscience nagged her. She sighed. Well, all right. Staying here wouldn't be ethical. Not if she planned to shoot Cass on sight. She couldn't very well kill him in front of his mother. She owed Lilly that much. No, she would have to make other arrangements.

The pearl ring the sheriff had returned would be her ticket to freedom. She would walk into town first thing tomorrow morning and see if the bank would accept the jewelry as collateral on a loan.

Wynne felt better now that she had a plan. The bank would lend her a small sum. She'd only need enough to live on for a few weeks while she continued her search for Cass. It wouldn't take a great deal. Only enough for food and lodging, and she would assure the banker that she ate very little and required a minimum amount of sleep. She was aware it was a rather slim hope that she might encounter Cass while he was on the trail, but at this point she really had little other choice.

And who knew? Maybe she would be lucky and find him right away. Wynne sat up straight. She might get even luckier and he would still have a portion of her money on him. After all, she was overdue for a stroke of luck. She glanced back at the Claxton farmhouse. Long overdue.

Her stomach felt slightly queasy at the prospect of removing personal belongings off a dead man, for that's exactly what Mr. Claxton would be two minutes after she found him. She'd come this far, so she supposed she could do anything she had to do. At least if Cass was dead, she could search his pockets without fear of his objecting.

Once her mission was accomplished, she could return to Savannah and try to rebuild her life. She'd have to make some recompense to God for carrying out her plans for revenge. Wynne had an uneasy feeling that simply admitting she was sorry wouldn't be quite enough for the Almighty.

Her mind went back to her Sunday school lessons and the Ten Commandments. "Thou shalt not kill." That was rather plain speaking on God's part. But it wasn't as if she really *wanted* to kill Cass. Killing a man, even if he did deserve to die for what he'd done, did not please her. But death was the only suitable punishment for a man like Cass. Left to live, he'd do the same thing to yet another unsuspecting woman with stars in her eyes. Surely God wouldn't want that to happen.

Looking at it another way, God probably knew Cass needed killing, and Wynne was the weapon He chose to use. In that sense, she had a *responsibility* to shoot the sorry excuse of a man on sight.

Why had she not realized immediately that Cole was Cass's brother? Why had she thought the similarities were only coincidental? The brothers looked so much alike it was almost scary, but she had been so preoccupied with all her other problems she never dreamed fate would throw another Claxton in her path! What were the chances of something like that happening? Wynne fixed her eyes on the first star of the night. She had delayed long enough. Tomorrow she would take up her search for Cass Claxton again, and with God's help, she would find him.

Cole strode toward the orchard, his eyes on Wynne as she sat staring at the branches of the cherry tree overhead. She appeared to have calmed down, but something had upset her. He waited to see if she would bolt and run when he approached.

The muggy air had a hint of reprieve. The sky was clear, the evening stars barely visible. It was his favorite time of the day. He decided he'd wasted enough time watching a sharp-tongued female who barely had a passing acquaintance with the truth. She may have Ma and the others fooled, but she wasn't getting anything by him. He could smell a liar at twenty paces. Wynne Elliot was up to something, and he meant to find out what.

"You didn't finish your supper."

She started at the unexpected intrusion, then stiffened, her body language indicating the last thing she wanted was to put up with his company. "I suddenly lost my appetite."

"So I noticed." He leaned against a tree opposite her, his gaze narrowed on her averted face. "I hope it wasn't anything we said that caused your sudden . . . indisposition."

Defiance gleamed in the eyes she lifted to meet his. "Certainly not. What would make you think that?" Her chin tilted at an angle that said she didn't care what he thought, and the sharpness of her voice indicated that it was none of his business.

He shrugged. "No reason—just thought it a shame to leave so much food on your plate when others are going to bed hungry." He tipped his hat back and crossed his arms over his chest.

She shifted beneath his penetrating gaze, staring down at her hands, which now rested primly in her lap. Finally she raised her eyes to meet his scrutiny. "Do I have food on my face?"

"No."

"Then why are you staring at me?"

Cole's shoulders lifted. "I was just wondering how you could keep such a straight face and lie the way you do."

Her gaze dropped back to her hands. "I have no idea what you're talking about."

He made a clucking sound with his tongue and shook his head. "Didn't that fancy school you went to back East teach you that a lady never tells stories? At least not the big whopping ones you've been telling lately."

Anger flared in her eyes before she looked away. "Mr. Claxton, did you want anything in particular, or are you here merely to heckle me?"

"Heckle you? My time is more valuable that that. A prissy little old thing like you bothers too easy." He watched her face redden under the impact of his words and wondered if she would flare up in a temper fit. He hoped so. Sometimes people said more if they were angry than they ever would when they were calm.

"I'm not prissy." She absently picked at a loose string around her waist. He watched as she jerked at the thread, unraveling it a bit further.

Cole studied her as she sat under that tree, picking at a string on her dress. Soft hands, pale skin—never did a day's work in her life. All fluff and ruffles with a bird on her hat. She wasn't wearing the hat now, of course, but any female who would pick out something like that and no doubt pay good money for it . . . He pitied the poor soul who hitched up with her, and the words were on the tip of his tongue to say so, but he wasn't inclined to start another argument. He had more important issues to discuss with Miss Elliot.

He pushed away from the tree and edged closer to where she sat absently wrapping the loose thread around her finger. "Mind if I set a spell?" he asked.

She shrugged. "Never known a polecat to ask for permission to do anything."

Well, now, he was going to ignore that remark. They sat in silence, gazing at the hovering clouds brushed with rose and pearl gray by the fiery blaze of the departed sun. "Going to be a nice night," he observed pleasantly.

She shrugged again.

"Willa can sure fry chicken, can't she?"

Wynne slid a sideways glance at him as if she wondered why he was being so cordial all of a sudden. She jerked another string off her dress. "Yes."

He removed his hat and laid it on the grass beside him. It

had been a long day, and he was tired. He leaned back against the tree trunk, gazing off into the western sky ablaze with purples and oranges and golds where the sun had disappeared from view. "It's good to be home."

"Were you away long?"

"Four years. Seemed like a lifetime."

"And Beau was gone that long too?"

"We left about the same time." Cole studied her from beneath lowered lashes, watching to see how she reacted. "My youngest brother, Cass, hasn't returned yet."

Wynne's back stiffened perceptibly. Her voice sounded remote, as if she was totally detached from the subject. "How sad. Where is he?"

"Fighting—like Beau and I. Last I heard he was in South Carolina."

Her mouth dropped open, and she shot him a surprised look that didn't quite come off. "He's been away fighting?"

Cole hunched down more comfortably. "When I left, Cass was supposed to stay around and help Ma with the farm. We even paid to have a man fight in his place, but it seems he took off a while back to visit family in Savannah, and then all of a sudden he decided to join up." He glanced at her, watching her expression. "You sounded a little surprised, Miss Elliot. Any particular reason?"

"No, I—I'm just surprised. I thought he was just away— maybe on business . . . somewhere."

"No, he's been in the war," Cole repeated. "He didn't join until late in the conflict. Ma's pretty worried about him. You heard her at the supper table. She's hoping he'll ride in any day now."

Wynne pulled at another string on her dress. "She hasn't heard anything from him lately?"

"No, but he'll not keep her worrying for long." Cole observed with interest the rising flush of color staining her cheeks.

"How gallant of him!"

Cole's eyes snapped up to meet hers. Sarcasm? "Gallant?"

She shot a look at him that he didn't have any trouble reading. She knew Cass; she just didn't plan to admit it.

"I mean, that will be very considerate of him," she amended. "I hope he's fared as well as you and Beau."

Cole momentarily turned his attention back to the fading sunset. "Yeah, that's what we're all hoping. How old are you, Miss Elliot? Seventeen, eighteen?"

"Nineteen," she said curtly.

"Nineteen? I didn't think you were that old. That's about Cass's age. He's twenty-two."

"I suppose he followed your leadership and became one of those Yankees." She turned an accusing gaze on him, and Cole remembered the blue uniform he had been wearing the first day he met her. She probably had reason to hate the uniform. Georgia had borne the brunt of the Union offensive. He wondered absently if her home had been destroyed in the fighting. Truth be told, both sides had done plenty to dishonor the colors they wore.

"Yankee?" He shook his head. "As a matter of fact, Cass chose to fight for the South. If you'll recall, Missouri was divided in its opinion of the war, and so were the Claxton men."

Wynne nodded. "Cass was the only one of you who knew right from wrong. He worried about the war all the time, even though he'd paid someone to fight in his place. He fretted over how it was going, about getting back to take care of your mother. . . ."

Her voice trailed off lamely, as if she suddenly realized what she'd said.

"Really." Cole's brow lifted thoughtfully. "Do you know my brother?"

"Oh, heavens, no," she said, a shade too quickly to be believable. "I was . . . just guessing." Her laugh sounded nervous.

"Amazing." His lips pursed thoughtfully as he studied her. "For a moment there you sounded exactly like you might have met him—even been friends. You did say you were from Savannah, didn't you?"

"Yes."

"Cass was in Savannah for a while," he mused.

"Really, Cole." Her laugh sounded more confident this time. "Savannah is a large city. I couldn't possibly know everyone who goes there."

He watched as her fingers flew over a stone she held in her hands.

In the blink of an eye he grabbed her shoulders, pinning her back against the tree. She looked up at him, eyes wide, lips parted as if to scream. His eyes locked with hers, and even he was startled at how deadly he sounded. "Then explain what you're doing with his worry stone."

"His . . ." She dropped the stone like hot lava.

Cole's voice was menacingly low when he spoke again. His face so close to hers he could feel the warmth of her breath, see the gold-tipped lashes framing her eyes. Her shoulders were warm and soft beneath his hands. He jerked his thoughts back to the business at hand. "Come on, Miss Elliot. I'm dying to know how you happen to have my brother's worry stone, yet you say you've never met him." He kept his eyes pinned on hers, his fingers relentlessly pressed into her shoulders.

"You're *hurting* me," she gritted between clenched teeth. She struggled, attempting to break his hold, but her puny efforts were useless. He wasn't about to let her go until she told him the truth.

They glared at each other defiantly. Her breath was soft and sweet against his face, and she smelled fresh, like soap and water. Good clean smells, the way a woman ought to smell, and like a scent of heaven to a man who had lived too long with the stench and decay of the battlefield.

He threatened her again in a stern tone. "I can stay here as long as you can, lady." He didn't want to hurt her, but if she knew anything about his brother, she wasn't leaving here until she told him, no matter how appealing she happened to be.

She lurched toward him, her curved fingers clawing at his face. Caught by surprise, he stepped back out of her reach then caught her wrists, holding them tight as she struggled to get away.

"Let me go, you brute!"

He laughed in her face.

Suddenly her body went limp. For a moment he thought she had fainted, but she batted her big green eyes at him prettily. "Is all this brute force necessary, Cole?"

Her voice was soft and her drawl as sugarcoated as those special cookies Ma used to make. It made him sick to hear it. Warning bells were sounding in his head. All this sweetness and light wasn't like her. She was acting like that Penelope who had come to work at Hattie's.

"I do declare, you're crushin' the little ol' life right out of me."
She blinked coyly. "Surely a big, strong man like you doesn't have
to threaten a poor innocent girl just to ask her a simple question."

He blinked back at her mockingly. "Coming on a bit too
strong, aren't you? You tell me where you got Cass's worry
stone, and I'll let the 'poor little innocent girl' go about her business—but not until she learns to tell the truth," he snapped. "If
she doesn't tell the truth, she just might get her pretty little ol'
behind whipped right here and now."

"Why, you big lout! Let me go!" Feminine wiles flew right
out the window. Because he was momentarily surprised by the
way she lurched away from him, he lost his grip on her wrists.
Wynne doubled up her fists and hit him squarely in the rib cage.

Deciding retreat was the best maneuver at this point, Cole
covered his head with both arms, but when her blows continued
to rain, he lost all patience with this contrary female. With one
swipe of his arm he moved her aside, out of hitting reach. Before
he could grab her shoulders and pin her down, she twisted
away from him and landed on her knees. She tried to struggle to
her feet, but he caught her around the waist and pitched to one
side, pulling her with him.

Wynne broke his hold, but this time she lost her balance
and rolled over the edge of a slight incline. Cole's arm snaked
out and pulled her back. His hands pressed against her shoulders, pinning her to the ground.

"I am out of patience with you!"

She glared up at him, all fire and fury. "You get your hands
off me!"

"I will," he said pleasantly, "as soon as you answer my question. Where did you get Cass's worry stone?"

"What makes you think that silly stone belongs to your brother?" she grated.

"Because I *gave* it to him, and Beau and I have one to match. I found all three stones in a riverbed not too far from here when I was just a kid. Cass would never willingly part with it, so save yourself another lie."

"He gave it to me!" she shouted in a most unladylike display of temper.

Cole relaxed his grip in brief surprise at her outburst. He blinked at her. "He *gave* it to you?"

"That's right. He gave it to me. Now leave me alone."

He studied her hot, flushed face. So she *did* know him. "Not yet. When did he give it to you?"

"In Savannah. Two days before we were to be married."

He felt his mouth go slack. His hold loosened. Wynne quickly seized the opportunity to escape. She pulled away from him, and Cole let her go. He stared at her in disbelief.

"Cass was going to *marry* you?"

"That's right." She drew a deep breath and reached up, trying to straighten her hair, which by now had tumbled around her shoulders in a fiery mass. "But don't worry, Cole. He didn't marry me. Your precious little *brother* left me standing in front of the church. But not before he made off with almost every cent I had in the world."

By now Cole had managed to regain his composure. If she thought he was going to believe this tale, she was off the mark. No brother of his would do anything like that. He'd helped raise Beau and Cass and he knew them to be fine, decent men, not the type to take advantage of a woman.

He tried to keep his voice under control. "Now I know

you're lying. Cass wouldn't steal anyone's money, let alone a woman's."

"Well, that just goes to show how much you know. He *did* take my money and when I find him, I'm going to shoot him first, ask questions later."

Cole's eyes narrowed in sudden realization of what was going on here. "Then Cass is the man you're looking for?"

"That's right." Her defiant gaze met his and he wanted to shake her.

"And you're going to shoot him when you find him?"

"That's right."

"So . . . that's what you're doing out here," Cole mused. "Looking for my little brother so you can kill him."

"So I can blow his thieving head off," she said.

"I doubt that."

"Don't. I'll do it. I promise."

"Not if I can help it, you won't."

"You won't be able to do a thing about it." She looked as smug as a cream-stealing cat. "First thing tomorrow morning I'm going to take my ring to the bank and get a small loan. Then I'll buy another stage ticket and be on my way. Unless you want to trail me all over the countryside, there's not one blessed thing you can do to stop me."

"Just where do you think you're going to find Cass?" he asked. "None of us know where he is."

Wynne pushed to her feet, not looking quite so assured. "I—I know that, but I inquired about his whereabouts everywhere the stage stopped, and I know he was seen in Kansas City a few weeks ago, and he was supposed to be on his way home. That's why I came to River Run. Obviously he hasn't made it yet, so now I'll just head west toward Kansas City and hope to find him somewhere along the way."

Cole sagged with relief. "Then he's alive?"

She glanced at him, looking guilty. "For now."

Cole shook his head and thrust his long fingers through thick hair. "Ma will be relieved to hear that." She could have told them sooner, knowing how worried they all had been. But he guessed if she had passed out that information she would have had to say how she knew and what she was doing here. Evidently she hadn't realized they were his family.

"Are you—" Wynne straightened her spine defensively—"are you going to tell Lilly about me? She's been awfully good, and so has Beau. I wouldn't want to cause them any more worry, although Cass has handed me more than my share of trouble."

Cole studied her for a moment and then chose his words carefully. "I don't know what happened between you and Cass, but I do know my brother is an honorable man. Whatever he's done, he had good cause to do it. That's why I'm not going to say anything to Ma about any of this, but not because of you. Number one, I don't want her to worry any more than she already is. Number two, I think my brother can take care of himself." He let his eyes skim over her, showing his contempt. "Especially when it comes to little Eastern finishing-school girls."

She pointed her finger at him. "You'd better fear for his life."

"Like I said, Cass can take care of himself." Cole rolled to his feet. "And number three, you haven't a prayer of finding him in the first place. In case you haven't noticed, lady, there's a lot of territory between here and Kansas City, and a woman traveling alone is asking for trouble."

"I'm nineteen years old, and I am perfectly capable of taking care of *myself*. I made it out here alone, didn't I?" Wynne pushed at that fiery mop of hair that kept falling in her face.

"You did—barely. But I'd have to argue with you about being able to take care of yourself."

"Why?" Her mouth firmed, and her chin rose automatically to challenge his statement.

"For one thing, you're standing there in nothing but those frilly little breeches you women wear—"

"Frilly breeches! What are you talking about?"

He grinned as Wynne's gaze dropped to her waist, and her mouth gaped open with astonishment. The skirt of her dress had slipped to the ground and lay in a puddle around her feet. Apparently the loose strings she had been jerking away at had been there for a purpose, and in all the scuffling the material around the waistband had given way, leaving her standing in nothing but her linens!

"Oooooooh! How dare you!" Her face flamed as crimson as her hair. She swooped down to pick up her skirt and step back into it, shooting him a glare that would have felled a lesser man. "I hope you were enjoying yourself!"

A smile played about his lips as Cole observed her growing frustration. "No, as a matter of fact, I wasn't. You're not my type. And if you call getting robbed and being stranded in a strange town without a penny to your name taking care of yourself, then I guess you have," he said, going right back to the conversation as if nothing unusual had happened. "But the next time you might not be so lucky. Next time you might run into highwaymen who are looking for a little more than money, or you might meet up with Bushwhackers who haven't seen a woman in a few months, or there're still splinter groups of Quantrill's Raiders riding in these parts. One of them might take a fancy to a pretty face."

The more he talked, the more uneasy Wynne looked. "You're—you're just trying to scare me."

"You think so?" Cole kept his expression as solemn as a preacher's. "There're a lot of men riding these roads nowadays. Most of them have been away from home for a long time, and they wouldn't be too particular how they treat a woman."

A rosy blush painted her cheeks. "You can talk all you want, but I'm leaving tomorrow morning."

"Fine." He shrugged indifferently and reached down to pick up his discarded hat. "If you want to be bullheaded about it, then it's your skin you're risking, not mine. Have it your way." He turned and started to walk away, then had second thoughts. "Oh yeah. Tell Cass, when you see him, that Willa's keeping his supper warm."

"I'm not about to give that no-good man any message," Wynne snarled. She gathered the waist of her skirt in one hand, the hem in the other, and marched to the house.

Cole followed, feeling like Missouri's biggest villain, but she had it coming. Maybe he'd been a little rough on her, but Cass was his brother. She had no call to lie about him. Miss Wynne Elliot needed to be taught a lesson and he was in a mood to teach.

CHAPTER 8

The sun was grazing the horizon when Wynne stole silently out of the Claxton house the next morning. She tripped lightly over the rutted path, carrying two brown valises, her mood brighter than it had been in days.

It was going to be another scorcher, but she comforted herself with the thought that it couldn't be a very long walk into town, and she would enjoy the peace and solitude.

She choked back a laugh when she thought about the way Cole had accused her of being incompetent—incapable of coming in out of the rain. She'd show him she could take care of herself. He looked so much like Cass it was easy for her to muster up true revulsion. And it wasn't just the way he looked. Cole Claxton was the meanest . . . the most aggravating man she had ever met. But as much as she detested him, she despised his brother more.

Wynne sighed and shifted her grip on her valises. She wished she could catch up with Cass and get this entire episode behind her. This urge for revenge surely did tire a soul out.

Her thoughts turned to the man she was leaving behind at the farm. If Mr. Cole Claxton could see her now, he'd strangle on his own smugness. She was properly dressed in a pale blue, sprigged dress with tatted lace trim, the waist nipped in to emphasize its narrowness. Her hair was upswept with miniature curls nested at the crown, *and* she was on her way into town to take care of her own affairs.

She was a lady well versed in running a plantation—Papa had made sure of that—so dabbling in the business world wasn't new to her. She knew Cole thought she was a pampered Southern belle, but she'd had her share of work. Oh, maybe not cooking and cleaning like Lilly and Willa did, but she knew the workings of a plantation and how to manage servants. He'd see just how helpless she was.

Granted, the superintendent at Moss Oak had been experienced and conscientious, considering that many overseers had up and deserted the plantations during the war, leaving their employers helpless in the care of the few servants left behind and the crops in the field. Many landowners had sat and watched their heritages disintegrate before their eyes.

But Moss Oak had survived, not without a great many problems, but the land was still there and in the Elliot name. The fields were parched, no crops in the ground other than the small truck garden, which fed the servants who remained. Her childhood home would eventually be coaxed back to fertile land; she'd see to that. And she sincerely hoped that whoever bought the plantation would love it as much as Wesley Elliot had.

She sniffed disdainfully. Though she had been stripped of her personal belongings and set afoot in a Missouri town, she was still an Elliot of Savannah, Georgia. The Elliot name counted for something back home.

Dust puffed up with every step she took. An irritating gnat hovered around her sweat-slicked face. She used her handkerchief for a fan. Mercy, it was hot! Wynne glanced at the sun, beating pitilessly down on her and it barely seven in the morning. Already the lace collar chafed her skin. Her black, high-top, buttoned shoes were fashionable, but the footwear was not intended for long-distance walking. She had progressed only a short way when the fact became achingly evident. If Cole Claxton had cretin manners he'd have offered to drive her into town. Considering he'd be rid of her that much faster, she would have thought the idea would have appealed to him.

Even the perky bird sitting serenely on top of her hat looked slightly more wilted than when her journey first began. And the humidity! Her hair straggled down her neck in limp strings.

The sun was a blazing ball of fire now. Wynne used her handkerchief to mop ineffectually at the perspiration pooled on her brow. She thought of the cool veranda at Moss Oak and how she used to sit there, rocking gently, sipping fresh lemonade. Right now her mouth was as dry as a cotton boll. Why hadn't she thought to bring water? Fresh water, drawn from the cool depths of the Claxton well. She stiffened her back and marched on.

She had only a meager amount of clothing in her valises, but they seemed to weigh ten pounds more than they had when she started out. Her arms ached from carrying the cases, and these shoes were ruining her feet. She hadn't realized exactly how far it was to River Run from the Claxton farm.

Another mile down the road and a large blister started forming on her right toe.

Another two miles found her angrily sorting through the valises and stuffing only the essentials into one, then discarding the other in the middle of the road.

By the time the town of River Run came into view, her disposition could best be described as something less than sunny. It was a good thing she didn't meet up with Cass in this mood; the way she felt, she would have shot him on sight even before she told him what a rotten hound he was to have treated her so shamefully.

The sound of approaching hoofbeats reached her. The animal wasn't moving very fast, just a smooth, ground-covering lope. Curious, Wynne turned to see who it might be. Perhaps whoever it was would give her a lift.

Oh, no! She groaned. Him! She'd recognize Cole Claxton's arrogant bearing anywhere. What was he doing here? Coming to drag her back, no doubt. Well, he had another think coming. She turned around, eyes on the road, and stepped out at a good clip, unwilling to let him see how tired and hot she really was.

The horse drew nearer. Her chin lifted a notch higher and she mentally prepared a scathing rebuttal for when he demanded she return to the Claxton homestead.

When his mare was abreast of her, her mouth shot open to refuse his offer, but he rode right past her! Didn't even look her way.

Before she realized it, she had been standing in the road for a full five minutes watching him disappear from sight. Her cheeks bloomed scarlet. That wretched man was playing with fire! Didn't even wave, passed her like she was a fence post. She harbored a furious thought about taking care of her business with Cass and then making Cole pay for the way he had ignored her.

She shot an apologetic glance heavenward. *Sorry, Lord. I don't know what I was thinking. I know vengeance is Yours, and I shouldn't be having such thoughts about Cole, but he is certainly the most arrogant . . . ignorant . . . well, words fail me when I try to describe him. I won't shoot him, honest I won't. Just Cass. And You know he's got it coming.*

She trucked on down the road, more determined than ever to accomplish her purpose. The farther she got from River Run and the Claxton family, the better for her. She'd meet up with Cass between here and Kansas City. There weren't that many roads, and he'd have to be traveling on one of them. A no-account man would be no competition to a determined woman. And she was getting more determined by the minute.

Cole stood in the window of the general store drinking a cold sarsaparilla when Wynne trudged into town an hour later. He probably should have stopped and offered her a ride, but she would have refused. Besides, she was out to kill his baby brother. Not that he thought she could shoot straight enough to achieve her purpose, but so far her luck had been so bad she was overdue for a victory. It was a wonder she hadn't shot someone the day the stage had been robbed, waving that gun around like a drunkard. He took another low swallow of the ice-cold drink.

"Three pounds pinto beans, sugar, and flour." Nute Brower laid the items out on the counter. "Anything else I can help you with today?"

"That should do it, Nute. I'm killing time until Tal gets here." He didn't really have any business with the sheriff, but one excuse was as good as another, he supposed. As a matter of fact, he needed to be home working, but he'd gotten to worrying about the Elliot female so he'd ridden behind her—to see if she made it to town all right. But seeing she was safe didn't mean he had to coddle her. She'd chosen to walk to town—so let her walk.

"Tal's not in town," Nute said. "He rode out with a posse before dawn to look for the Beason gang. Thinks they might be the ones who killed the stage driver and the guy riding shotgun."

Cole finished off the last of his drink. "I doubt that he'll have any luck."

Nute shook his head. "Something's got to be done about that bunch. They're getting real dangerous."

Cole set the bottle back on the counter. "Might not be the Beasons. The witnesses weren't too clear on who'd done the robbing. Could be the James gang. Heard they were operating in this neck of the woods."

"Last I heard the James boys had moved their operations farther west. Seems they're getting their kicks robbing banks these days. Some say the boys are heroes, robbing from the rich and giving to the poor, but I've got money in that bank across the street, and I'd hate to see it wind up in the James boys' pockets."

"I'd have to agree with you." Cole watched Wynne limp up the steps to the bank's front door and wondered if Elias would be fool enough to loan her money on a ring. Once she had cash in her hand, she'd be out of town faster than a scared rabbit, and he'd bet his last dime that she wouldn't be back to pay her bills. A woman who would deliberately set out to kill a man wouldn't be too concerned about her credit rating.

He glanced at the bag sitting on the mercantile floor; he'd picked up the valise she had abandoned. What was he going to do with it?

Wynne staggered through the bank door, dragging her dust-covered valise. She blew a strand of hair out of her eyes as she caught a glimpse of herself in the mirror hanging on the back wall. No doubt the mirror was installed so the banker could keep a close eye on employees and customers, but her reflection didn't do much to boost her flagging self-esteem. Her face was as flushed as one of the stripes on Old Glory flapping in a lackluster wind atop the courthouse. Her hat was cocked crazily to one side, and the bird she had thought was so fashionable when she had purchased the thing now looked as if it had been shot at and hit. Her dress was soaked with perspiration, her hair hung in limp strands around her face, and her eyes were so ringed with dust she looked like a rabid raccoon. Not a spectacle guaranteed to inspire confidence in a banker. She wasn't much of an endorsement for Miss Marelda's school either. No one looking at her would take her for a finished young lady. In fact, she looked decidedly *un*finished.

She dabbed her cheeks and neck and sagged weakly against the polished pine railing, letting the cooler air of the bank's overhead fan wash over her. If it hadn't been for making a spectacle of herself, she would sit right down on the floor under the revolving blades and stay there until her temperature dropped.

Elias Holbrook, bank owner, approached, speaking pleasantly. "Howdy, ma'am. It's going be a warm one."

She smiled lamely. Yes, you could certainly say that. She forced herself to respond politely. "Quite warm. It isn't nine o'clock in the morning, and the heat is suffocating."

Elias poured a glass of water from a pitcher sitting on his desk and handed it to her. Wynne accepted it gratefully. The tepid water felt cool to her parched tongue. She emptied the glass in one long swallow then drew a deep breath and returned it to the corner of Elias's desk. Air from the fan and the drink of water had restored some of her sense of well-being. She breathed the way Miss Marelda had taught her. In, out, in, out—guaranteed to calm nerves. And she was about as stretched out as she could handle.

Her foot throbbed like a sore tooth. There was a chair right next to the oak desk, and without thinking, she sat down and peeled off her right shoe, exposing a throbbing blister the size of a silver dollar covering her big toe. She sighed in relief as she wiggled the smarting appendage. Land sakes, the last mile had been so painful she had been afraid she would be reduced to crawling the rest of the way. She tucked the skirt of her dress around her legs and then brought the injured foot up to her lap. Blind to her surroundings, she cradled her foot, poking gingerly at the puffy spot.

Elias leaned forward, peering at the proceedings with growing interest. "My, my. That looks terrible." He clucked sympathetically.

"It hurts like the blue blazes," she said. Immediately she realized her unbecoming posture. Her jaw dropped. What must he think of her?

She slid her foot slowly off her lap and, as circumspectly as possible, tucked her bare foot and her shod one beneath the dusty hem of her skirt. A lady would never enter a bank and take her shoe off in front of a man. She could just hear what Miss Marelda would have to say about that! Papa would have had a fit, and Miss Marelda would probably have collapsed in such a swoon it would have taken a bucket of smelling salts to bring her around. Wynne never would have imagined this quest for revenge would mean such a lowering of her standards.

She cleared her throat and crossed her hands in her lap, trying to restore a shred of her lost dignity. Elias waited, looking patient, as she drew a deep breath and pasted on what she hoped was an utterly charming smile. She figured she needed to change his first impression of her as quickly as possible. She kept her voice sweet and genteel, the mark of a true lady. "Would you perhaps be the man I would talk to about obtaining a small loan?"

Elias straightened his vest. His face brightened. "Why, yes, my dear! I certainly am." He extended a cordial hand. "Elias Holbrook, at your service."

"Mr. Holbrook." Wynne accepted his hand with a graceful nod. "Charmed to make your acquaintance, sir. My name is Wynne Elliot." When she shook his hand, her hat tilted dangerously to one side. Probably made her look like a scatterbrained female. Cole's favorite word rose to her mind. *Addlebrained.* She hurriedly reached up and adjusted the offending headgear.

Elias beamed. "Wynne. What a lovely name, my dear. You're staying at the Claxton place, aren't you?"

"Yes . . . I don't know if you heard about my misfortune. . . ." Of course he had; nothing in a town this small went unnoticed and most certainly not a stage robbery that took the lives of two men.

"Yes, yes, I did." He frowned. "I'm terribly sorry."

For a moment her smile dimmed. If he knew about the robbery then he was also aware of the spectacle she'd created when she fell out of the stage with the rifle. Her cheeks burned with embarrassment. If Cole Claxton had been gentleman enough to assist her—the way he had Penelope—she wouldn't have fallen on her . . . well, fallen in the middle of the street.

"Yes . . . well, about the loan. Your establishment comes highly recommended," she said, hoping he wouldn't suspect how desperate she was. Actually, the suggestion about someone recommending his bank was not entirely true. Not a single soul had suggested she try the bank, but she thought she might sound more businesslike if she took a professional approach.

"Oh, my. Why, that's wonderful," Elias exclaimed. He scurried around his desk and sat down, reaching for a pen and paper. "Now, what amount did you have in mind, Miss Elliot?"

"Well . . ." Wynne twisted her handkerchief in her lap. "I think perhaps ten dollars would be sufficient." She hoped that amount would be enough. Papa had always taken care of purchasing what she had needed, so she had very little idea of what it would cost to travel by stage to Kansas City. There would be food and other travel expenses. The amount didn't seem to shock the banker, so she relaxed a little, enjoying the thought of soon having her financial problems under control.

"Hmm . . . ten dollars . . . yes . . ." Elias scribbled as they talked. "And other than the Claxtons' cosigning the note, what sort of collateral would you personally be able to offer?"

The Claxtons' cosigning the note? Wynne stared at him as if he had suddenly started spouting a foreign language. He had most certainly misunderstood her. As if she would accept help from the Claxtons! Well, any more help than they had already given, that is.

She cleared her throat and smiled sweetly at him. "I have this lovely pearl ring my father gave me on my sixteenth birthday." She hurriedly slipped the circle off her finger and handed it to him. "Isn't it nice?"

Elias stared at the tiny loop resting in the palm of his hand then glanced back at her. He didn't look as impressed as she'd hoped. "This is the collateral you have?"

She mustered up her most engaging smile. "That's all I have with me right now, but it is truly a lovely ring, don't you think?" She scooted to the end of her chair. "See? The natural pearl is large, and the gold setting is stunning. Wouldn't you agree? Are you aware that a pearl signifies love, happiness, affection, and generosity? I'm sure the ring would bring half as much again as Papa paid for it."

She could see the seed of doubt begin to sprout in his eyes, and her heart sank.

He bent and closely examined the token. "It is lovely, but I would need more than the ring to make such a loan," he said, handing the ring back to her. "Have you nothing else of value?"

"I have a whole plantation back in Savannah," Wynne said. Surely mention of Moss Oak would reassure him that she was a woman of means.

"A plantation, you say?" Elias seemed more interested. "Well, that's more like it. May I see the deed, please?"

"Deed?" She stared at him, her heart sinking for the second time.

"Proof of ownership. You do own the land free and clear?"

"Yes, but I don't have the deed with me." Did anyone carry a deed to their land?

Doubt clouded Elias's face. "No deed."

"But I *do* own the land, and I could send for the proper papers—"

"That might take months," he pointed out gently. "Perhaps the Claxtons' signatures would suffice—"

She interrupted. "The Claxtons will not sign a promissory note for me." When they found out what she intended to do with the money, they'd burn in hades before they'd help.

Elias carefully placed the ink pen back on his desk.

"But the ring is collateral. . . ." Her voice trailed off when he began to shake his head negatively, and she realized with a sinking heart he wasn't going to give her the loan.

For over ten minutes she argued everything she could think of to make him change his mind, but he remained firm. The bank could not issue the loan in a woman's name.

"But that's not fair," she spluttered. "I own land—a fine plantation. The fact that I'm a woman shouldn't come into it at all."

"Miss Elliot, may I make a suggestion?" he said gently. "Why don't you talk this over with Cole Claxton, and then you and he come back tomorrow morning? Perhaps something can be worked out—"

Wynne flew to her feet. "Cole Claxton! Never!"

"Now, my dear—" Elias stopped and started over. "It pains

me greatly to refuse you a loan, but you must realize the bank is not in the habit of making loans to women—"

"It pains me too," Wynne snapped. She stuck her foot in her shoe and sucked in a painful breath when the leather grazed the blister. "Thank you for your time, sir."

"Miss Elliot . . . perhaps a private investor? Nute Brower, owner of the mercantile, sometimes makes small loans. . . ."

She limped across the bank lobby, snatched up her valise, and slammed out the front door.

The temperature felt as if it had shot up ten more degrees when she stepped out of the bank. Wynne slipped the ring back on her finger where it would be safe and surveyed the crowded street, people going about their business, and no one paying the slightest attention to her. No one cared about her dilemma. Oh, it was a cruel, cold world when a banker wouldn't do business with a fine, upstanding customer just because she was a woman. Someone needed to do something to correct such an injustice.

Oh yes, Banker Holbrook had thought the ring was lovely, but completely insufficient collateral for a ten-dollar loan. And he wouldn't give her a loan because she was a woman! But it wasn't until he suggested that Cole come talk to him, that perhaps *he* would be willing to cosign the note, that she'd known her goose was cooked. She could well imagine the arrogant Claxton sneer he'd flash if she even suggested such a thing.

No matter how she'd argued—presented her case, she amended for Miss Marelda's sake—Banker Holbrook had not been persuaded.

Well, she wasn't whipped yet. She shifted the valise to her other hand, stepped off the sidewalk, and limped toward the mercantile.

Mr. Holbrook had suggested that she find a private investor. He'd said Nute Brower sometimes made small loans in exchange for personal property. But Mr. Brower didn't need a pearl ring.

Neither did Tom Clayborne or Jed McThais or even Avery Miller, for that matter. Not one person in River Run had use for a lovely pearl ring or any money to lend, either.

Wynne slumped down on a bench in front of Hattie's Place and glumly surveyed the pearl on her right hand. Hot tears sprang to her eyes. She thought it was the prettiest ring in the world and she'd been so sure it would be an easy task to exchange the priceless trinket for the cash needed for the journey.

The saloon was extremely quiet this morning. She supposed Penelope would still be sleeping. Wynne toyed with the idea of marching right in there and rousing Hattie out of bed and asking for a job. She was completely alone, broke, in a strange town, and didn't know where her next meal was coming from.

Time had come for desperate measures.

She stood up and edged to the saloon door, hoping she wouldn't see anyone she knew. How could she bear it if Cole Claxton should see her peering into Hattie's? He'd mistaken her for one of the madam's girls before. Her anger kindled at the memory.

She raised herself on tiptoe and peeked inside at the dark interior. She couldn't ever recall seeing such an establishment before. Papa would never have permitted it, and it was quite possible he was turning over in his grave right now because of her shamelessness. Ladies of her acquaintance back in Savannah would have swept past a place like this, pretending it didn't exist. But then those ladies hadn't been alone and broke with no place to go.

She could barely make out a lone man sweeping the floor. Chairs were stacked neatly on top of tables, and a low ceiling fan was trying its best to move stagnant air. The stout odor of stale smoke and brackish beer stung her nostrils. She wrinkled her nose, thinking what it would be like to work here. She was desperate all right, but not that desperate.

If you're going to kill a man, Wynne, then you certainly should be able to go inside a saloon, she reasoned.

For a moment she felt an insipid stirring of apprehension. The thought of actually murdering a man turned her stomach. What would it be like to walk up and point a gun at Cass's big, broad chest, then deliberately, coldly, cruelly pull the trigger? Revulsion snaked through her. Actually she'd been so consumed with bitterness that she'd never really stopped to think about the act itself.

She stood there, holding on to the saloon door and thinking of what it would be like to shoot someone. When it happened, would Cass look at her with amusement or with scorn or maybe even with a hint of remorse? Or would he throw his dark head back and laugh at her, his even white teeth glistening in the sunlight, having his own revenge, even as he stood at death's door?

Could she really take another's life?

Tilly had taught her the Ten Commandments, and she could recite the Scripture by heart. One of those commandments was a stern warning: "Thou shalt not kill."

Her resolve wavered. Would God punish her the way she planned to punish Cass? She'd tried to reason away her doubts as to God's acceptance of her behavior, but she had an uneasy feeling He might not agree with her assessment of the situation. And what about Cass? What would he do when she showed up breathing fire and accusations? She knew he was enough like Cole that he might be hard to kill, but she'd cross that bridge when she reached it.

She stepped away from the door and sat back down on the bench. She wouldn't know Cass's reaction until she found him, and she couldn't find him until she had a mode of transportation, and she couldn't get that transportation unless she sold her ring.

Across the street a small crowd had gathered at the general store. A sign advertised a wagon train leaving the following morning. Mr. Brower had suggested she try to sign on, but when she'd inquired about the prospect, she'd been told she would have to have a husband or a guardian, preferably a family member. It was a man's world all right. A woman like her didn't have a chance.

She heaved a deep sigh. Obviously, she didn't have a spare "uncle" around, and her chances of finding a husband by daybreak tomorrow were about as slim as selling the pearl ring.

Her gaze fell on the livery stable, and it occurred to her that she hadn't tried there yet. Now here was a possibility she hadn't thought of before. Of course, how stupid of her! She probably wouldn't be able to sell the ring there, but perhaps the owner would have a horse he would trade for it.

Riding a horse wouldn't be the most comfortable way to travel to Kansas City, but she supposed she could do it if she had to. She'd ridden nearly every day before she'd gone away to school. And other women braved their way across the rugged frontier, didn't they? She'd gotten this far on her own, hadn't she? She lifted her chin. Women were a lot smarter than men gave them credit for; she wasn't whipped yet.

Feeling slightly easier about the whole situation, Wynne picked up her valise and hobbled across the street.

The blacksmith was busy shoeing a horse as she approached. He was a huge, burly sort of fella with a big gold front tooth. He towered above her small frame.

Combined with the heat of the day, the inside of the stable felt insufferable. The forge gave off a hot blast. Not a thread of the smith's clothing was dry. Rivulets of sweat poured off his forehead and ran in streams down his neck; his muscles bunched and relaxed as his hammer beat a steady rhythm to shape a red-hot horseshoe. He threw her a brief glance then refocused on his work.

Wynne cleared her throat and smiled. "Good morning, sir."

He answered with a grunt.

"It's extremely warm," she said and then realized how absurd she sounded. It was hot as a summer skunk in here. How on earth did the man stand it? She had thought it was hot outside. It made her think of Pastor Burke back home. He had a habit of preaching on hell so convincingly, Mattie Pearson said you'd have thought the man was born and raised there. Well, he'd probably gotten his inspiration for his sermons in a blacksmith shop.

The smithy grunted again and moved aside to pick up more shoeing nails, cradling them in his large, soiled apron.

"Could you tell me how far it is to Kansas City?" Wynne asked.

"Over two hundred miles."

Wynne squinted. "That far?"

He nodded and drove another nail.

She glanced around the stable. There was a solid-looking horse standing in one of the stalls. The animal was large *and* sturdy-looking, and had a glistening coat of the most beautiful rust-colored shade. The mare looked as if she would have a gentle gait—and Wynne desperately wanted a soft ride if she had to travel two hundred miles!

Wynne cleared her throat again. "Sir, I was wondering . . . would that horse over there happen to be for sale?"

The blacksmith's gaze followed her finger. "It is." He returned to the job of shaping another horseshoe.

Wynne set down her valise and walked over to the stall. The horse stuck its head over the gate and whuffed at her. She smiled and rubbed its velvet-soft nose. "Pretty girl," she whispered. *Oh yes, this one will do nicely.*

She quickly stiffened her resolve and turned back to the smithy. "Well." She spoke again, more loudly.

He didn't even look up.

"I'm sure you've heard about the stage robbery. I was on that stage and the thieves stole my money and now I have no way to get to Kansas City," she explained in a rush of breath. "But I do have this lovely pearl ring; I'm sure you'd like it. I would trade the ring in even exchange for this horse—"

The blacksmith's eyes promptly narrowed; his mouth firmed.

Wynne's mouth went suddenly dry. "I didn't mean that *you* might be interested in the ring," she hurriedly added. "I thought maybe you might know someone you could give the pearl to—like a wife? Daughter . . . ?" She trailed off hopefully when she saw the man's attention unwillingly drop to the ring on her right hand. Quickly she thrust the jewel toward him. "See? It's very appealing."

His dark eyes took in the fragile object with little sign of interest. She waited, and he leaned toward her a fraction more, studying the piece of jewelry more closely. Wynne held her breath. Her heart beat so strongly she was sure he must see it beneath the cotton fabric of her bodice. If he wouldn't trade the horse for the ring, she'd have no choice but to go to Hattie's and ask for a job.

The blacksmith straightened and scowled. "What would I do with a little play pretty like that?"

"You could give it to your wife—"

"Don't have a woman," he interrupted.

"Well, then, you could give it to—to a lady friend," she suggested. She flashed the ring, waiting for him to deny he had a lady friend. That probably was a bad suggestion. It would be a miracle if he even had a female acquaintance.

But apparently he didn't find the suggestion preposterous, because his gaze had switched back to the ring, lingering there. For a second he seemed to be seriously considering the offer.

A stream of tobacco juice whizzed by her ear. The spittle had come so close to her face she was positive that a remnant of the repulsive spray hit her left cheek.

"I don't know . . . ," he said.

Wynne tried to keep from gagging (because Miss Fielding had repeatedly warned that a lady does not gag in public). She fumbled hastily in her pocket for her handkerchief and wiped her face. She had to have that horse!

"Any lady would adore the ring," she encouraged, turning her hand from one side to another to catch the light.

Fifteen minutes later she rode out of the stable on the back of a glorious white mule, grinning ear to ear. She'd made a deal and she'd done it all on her own.

The blacksmith wouldn't trade the horse for the ring, but he would trade the old mule. It seemed the animal had wandered into town a couple of weeks ago, and it was widely speculated that it had once belonged to a prospector. Perhaps he'd died somewhere out on the trail, and the mule had wandered wild for a while. The animal was of no value to the smithy, just one more mouth to feed, and the ring didn't eat anything.

The trade had come complete with the prospector's pack equipment. Two filthy blankets, various mismatched eating utensils, a pick and a shovel, three pie-shaped pans for gold panning—should she happen to run across a gold mine, here in Missouri—and an old rusty pistol. The unexpected weapon would be a godsend if she were to complete her mission successfully, for she had wondered where she would get a gun. She was sure she couldn't run Cass down and club him to death, although if it came to that alternative, she'd do it.

Once again, she pushed thoughts about God aside. Seemed like her anger at Cass overrode everything else. She didn't use to be like this. Back at Moss Oak, she had sat in church and thought pure thoughts. Now all she thought about was how badly Cass had treated her and what she intended to do about it.

She was proud of her mule and all the equipment though. There was a lot of other paraphernalia that she couldn't readily identify, but she was sure everything would come in handy once she was on the trail. All in all, she thought with a satisfied smile, she'd driven a very shrewd bargain.

The only problem was that she'd always ridden sidesaddle. Because, she suspected, he had felt sorry for her, the blacksmith had thrown in a worn saddle with the deal, and she had to ride astride. Adapting was going to be a little tricky, and the animal had a peculiar gait, more of a lurching from side to side than the smooth horse stride that she was accustomed to at Moss Oak.

The blacksmith had helped her mount. At first she thought

about insisting upon riding properly like a lady, hooking her knee around the saddle horn, but the smithy had warned her that would be a poor choice.

"You'd best set like a man," he'd said, "or the ornery thing will pitch you headfirst in the middle of the road."

Of course she didn't want the "ornery thing" to do that, so she'd primly tucked her skirt around her legs and shinnied up on the back of the mule as gracefully as shinnying allowed.

"Excuse me. Exactly what direction is Kansas City?" she'd asked moments before she started out on the long journey.

The blacksmith had absently scratched his head and then sent another brown stream of juice flying by the mule's head. "You sure you ought to be doing this, lady? If you don't know what direction Kansas City is in, I don't think you should be setting out for it by yourself."

She adjusted the bird hat. "Thank you for your concern, but if you would kindly point the way?"

He shook his head, then pointed due north. "Keep bearing north, little lady. Just keep bearing north."

Cole leaned against the porch railing of the general store and watched Wynne ride out of town on the back of a mule. It would be hard to miss her departure. Pots and pans clanging, skillets and gold pans banging. The procession made as much racket as a marching band. The pack was fastened firmly behind the saddle, but the utensils were tied on loosely and clattered noisily when the mule and its rider ambled slowly down the street.

Elias Holbrook had refused to loan money on that ring. You had to get up early to catch an old fox like Elias. Banks weren't in the habit of loaning money to women, particularly to strange women with birds on their hats and no apparent roots. The here-today-and-gone-tomorrow type didn't inspire a banker's heart.

Cole guessed she'd traded the ring for the worn-out mule and that pile of junk she had tied on it. One thing for sure: Cass didn't have to worry about her taking him by surprise. Little brother would hear her coming a mile away. He sighed.

He didn't actually think she had the skill to kill his brother, even on the remote possibility that she could find him. But there was always the chance she could accidentally kill him if she came upon him unexpectedly. Cass probably wouldn't know he was in danger until it was too late.

Cole pushed away from the post. He'd have to follow her and see that she didn't achieve her purpose.

The last he saw of Wynne Elliot, she was bouncing in the saddle like a proud prairie hen, heading for Kansas City.

She had about as much chance as a snowball in August of getting there.

Oh, what a *glorious* feeling it was to ride down the center of town knowing she was once again in charge of her own destiny.

The only thing that spoiled her newfound paradise was the fact that *he* was there outside the general store taking note of her departure with an irritatingly cool detachment. He didn't even wave as she rode past him.

Wynne didn't care how blue his eyes were against the dark tan of his face. It didn't matter that his white muslin shirt was open at the neck to reveal the shadow of a patch of thick, dark hair across his chest. Or even that his sleeves were rolled up to reveal corded forearms. His hat was tilted rakishly to the back of his head, and a fringe of hair that was a bit too long framed his strong face.

The cad was so handsome it nearly took her breath away.

Cole Claxton was ill-tempered, arrogant, and a complete egotistical old goat. But there was something about him that commanded her respect. Maybe it was his posture—or his attitude—or even the impenetrable stance he'd shown toward her. She liked a man who knew his own mind.

Feelings ran deep in the Claxton household; that was evident. The family came from a background of wealth and gentility. Their home reflected pride, and Lilly's ingrained Southern mannerisms left no doubt of her heritage.

But then, Wynne came from a similar background. Only trouble was, she was alone. She didn't have family to love her, support her, or defend her from men like Cole and Cass Claxton. The thought hurt but was nonetheless true. If there was any defending to do, she'd have to do it. She firmed her lips. Well, she was up to the challenge. Wynne Elliot was capable of taking care of herself.

With a decisive lift of her nose, she kneed the old mule to a faster gait and loped out of town, aware that a smirking Cole

Claxton stood on the mercantile porch, arms crossed, silently laughing at her. Good riddance, he was undoubtedly thinking.

The same to you, sir.

She was glad to be rid of the troublemaker.

CHAPTER 9

"Guess we could always cross the street and wet our whistles." The old-timer shot a wad of tobacco juice off the porch, then wiped the brown stain outlining his mouth on his left shirt shoulder.

It never ceased to amaze Bertram G. Mallory that a man could be so disheveled. It wasn't that he dressed all that upscale himself. He was no dude, but a man could keep himself clean.

"Better not. We were over there earlier." Bertram winced and shifted his broken ankle to a more agreeable position. The heavy splint encasing his foot was cumbersome, and his leg itched like crazy. And the insufferable heat wasn't making conditions any better.

"We could go wet a line, if you were of a mind to."

For some reason the old-timer thought Bertram was his responsibility. From the moment he'd taken a headlong plunge off that porch, Jake had befriended him—stuck closer than wool underwear on a hot day. The old codger insisted Bertram stay with him until the break healed. Since Bertram was once more at the mercy of fate—and low finances—he had little choice but to accept the offer.

Jake lived alone in nothing more than a shack on the outskirts of town. The accommodations weren't great, but Bertram had stayed in worse, and Jake was friendly and wouldn't take any money for his help. His wife had died back in '51, and his only son had been killed in a gunfight the year after. In short, Jake was a man starved for company, and he welcomed the young stranger's companionship. And it hadn't been all that bad, except Jake talked a lot and got on Bertram's nerves something awful. Still, the old man was salt of the earth. Bertram couldn't complain.

"I could put you on the back of old Millhouse and walk you down to the river," Jake offered.

Every morning Jake unceremoniously hefted Bertram atop the old mule's back and led him into town. Bertram was fond of good horseflesh, and it hurt his pride to jolt along on a jenny, of all things. The animal's rough gait wasn't comfortable, but Jake insisted, and the ride was better than lying in bed all day. For the rest of the day, the two men sat on the plank porch in front of the café. Sitting and talking with Jake, chewing and spitting, got a mite old real quick. Bertram counted the hours until he could leave Springfield and resume his mission—one he wished he'd never accepted.

"Not in the mood for fishing," Bertram said. "Just want to sit here and finish this cow I started." He held up a piece of pine, poorly fashioned to bear a mild resemblance to a four-legged bovine. Jake could turn out a pretty good piece of whittling. You could almost always tell what it was. Bertram eyed his cow. Could be a horse, or an ox. Could be anything you wanted to call it, but it took a lot of imagination for anyone to see a cow in his work.

He appreciated the way the old-timer tried to keep him busy, but he was getting mighty bored. He needed to find the Elliot woman and get this business over with once and for all. Once he was through—and only then—would he be able to resume a normal life.

"Why, that's right nice, boy." Jake studied the carving Bertram was holding.

Well, it wasn't, and Bertram knew it. The miniature carving didn't look anything like a cow. More like an old, notched-out piece of wood, but Jake had worked hard to teach him to whittle. Bertram didn't have the heart not to at least try. He appreciated the encouragement though. Seemed like there wasn't enough of that commodity to go around these days.

This afternoon the porch was full of Jake's counterparts, all whittling and spitting in unison. Bertram hadn't taken up tobacco chewing yet, but he suspected that would be next if he didn't get out of Springfield soon. Sometimes he had nightmares of himself sitting here for the rest of his life, stuck in this one-horse town like one of the old-timers. Woke up in a cold sweat a time or two. This wasn't any life for a young man.

An annoying jingling, jangling racket woke everyone up. Bertram blinked in amazement at the apparition headed their way. All eyes centered on the woman atop a white mule who seemed to have appeared out of nowhere. The animal lumbered through town, with the pans and other artifacts tied to it rattling and tinkling to beat the band. The young, pretty redheaded girl wearing a silly hat with a bird on top didn't look too comfortable, and she couldn't control that mule worth spit. It would be a miracle if she didn't get dumped on her . . . well, dumped in the middle of Main Street.

Bertram pushed slowly to his feet, wincing when he heard the woman shout a blistering command. The mule stopped dead still in the middle of the road, pitching the girl forward. She grabbed its mane to keep from falling.

"You *filthy*, stubborn piece of *dog meat*! I ought to—" She glanced toward the porch full of gawking men and stopped midshout, as if she had suddenly become aware of the exhibition she was making of herself. She reached up to push a lock of hair out of her heat-flushed face and flashed an enchanting smile. "Afternoon, gentlemen," she trilled.

One by one the men left their chairs—all except Bertram; he couldn't leave that easily. A couple tipped their hats and offered toothless grins.

The girl sat astride the mule, holding court. The men gathered close, engaging in friendly introductions. *Act like they've never seen a female before*, Bertram thought.

He leaned back in his chair and grinned at her obvious dilemma. "May we be of assistance, ma'am?"

She shot him a lame smile, but about that time the mule decided to move on. Without warning the contrary animal lurched ahead. The girl grabbed for the reins and yelled, "Whoa!" but the mule ignored her. By the time they hit the end of the street, the mule had worked up a full gallop.

The last Bertram saw of the girl was a white streak bounding out of town in the midst of the banging pots and pans. The old-timers stared after her, looking dumbfounded.

Jake climbed the porch steps and sat down in his usual chair. "You see that?" he demanded.

"Yep. I saw her." Bertram shook his head in amusement. He picked up the wooden cow once more. "Sure was an unusual method of transportation for a lady, wouldn't you say?"

Jake grinned. "Didn't seem like she had much to say in the decision to go or stay, did it?"

Bertram laughed. "No, I'd say the mule was driving."

A few minutes later Jake said, "Here comes Fancy Biggers."

Heads pivoted to watch the young woman crossing the street. Fancy worked at the saloon, and Bertram had observed, in the two weeks he had been in town, how the other women picked up the hems of their skirts and made sure they didn't touch any part of Fancy's gown when they passed.

Bertram was concerned for Miss Biggers's soul. Clearly, she wasn't living by the Good Book, but other women had no cause to treat her like a bad smell.

Miss Biggers couldn't be much older than eighteen, maybe nineteen, he guessed—hard to tell with all that war paint on her face: heavily rouged cheeks, black kohl lining baby blue eyes. She was pretty; he was certain of that. Her hair shone like a shiny new copper penny in the afternoon sunlight.

She was thinner than most. Looked to him as if she could stand a few square meals under her belt. The emerald gown she was wearing was indecent by any standards; couldn't argue that. The shiny satin made her waist look tiny—why, his hands could span her waistline and still have room left over. And the neckline—well, the material dipped way too far to be modest. Course, he didn't mind the dress all that much, but he could see where the other womenfolk might get a little upset with Fancy's style. This morning she was carrying a matching green umbrella, twirling it absently between her hands as she walked.

Fancy stepped onto the porch, and the men's chairs came back down on all four legs with loud thuds. "Afternoon, gentlemen," she drawled.

Bertram witnessed a second outbreak of toothless grins and nervous twittering at the men's appropriate responses. Yep, he needed to be moving on in case that sort of behavior was catching.

Fancy focused her smiling attention on Bertram. "Afternoon, Mr. Mallory."

"Afternoon, Miss Biggers." Bertram managed to struggle respectfully to his feet when she approached. His stomach fluttered. He didn't know why.

"Lovely day," she remarked, meeting his direct gaze.

"A mite hot."

"Yes. Surely could use a good rain."

"That we could. Looks kinda threatening to the south. Maybe we'll get a shower before the day's over." Jake grinned at her as he butted into the conversation.

"I wouldn't mind rain at all, but it's such a lovely day for a drive, wouldn't you think?" Fancy's eyes refused to leave Bertram's, and he felt his face grow hot when he heard the other men's knowing chuckles behind him.

"I guess it is. Real nice." Was she inviting him for a ride?

"I know you're not exactly up to driving a team at the moment, but the saloon has a buckboard I could borrow. I was wondering if you might like to go for a ride with me."

Well, you could fell him with a two-by-four. Would he like to go for a ride with her? Was the earth round?

"Why, yes . . . a ride would be real nice," Bertram said, wishing the other men would stop their dad-blasted giggling. They were worse than a bunch of old women.

"Oh, that's lovely." She smiled, showing her pleasure. "I'll get the buckboard and be back for you in a few minutes."

Bertram endured the usual male ribbing before Fancy finally reappeared, driving a horse and buckboard. He gazed up at her, sitting up there behind the horses looking so pretty and so friendly, and decided the affable jesting was worth it. The old-timers hoisted him aboard, and shortly he and Fancy were leaving the town behind.

Those old geezers could laugh all they wanted to, Bertram thought when he sent an admiring glance in Fancy's direction. A warm summer ride in the countryside with Fancy Biggers was a whole lot better than carving another one of those blasted cows. And Fancy was prettier and better company than he'd been accustomed to lately. He settled back against the seat. Yes sir, things were looking up.

Wynne shoved her hat out of her face and stared up at the sun. Sakes alive. She was burning up! The mule had turned stubborn again, and she rued the day she'd traded the pearl ring for a misbegotten, ill-tempered piece of meat and hide that was going to be the death of her.

She'd gotten the short end of the deal.

That mule had been nothing but trouble from the moment

she left River Run. It didn't want to walk, and it didn't want to sit down. It wanted to exist—nothing more.

Two miles out of Springfield she'd had to slide off and drag the contrary beast several hundred feet before Wynne made up her mind that they were going to have to get a few things straight, one being that she was the boss, and the mule was not.

The sun was hotter than a two-dollar stove burning pitch-pine bark. Another hour and she would be baked to a crisp, basted with her own perspiration. She knew from Miss Marelda's teaching that a lady didn't sweat. Men sweat. Ladies glowed. Well, if she glowed any more, they could use her for a lamppost. She angrily jerked off her hat and fanned herself, trying to catch a breath of air.

The blister was paining her something awful, so she hobbled to a grassy patch and took off both shoes, wiggling her toes. After a few moments of blessed relief, she hobbled back and stuffed her shoes into her valise, which she had tied on the mule's back along with all of her other newly acquired possessions.

After a sip of tepid water out of the canteen, she turned her attention back to the mule, her current problem. She'd heard animals were smarter than they looked. Well, when they looked as ignorant as the mule did right now, you still might not have all that much to work with. Maybe if she tried to explain her predicament, this poor excuse for a beast of burden would be more cooperative. At least it was worth a try. The horses at home had liked to have her talk to them.

"Now, mule, you and I have got to have an understanding," she began in her most cajoling voice. "I've got a job to do, and you're here to help me do it."

The mule didn't look overly interested.

"I know you had a nice stall in that stable, and I've brought you out here in the hot sunshine, which you probably resent, but we're going on an adventure." That was it. Lie to it. Perhaps . . . oh, fie! It didn't really matter what she said. This worthless animal didn't understand a word she was saying! And couldn't care less.

Besides, who was she trying to fool, herself? Adventure, ha! She was out to kill a man, and she was beginning to wonder if she was really equipped to handle the job.

Wynne sat down again, holding one rein while the mule stood facing her with a simple, placid look on its face. Whatever smarts were floating around out there in the mule kingdom had evidently bypassed this animal. She was glad no one had seen her trying to hold a conversation with this misbegotten reject from the equine race.

Cold reality was beginning to appear on her horizon, and some of her earlier enthusiasm for the task she'd set herself was beginning to seep away. "If the truth be known, mule, I think I may have bitten off more than I can chew," she confided.

Miss Marelda was very strict about things like serving tea properly and carrying on a charming conversation, but her course of education had been lacking somewhat on the subject of the proper way to kill a man. Even one you hate with all your being, which should add enough incentive to help Wynne develop her own method—preferably something quite painful. She'd done a lot of thinking about how painful it should be. She was sure even *Godey's Lady's Book* had absolutely nothing to say about the way to handle that task. In fact, it probably said quite the opposite. A proper young woman did not attempt revenge. She was supposed to be above that.

"Such trifling with a lady's heart should be avenged by the men in her family," Wynne assured the mule. A deep sigh escaped her. There were no men in the Elliot family now. They all were gone. A tear rolled down her cheek.

A long rumble of thunder—like dominos falling over—rolled across the horizon. "Oh, flitter, mule. If it rains, I don't know what I'll do." She stood up and tugged on the reins. "Come on. Please, please cooperate," Wynne begged but the mule didn't budge.

She searched for shelter. Other than the ominous-looking dark clouds on the horizon there was nothing but trees and scrub brush and hundreds of grasshoppers, surrounding her like a miniature spitting army. The lack of rain had made the pesky creatures abundant this year. They clung to her skirt and hopped around her feet and made a squishy sound when she accidentally stepped on them.

A grove of hickory trees off to the right looked promising. Her eyes narrowed when they focused on what seemed to be some sort of primitive dwelling hidden among the trees. Dense foliage almost obscured the sight, but on closer inspection Wynne decided that it must be an old log cabin.

If she were fortunate, the owners would allow her to take refuge when the storm broke, but the first thing she had to do was get the mule to move.

She turned her attention back to the animal, tugging on the rope halter as she tried to force the beast back to its feet. The beast, of course, enjoyed his sit. "Ohhh!" Wynne jerked the halter and the mule brayed louder than Gabriel's last trumpet.

"My word!" She dropped the reins to cover her ears. She'd never heard a mule with such lungs. So far that bray had been the only part of this animal that had consistently worked.

Cole slowed his horse to a walk as he zeroed in on the scene below him. He rested his arms on the saddle horn and watched the spectacle with budding amusement.

Wynne had the mule in front of her. The contrary thing had planted itself squarely in the middle of the road. The two of them hadn't made it much past a couple miles out of Springfield, but somehow that didn't surprise him.

What did surprise him was that she was standing there shaking her finger in the animal's face and, from the look of it, preaching a sermon.

Fool woman, he thought irritably. Why was he wasting precious time following her, time that could well be spent on a hundred other things? While he was away, the farm had gone steadily downhill. Ma had done her best, and he'd hoped Cass would stay there to help out, but he'd gone off and left the farm to go to ruin. Fences to be mended, ground to be tilled, crops to be planted, and what was Cole doing? Chasing a crazy female, that's what.

He'd blamed himself all afternoon for giving her a second thought. He'd told himself that whatever happened to her was just due, but as the day wore on, her pitiful plight kept coming back to him. She was a city woman, unaccustomed to the Ozarks terrain.

The thought had nagged at him all day, and by late afternoon he'd decided to follow her another few miles. So, instead of mending fences, he was trailing Wynne and an ornery mule.

And it was getting ready to pour. He glanced up, studying the churning clouds.

Stubborn female. She'd been nothing but trouble from the day he and Beau had come across her, and now he was going to be following her across half the state. He was not her protector, and she wasn't his responsibility.

He found it hard to believe that Cass had actually left Wynne standing in front of the church, but if he had, the boy would answer to Cole. Cass was the baby; Cole had always been overly protective of him since he'd never known their pa, but neither of his brothers would get away with breaking his word. If a Claxton man gave his word, then he'd honor it. Although he'd hate like blazes to see Cass, or any other man for that matter, bound to the Elliot woman. No man deserved a fate like that.

He sighed and shook his head when Wynne's frustrated screeches filled the air. Seems like there was no end to the trouble she could cause. Now he was going to have to lie to Ma. Wire her some far-fetched story about unexpected business that would take him to KC for a few weeks. His conscience hurt him. He didn't make a habit of lying. It surely wasn't the Christian thing to do, and to lie to his mother seemed to double the guilt. And it was all because of that fickle female. Now was that fair?

The little twit sat in the road, her feet firmly planted as she pulled on the mule's halter. The animal lurched up, knocking her flat on the ground, and then stood over her, braying.

Cole grinned when Wynne screeched with indignation. She was living up to redheads' reputation for bad tempers. He kneed the mare forward and walked it down the slope, pulling up a scant five feet from her. His eyes skimmed her pitiful condition:

rumpled dress, filthy hands and face. She raised her eyes and sent him a disparaging look.

Cole eyed her bare feet. Surely not Southern ladies' proper attire. He casually leaned forward and peered down at her. "The mule a little disobliging, Miss Elliot?"

"What are you doing here?" she snapped.

He let an ornery smile trace the corners of his mouth. "Why, Miss Elliot, you act as if you're not happy to see me."

"How astute of you. I'm not." She got to her feet, brushing the dust and grasshoppers off her skirt.

Cole watched while she fussed with her appearance, trying to conceal her bare toes beneath the hem of her dress. Her hair had come loose from its pins, and limp curls hung down her back.

"I thought you were going to take the stage to Kansas City," he said.

"I decided it would be better to travel by . . . mule. If I'd gone by stage, I might have missed Cass on his way home."

"Well, here I was thinking maybe you couldn't get a loan at the bank, so you went all over town trying to sell your pearl ring, and that didn't work either, so you finally had to go to the stable and swap the pretty little thing off for this old mule and back-pack."

"Well, you thought wrong," she said, squinting. "Now how did you know all that? There are obviously a bunch of busybod-ies in River Run."

Cole shifted in his saddle, grinning at her growing frustra-tion. "Where's your little bird hat?"

Wynne strode to the side of the mule and jerked the hat out of her valise. She flung it at him. "Right here!"

He ducked when the bird sailed past his head, but he was

still grinning when he straightened and clicked his tongue. "Did anyone mention you have a nasty temper, Miss Elliot?"

"Mr. Claxton, I'm sure you have not ridden all the way out here to discuss my personality traits," she replied icily. "What do you want?"

"Oh, I don't know. Maybe I missed you, and I decided to ride out and see how you were doing."

"Very amusing." She wasn't buying that in the least.

"Maybe I wanted to make sure you had a rain slicker." His grin widened when he saw her getting madder by the minute. His gaze shifted to the south. "Looks like it's going to pour, and maybe I got to worrying about that little bird on your hat. I sure wouldn't want a little sparrow to get wet, so maybe I rode out here to—"

He ducked when a black shoe flew past his head.

Cole straightened in the saddle once more and clucked as if amazed at her behavior. "There you go getting all riled again. And I'm trying to be nice to you."

"Ha! That's a laugh! You have never been nice to me. Will you kindly move on, Mr. Claxton, and leave me alone?" She grabbed the mule's reins.

"No." The saddle creaked when he shifted. Suddenly the situation didn't seem so funny. "I can't do that, Miss Elliot."

"And why can't you do that, Mr. Claxton?"

"Because now that I know you're out to kill my brother, I have to stop you."

"Well, you can't stop me."

"Protect him from your . . . oh, shall we say, ineptitude? You're not a professional gunslinger, are you? Haven't made a name for yourself?"

Her face turned hard and impassive. Her eyes skimmed the area. "I'll have you know I can shoot a—a grasshopper's eye out at a hundred feet!" she boasted.

He whistled in mock admiration. "A grasshopper's eye at a hundred feet, huh? Well, I have to admit, that's pretty fancy shooting."

"That's right. It certainly is." Their gazes locked, and her lower lip jutted out until she looked as stubborn as the white mule.

"But you'll have to do better than that, because I can shoot a grasshopper's eye out at a hundred and fifty feet." He seriously doubted if he could *spot* a grasshopper that far away, and he didn't bother to point out the fact that there would be nothing left of the grasshopper to support this boasting should they actually engage in such a childish duel.

Wynne bulled up like a thundercloud and stared back at him. "I do not want your despicable company a moment longer. I don't care if you can shoot a hummingbird's eye out a mile away."

"I don't want yours either," he said. "But we're stuck with each other. Don't make the mistake of thinking I'm here for you. I'm here for Cass. So don't come running to me when you get yourself in a peck of trouble you can't get out of. I'll be right behind you all the way, Miss Elliot. I want you to be aware of that. And if you do happen to run into my brother, I'll be there looking over your shoulder." All trace of teasing had disappeared from his voice. "I'm giving you fair warning; I will not stand by and watch my brother killed, even if it means one of us gets hurt in the process."

Wynne paused in rearranging the pack on her mule, and he

was relieved to see she looked apprehensive. He was doing his best—using a stern tone of voice—to convince her he was not making idle threats. He would stop her from shooting Cass any way he had to.

He knew she was itching for a way to call his bluff, but he didn't plan to give her a chance. His eyes locked with hers. "One final piece of advice, Miss Elliot." He turned his horse and prepared to ride off. "It would be smart to quit while you're ahead."

Still, half a mile up the road he paused and dropped his canteen in the middle of the road. He had extra; she wouldn't think of refilling her canteen until she drank the last swallow.

If she walked right past the water, he couldn't help it.

CHAPTER 10

In the two days Cole had trailed Wynne Elliot, she'd been caught in a brief but drenching rain, fallen in the river twice, and shouted at the mule in a most unladylike manner. But even that had only been a prelude to the hissy fit she'd pitched when she discovered she couldn't start a campfire because she had insisted on swimming the mule through the deepest part of the streams during river crossings and invariably got everything wet, including her matches, her clothing, and her bedding.

The old adage held true: God made the rain to fall on the just and the unjust.

And on fools.

She must have slept in a wet blanket every night since she left River Run. The fool jenny wouldn't walk half the time, its obstinacy matched only by the pea-brained stubbornness of a Savannah tidewater belle toting a grudge a mile long.

Cole rested in the saddle and observed Wynne on the trail ahead of him. As far as he knew, she had eaten very little since her trip began. She had found the water he'd left—he'd doubled back and made sure of that—but he'd bet she was getting mighty hungry.

She was a mess by now, clothes limp and permanently wet, her hair hastily piled up on top of her head. But he was not going to help her. Helping her wasn't part of his plan. He wanted her to get discouraged enough to quit this crazy vendetta of hers and go home—back to that Georgia plantation where she belonged.

During the day, he had trailed her at a safe distance. At night they had made camp not two hundred yards from each other. Every night he had a fire going in minutes, coffee bubbling over the coals, and bacon and beans sizzling in the pan. The aroma of the simple but filling food drifted on the humid air.

Wynne had steadfastly ignored his presence. And he had ignored hers.

Tonight was different; tonight, he noted with disgust, she had chosen the most exposed location she could find. Anyone with a lick of sense would have known better, but he guessed they hadn't taught survival skills at that fancy women's school she had attended. She'd picked an open space, too far from water and without protection should an enemy approach. If she did happen to get a fire started, anyone could spot the smoke a mile away.

Why didn't she give up and admit that she was beaten? Why was she so all-fired intent on killing a man anyway? He wouldn't have expected her to be the type to let revenge eat her alive. She wasn't the first or the last woman to be wronged by a man. If a woman had left him at the church, he'd have said good riddance and thanked the Lord for saving him a lot of heartache.

Cole picked a campsite deeper into the brush. Wynne had

already pulled her pack off the mule and spread her blankets. From the looks of them when she tried to shake them out, they were sopping wet. He studied her unraveling hem, and the sight reminded him of the night in the cherry orchard when she'd accidentally unstitched her skirt from her bodice. There she'd stood in her bodice and white cotton bloomers, the crimson cloud of hair making her look even younger than her nineteen years.

He'd never seen a woman look more vulnerable—or more attractive.

Waiting for his supper to cook, he clasped his hands behind his head, leaned back against his saddle, and closed his eyes. The campfire's gentle hiss soothed his weary bones. His muscles slowly begin to relax. During the war he'd ridden as much as two days without closing an eye, but sometimes he thought he was getting older, and his body wouldn't take the strain anymore. Sleeping on the hard ground wasn't as easy as it used to be. If it wasn't for Miss Pain-in-the-Neck Elliot, he could be home, sleeping between sun-dried sheets, eating Willa's biscuits and gravy every morning. . . .

The stars twinkled overhead like diamonds, but toward the west, occasional flashes of heat lightning marked the sky. The smells of rabbit roasting over the fire and coffee boiling in the pot softly infiltrated the twilight.

For some reason he felt guilty that she was sitting in the dark beside an unlit pile of sticks, hungry and scared. After all, it wasn't his fault. All she had to do was give up this insane idea of killing Cass and ask for help. The town would have been glad to take up a collection to send her home—come to think of it, he'd have been one of the major contributors. But she wouldn't accept help—oh no, not her. Pride. The woman had more pride than a lizard with two tails.

He shifted on the hard ground, ignoring his conscience. He'd warned her about making this trip, but she'd refused to listen. The chances that she would find Cass were close to nil, and every day he expected her to give up her crazy jaunt and go back to Savannah where she belonged. Maybe after she'd spent another night on the hard ground, hungry, listening to the coyote's howl while she sat alone in the dark, she would reconsider what she was bent on doing.

He didn't have to be told that Ma wouldn't approve of the way he was behaving. She had brought her boys up to respect women, and to live by the Good Book. Ma firmly believed the man should be the head of the house in spiritual matters, but when she had been left with three small boys to raise, she had done her best by them physically and spiritually. Cole couldn't remember a time he ever went to bed hungry, or a time when his mother hadn't thanked God for her blessings. She'd made sure he learned about Jesus and salvation at an early age too, and she'd wept tears of joy the day he was baptized. He wondered if Wynne Elliot was a Christian. Likely not, or she wouldn't be so blamed determined to kill a man.

He let his thoughts drift aimlessly, ignoring the waif who sat next to a cold pile of logs while he basked by the dancing flames of his own campfire. He couldn't imagine what had gotten into his younger brother. If anything, Cass was like Beau, generous to a fault. He wouldn't think of stealing a woman's money. The Claxton men were gentlemen, with Cass being the gentlest of the three.

Beau had his soft side. He was always the one to take in

injured animals and defend the smallest child in school. Then again, like Cole, he could be angered when provoked. Cole had to admit that Cass was the ladies' man of the three. Being the youngest, Ma had spent more time with Cass—taught him more of the Southern way than he and Beau had absorbed. That was one reason Cass had gone to Savannah to visit relatives Cole and Beau had never met, and the reason Cass had joined the Southern sympathizers when he'd enlisted.

Cole sat up and tested the rabbit on the spit, now tender and dripping with fat. He settled back against his saddle, pondering what he was going to do about Wynne Elliot. How long would it take for her to give up and give in to the fact that she wasn't going to achieve her purpose? And what would he do then? She wasn't his responsibility, but he knew he couldn't walk away from her. It wasn't in him to abandon a woman without money or any means of support. After he'd gotten to know her, he had been convinced she wasn't the type to work at a place like Hattie's. That meant someone was going to have to help her get back to Georgia, and it looked like he was elected—unless she managed to kill his brother. Then all bets were off.

He sat up again and gingerly tipped the cross stick loose and off the forked stands of the spit. He couldn't get Wynne's purpose out of his mind. Someone other than Cass had jilted the woman. Maybe someone was using his name. Whoever had taken advantage of Wynne had not been a Claxton. Cole knew that better than he knew his own name. No Claxton would do anything so despicable. That was the only logical answer. But if that was the case, where was his brother now?

Cole pulled a leg free from the rabbit and tasted the succulent meat. His conscience bothered him so much he couldn't enjoy the tasty fare. Wynne had to be hungry. And while the days were blistering, without a fire the night air could seep uncomfortably into the bones. Maybe he should give her a few of his matches.

One match couldn't hurt anything. The simple gesture wouldn't be contributing to his brother's imminent death.

Wynne was miserably hungry—wretchedly, pathetically starved.

The aroma of roasting rabbit saturated the air. She sat huddled next to the unlit pile of sticks and envied the flickering glow of Cole's campfire. It looked so warm, so comforting. She shivered as a cool breeze rippled through the underbrush. If only she could dry her blankets so she could at least get warm. She was apt to catch her death out here with no shelter. And hungry—so hungry.

Her stomach growled, and she drew the blanket more tightly around her shoulders. Her skin felt clammy and dirty. Her head itched, her face was gritty with trail dust, and her dress was destroyed—and all because of that horrible mule.

She glared at the animal, standing not ten feet away, looking placid and docile. "Why can't you act like that in the mornings when I'm ready to ride instead of being so blamed stubborn? Wretched mule." She had traded her pearl ring for this? And thought she had gotten a bargain. That blacksmith had taken advantage of her. He had her lovely ring, and she had this white, long-eared, misbegotten son of Beelzebub.

Her stomach rumbled. That rabbit smelled heavenly, and the coffee's rich, full aroma drove her crazy. *He's torturing you, Wynne*, she argued with herself. *It probably isn't even coffee, just some old stuff he's made with chicory.*

But she wouldn't have minded having a cup if it were made with weeds. Something warm in her stomach would be heavenly. And rabbit? Real food? Just thinking about it made her dizzy. For the past two days she'd lived on nothing but the tough jerky she'd found in the miner's backpack. At first she had been too squeamish to think about eating it, but as the hours had worn on she'd decided that eating the leathery stuff was better than starving to death.

She rested her head against her knees and fought back bitter tears. She wasn't one of those crying ninnies. It took a lot to make Wynne Elliot cry, and it sure wouldn't be over the smell of Cole Claxton's coffee.

Wetness trickled down the sides of her cheeks as she sniffed and swiped at the unwanted tears. She pulled the blanket up tighter. Why was he following her anyway? Did he really think he could keep her from killing his worthless brother? If so, then he'd never dealt with an Elliot before.

Tomorrow she would practice shooting. The blacksmith had been kind enough to include bullets in the trade, so she didn't have to worry about running out of ammunition. And she couldn't argue that she needed the practice. She had to make certain that when she found Cass, she could outshoot him and his contrary brother.

Her gaze returned to his firelight, and she absently licked

the salty wetness trickling into the corners of her mouth. By tomorrow night she would be a good enough shot to kill her own supper, and then she'd just see whose mouth was watering!

She would get a fire started, even if she had to resort to rubbing two sticks together. She'd already tried that numerous times in the past two days, and the method hadn't worked for her, but tomorrow night she'd keep at it until she had a nice roaring fire. Mr. High-and-Mighty Cole Claxton wasn't about to get the best of her. She jerked at the blanket and winced when she felt water ooze down her neck.

She tried to pray, but she didn't have any sense that anyone was listening. Maybe God was through with her. When she was feeling discouraged, like now, she could admit this manhunt was wrong. The commandment about not killing haunted her waking moments. But then she would think of Cass spending her money in Kansas City, or see Cole sitting by his warm campfire, eating his rabbit and drinking his coffee, and she got mad all over again. And she guessed you couldn't be mad and repentant at the same time. God's forgiveness didn't seem to work that way.

But then, God's mercy didn't seem to work for her either. She'd lost everything and gotten nothing in return. Had the beliefs she'd learned in church been a lie? No, she didn't really think so. Her mother's faith had been strong even when she endured the horrible pain of dying. Wynne admitted the problem was probably with her and not with God. She just didn't know how to make things right again.

She eyed the fire, then sniffed the air, hoping to absorb the smell. Rabbit. Delicious, hot rabbit.

Oh, he thought he was torturing her, but he wasn't.
She could take anything Mr. Smarty-Pants dished out. He'd
see.

At daybreak the next morning, Cole was awakened by the
sounds of a gunshot and a bullet loudly ricocheting off his
coffeepot.

He was on his feet in a flash, gun in hand. As his heartbeat
slowed to normal, he realized he made a wonderful target standing upright like that. He took two steps backward and dropped
behind the large log he'd drawn up beside his fire. Cole stared
over the wooden barrier, still half dazed and trying to figure out
who was doing the shooting—and why were they shooting at
him? He hadn't done anything to anyone. At least nothing bad
enough to be jerked out of a sound sleep by someone banging
away at his coffeepot.

He peered cautiously over the log toward the fire. Black
liquid trickled out of the gaping hole in the coffeepot and into
the faintly glowing embers. Steam and the scent of scorched
coffee drifted on the morning air.

A movement to the side of his range of vision caught his
attention. His gaze swiveled upward in that direction to find
Wynne towering above him. Her red hair tumbled wildly about
her head, her green eyes sparkled angrily, and her mouth was
set with determination. "Hand over what's left of that *rabbit!*"
she demanded.

"What—" Cole, wide awake now, stared blankly up at her. Every muscle in his body was taut and ready for a fight, but instead of a bushwhacker standing over him, he saw a five-foot piece of fluff gripping a pistol. And she was pointing it straight at his head.

"Don't argue with me!" She took a menacing step forward, the metal of her gun barrel glinting wickedly in the early-morning sun. "I said, hand me that *rabbit!*"

Cole cautiously got to his feet.

"Don't come any closer," she warned. "I'll shoot—I mean it."

She looked hungry enough and mad enough to hand wrestle a bear.

"Easy." Cole leaned down and picked up what was left of the meat. "Here's the rabbit. Now put that gun down before you hurt someone."

She waved the barrel toward the coffeepot. "Pour me a cup of coffee before it all seeps out," she ordered.

He put his hands on his hips. "How do you expect me to pour you a cup of coffee when you just blew a hole the size of Texas through the middle of the pot! What am I suppose to do for coffee now?"

"You'll do just what I've been doing," she said without the slightest trace of pity. "Without. Now, pour that coffee before it all runs out on the ground."

If it hadn't been for the fact that she had the gun, he would have put a stop to this nonsense once and for all. But he valued his life more than he did the coffee, so he grudgingly obliged her request.

"Set the cup down on that stump."

He had hoped he could get close enough to take the gun

away from her, but he decided he'd better do what she said. He wasn't fool enough to mess with a woman in this mood.

He placed the cup where she indicated.

Wynne nodded. "Now, you stand over there out of my way."

He did as she ordered, silently gritting his teeth at his awkward situation. Wynne picked up the cup and started slowly backing away from his camp.

Cole stood with his hands on his hips, watching her. Robbed by a woman. It was too much.

"Oh—" she paused in flight—"give me some matches too."

"What?"

"You heard me!" She steadied the gun, holding the meat and tin cup with her other hand. "Give me some matches!"

And he had been about to give her matches the night before. "You steal my rabbit, shoot up my coffeepot, and now you want my matches? Lots of luck, lady."

She leveled the gun barrel directly at his chest and repeated in a low, ominous growl, "I said I want some *matches. Now.*" Her finger hovered near the trigger.

He wasn't certain how tight that trigger was set. Let her grip it too hard, and he could be dead where he stood before the fool woman realized what she'd done.

He bent and flipped open his saddle pack, then tossed a small packet of wrapped matches toward her.

When they landed in the dust, Wynne waved the gun. "Pick them up and put them where I can reach them. Do it nicely."

Moments later she had her matches and was backing her way out of camp. When she was in safe running distance, she whirled and fled.

Cole stood watching her, his jaw open in disbelief. She'd

done it *again*! How many times was he going to let her get the best of him? The woman was a menace to society!

Wynne dropped down on a nearby rock and began stuffing the meat in her mouth, keeping one eye on the enemy camp. She had to admit that what she'd done wasn't very nice, but right now she really didn't care. It was only after she had eaten her fill and drunk the barely warm, bitter coffee that remorse began to set in.

Her life of crime was increasing every day. She sighed, licking remnants of the tasty rabbit off her fingers. Just how was she supposed to explain this moral lapse to God? Another commandment broken: "Thou shalt not steal." Well, really, she hadn't broken the one about killing because she hadn't exactly killed anyone yet. But she certainly had plotted in her heart to kill, and Pastor Burke had insisted that holding the thought was the same as committing the deed. That didn't really make sense to her, but she was willing to admit he might be a bit more versed on the Good Book than she was. Still, it did seem that until she actually pulled the trigger, she hadn't broken the mandate.

Would she really have shot Cole back there in his camp? She didn't know. He had looked so . . . well, attractive . . . and vulnerable, waking up all surprised like that. Still, she had been terribly hungry, and he had that rabbit. Hunger did odd things to folks. If Cole Claxton had even the smallest scrap of manners he would have offered her some of his food. She rested the gun on her lap and stared off into space, wondering how she had come this far from the way she had been raised.

The whole mess had started with her simple—and completely understandable—determination to avenge herself and get her money back. Then she had decided to kill the man in the process, and now she had resorted to robbery.

Miss Marelda Fielding would swoon.

More to the point, Wynne had a feeling God was taking a dim view of her present behavior. Surely He would take into account that during the present atrocity she had been extremely hungry, if not actually starving, and irrational behavior had won out. And it should count for something that Cole Claxton had food aplenty but hadn't offered to share. Wasn't that a biblical command: to share with those who were in need? Well, she had been in need, and he hadn't shared. In that light, you could say that she had just taught him a lesson in Christian behavior. God was probably looking approvingly on the way she had handled the situation.

She sighed. No matter how hard she tried to justify her actions, she knew she had done wrong. There was no justification for stealing and shooting up a man's belongings.

If she felt this bad about shooting a coffeepot, what would she feel like after she shot Cass?

That woman was asking for trouble! Having Wynne Elliot best him didn't sit well with Cole. The very thought that a pint-sized woman weighing a hundred pounds less than him could waltz into his camp and demand he hand over his food at gunpoint was nothing short of humiliating.

If she had been a man, she would have lived just long enough to hear the sound of his gun explode. Cole squirmed uncomfortably in his saddle. He was hungry. Last night he had purposely eaten only half that rabbit so he could have the remainder for breakfast. But Miss Elliot had taken care of that.

Well, she wouldn't take him by surprise again. And the next time, the fact that she was a woman—and a pretty one to boot— would make no difference.

By evening he was too beat to ride another mile. The heat sapped his spirit and his energy, and when he noticed Wynne making camp earlier than usual, he did the same.

At least this time she'd chosen a decent camping space. She had stopped in a pine grove beside a clear stream. The peaceful setting looked cool and inviting. Much more so than the bare expanse of rocky ground he would have to bed down on if he was to keep her in his sights. But again, why should he be uncomfortable because she was in the lead?

Having made his decision, he rode to within fifty feet of where Wynne was bent over trying to start a fire. She glanced his way, then quickly turned her attention back to the sullen spark she was striving to coax into life.

He made camp and had a good fire going long before she had fanned the tiny flame to life. Remounting his horse, he tipped his hat to her in a mocking gesture and rode out. Game was plentiful here, and it took only two shots to bag a couple of plump rabbits. He was going to cook both of them and eat in front of her tonight. See how she liked that. He'd heard her trying to kill her own supper all day—it would have been hard to miss all the rounds of ammunition she had wasted. Made him nervous too. As unhandy as she was with a gun, he half expected to hear a shot come over his head any time. And if it had, he wasn't at all sure it would have been accidental. She had a redhead's temper all right. It was a shame that someone that pretty had such a cantankerous disposition.

Wynne straightened, placing her hand in the small of her aching back, and watched as Cole took two rabbits down to the edge of the stream and began to clean them. She didn't watch the process, knowing it would only upset her stomach and ruin any success she might have in killing her own dinner. She pushed aside any thoughts of having to clean anything she was lucky enough to shoot.

But the stream was inviting. She was tired and grungy. Her hair had been whipped and matted by the dry wind, and her skin felt about to crack from the heat. She had never in her life been this dirty.

She decided that since she would be going to bed hungry again tonight, she could at least be tidy. The old prospector's gear didn't offer much in the way of luxuries, but she gathered the scrap of soap she had packed in the valise and the last of her clean clothing and walked downstream in search of privacy.

Around a small bend in the stream there was an inviting pool deep enough to meet her needs.

The setting sun bathed the tranquil waters in a fiery orange glow. Wynne left her clothes in a pile lying on the bank and stepped into the creek, wearing only her chemise. The lowering sun gilded her dampened skin as she cupped water in her hands and let it flow over her shoulders and arms. It felt so good to wash away the trail dust. She'd sleep better tonight for bathing, even if she went to bed hungry.

When Wynne didn't return, Cole reluctantly went looking for her. He followed the bend in the stream and saw her standing in water to her waist with her damp red locks flowing around her like molten copper. She was lathering soap in her hair, working the rich creaminess through the crimson mass.

The sun had turned her fair skin to warm honey. It occurred to him that when he had seen her this morning up close, over a steel gun barrel, her nose had been sunburned and her cheeks sprinkled with freckles.

The deep water and the chemise she wore protected her modesty, and the fall of her hair reached to her waist, like a scarlet cape. She was the most beautiful woman he had ever seen. He wished for a moment they weren't enemies, then swiftly pushed the thought away. This wasn't a battle he had sought. Wynne Elliot might be a beautiful woman, but she had only one thought in her mind and that was to kill his brother.

He moved cautiously back through the underbrush, hoping she hadn't seen him spying on her. When Ma had brought him up to respect women, she hadn't divided them into categories. His mother was as cordial to Hattie and her girls as she was to the women in church. When she said *women*, she meant all women. He guessed that included Wynne Elliot. Ma had taught her boys their Bible too. He had a strong belief in God, and he knew what had happened to David when he had seen Bathsheba taking a bath. A man couldn't be too careful in these matters.

In a few moments he was back at his fire and spitting the rabbits, wishing he were anywhere but here. This was no place for a God-fearing man. If he wasn't careful, Miss Elliot could become even more trouble than he wanted.

He made certain the meat was roasting properly, then gathered his own clean clothing and went to bathe farther downstream.

That night Wynne lay in her bedroll and forced herself to ignore the smell of Cole's supper lingering in the air. His campfire had been banked, and she presumed he was fast asleep by now.

They had not exchanged one word since they'd made camp, but that wasn't unusual. They rarely spoke to each other unless it was to argue.

In a way she wished that weren't so. She was lonely, and maybe just a little bit afraid, if she would let herself admit it.

This miserable journey was the first time she'd ever been so alone, and she hated it. She glanced at the other campsite and wondered if Cole had ever felt so lonely. Since he had served in the war, he would be used to being out in the dark night, beside a campfire with only the sounds of crackling bushes and wild animals.

Did he ever wonder what those strange noises were, or if they were dangerous? Probably not. He was a man of experience; she could tell that. A man who'd experienced war and killing and death every day. She stared up at the stars, wondering how many times he had lain out on the battlefield wondering if he would see another day. It was difficult to imagine Cole Claxton being a man with natural fears, but surely he experienced his own devils. The only reason he was following her now was his concern for his brother.

She could understand why Cole felt resentful toward her, why he must hate her. She would have felt the same way if someone were trying to kill one of her kin; yet it would seem that since they were traveling in the same direction, alone, maybe it wouldn't hurt for them to talk a little once in a while. They could discuss the weather, or he could tell her where he had fought in the war, or maybe they could just talk about nothing in particular.

The ache in her stomach reminded her of her hunger. And the thought that Cole still had one whole rabbit left—for his breakfast the next morning—didn't help any.

She knew she didn't dare try to take it from him again. He had let her get away with robbery once, but she probably wouldn't be so lucky the next time, especially since he had witnessed her deplorable inaccuracy with a gun today. He'd no doubt laughed all day at her bumbling antics. How embarrassing. Her cheeks burned in the darkness. How utterly stupid he must think her.

She propped herself up on one elbow, squinting toward his campfire as she tried to locate the leftover rabbit. There it was lying next to the fire—all brown and juicy-looking.

Get your mind off that rabbit! She dropped back onto the lumpy bedroll. *He would break your arm if you tried to steal it from him again. Surely tomorrow you'll be able to kill your own supper.*

Her gaze switched involuntarily back to Cole's camp, and she sighed. She was so hungry. He had at least enough rabbit left for two people, and if he was any sort of gentleman at all, he would have offered to share his food with her.

She bit her lower lip, thinking. Maybe she could just sort of sneak over there and take a bit of the meat while he was sleeping. He would never miss it. She would take a piece so tiny he would never know it was gone.

Wynne slipped out of her bedroll and tiptoed on bare feet across the short space between her camp and Cole's. She crept closer to where he lay peacefully sleeping, holding her breath lest the slightest sound wake him. A soft snore quivered on the breeze and helped still her growing apprehension of what she was about to do. It appeared Pastor Burke was right: Once you committed a sin, the next one was easier. Right now it didn't bother her a bit to take part of Cole's rabbit. She was only afraid he'd wake up and catch her.

Her steps faltered. She'd best make sure he was actually asleep. He could be trying to trick her. She certainly wouldn't put it past him. She leaned over and studied his expression. His eyes were closed, the dark lashes a smudge against his tanned skin. Dark curls tumbled over his forehead, and her fingers moved involuntarily to brush them back, but she caught the gesture just in time. His lips were parted, lightly snoring. She leaned closer, listening to the even pattern of his breath. No, he wasn't trying to trick her. He was asleep.

The plump rabbit beckoned. Wynne tiptoed closer to the fire. One teensy little piece. Smarty-Britches would never know the difference, but the food would mean that she wouldn't have to lie awake all night with an empty stomach.

Cole opened his eyes and watched when Wynne approached the rabbit he had left out as bait. She had to be starving, and his conscience wouldn't let him be. He'd never let anything go hungry. Every stray dog or cat, every traveling saddle tramp knew they could find food at the Claxton farm. He'd tried, but he couldn't go back on his raising. Still, she had to be taught a lesson.

He carefully got to his feet as she reached out to snare a plump, succulent morsel.

Her fingertips were actually touching the rabbit when he yelled at her. "Oh, no, you don't, Miss Elliot!"

She whirled, staring at him, her mouth open, one hand clasped to her throat. He wanted to grin at her stupefied expression. He'd probably looked as thunderstruck this morning when she woke him by taking a shot at his coffeepot. Well, turnabout was fair play, and it served her right.

"You were trying to steal my rabbit again, weren't you?"

"I most certainly was not!" she said indignantly.

"Oh yes you were, and this time you're not going to get

away with it." He grabbed her shoulders and gently shook her. He was going to scare the wits out of her this time.

She stared up at him, sobbing, tears rolling down her cheeks. Cole released her, feeling like a whipped dog. He fought the urge to take her in his arms and dry her tears. What was wrong with him? This woman could turn him inside out just by looking at him.

Now he'd made her cry. She was a thief—and planned to be a killer—and he felt sorry for her. Was he losing his mind?

He reached in his back pocket and took out his handkerchief. "From now on, if you want anything that's mine, you come and ask me—nicely." He wiped the tears from her cheeks.

"You're . . . a . . . big . . . bully," she said, sniffling.

"I'm not a bully. I know that's what you think, but I'm only trying to help you. You can't go through life stealing from others. You're going to get yourself killed."

"But I was hungry and you wouldn't let—"

"I know, and I'm sorry I wouldn't help you shoot your meat." He put the handkerchief back in his pocket and reached out to lightly place his hands on her shoulders. His eyes met her and he tried to look stern. "From now on I'll see that you have enough to eat."

She sniffed, nodding. "And a fire. Please."

This time he couldn't hold back the grin. "And a fire." His gaze lingered on the soft curve of her mouth. She sure looked kissable.

He slowly bent his head forward until his mouth touched hers.

She sighed—a soft, kittenish sound—and her arms automatically wound around his neck. He pulled her closer, and his mouth closed over hers in a kiss that left him feeling shaken.

Cole dropped his arms and stepped away. He cleared his throat. "Please forgive me, Miss Elliot." He had no idea why he had done that! Well, yes he did, but he didn't plan on doing it again.

Wynne backed away from him, her eyes wide. "It's—it's quite all right, Mr. Claxton."

"Listen—" he moved over to the fire to retrieve the extra rabbit—"you take this and go on back to bed."

"I couldn't," she said politely. "It's your breakfast."

He glanced at her in disbelief. Females! Five minutes ago she was ready to steal it from him. "I insist." He generously extended the meat to her. "But this doesn't change our situation. I will do everything in my power to prevent you from finding Cass."

She shrugged. "A man's got to do what he's got to do. That's what my father always said."

He blinked, surprised at the platitude dripping from her honeyed lips. Somehow he could never second-guess her.

Her hand flew out to accept the gift before he could have second thoughts. "If you're sure . . ."

"Yeah," he said dryly. "I insist."

He watched as she sprinted back across the grass with an air of triumph and a sneaky smile on her face.

She probably thought she had brought him to heel with her tears. He grinned, feeling smug. He'd figured she'd come sneaking around tonight if she got hungry enough.

Little did she know that he had killed that rabbit for her in the first place.

CHAPTER 11

Wynne awoke minutes before the sky began to slowly shed its heavy mantle of darkness. She lay in her bedroll, watching the spreading light with a strange sense of detachment from the beauty unfolding before her. The sun sent out exploratory rays, brushing the few clouds with gold.

Her mind was still on Cole's kiss. The kiss he had taken would be the appropriate description. For she would never willingly have allowed that man such liberties with her! But she had to admit Cass had never kissed her like that.

If she was truthful, she had to confess, though it made her uncomfortable to do so, that she'd done very little to stop the unexpected embrace; in fact, she might have actually encouraged him in the matter. However, she much preferred to think of herself as the victim who had once again been made to suffer at the hands of a Claxton.

The longer she lay and thought about what had happened, the easier it was to convince herself that she'd had nothing to do with the kiss, and that Cole had had everything to do with contributing to her damaged pride.

Oh, she would grudgingly admit the kiss had been nice, but certainly not pleasant by any means; a bit stimulating, perhaps, but only mildly so. Nothing to make her lose sleep. She had only tossed and turned because the ground was hard as a stone. Her restlessness had nothing to do with Cole Claxton. She thought of the way he had looked while he had been feigning sleep. For a moment she had felt guilty about taking advantage of him while he had been vulnerable, but he had only been pretending. Acting a lie.

No, of course she hadn't wanted him to kiss her. In fact, a gentleman would not kiss a woman the way Cole Claxton had kissed her.

The man should be ashamed of himself!

Still, it had been . . . interesting. Being a proper young lady, she'd never been kissed all that much. In fact, her experience with Cass, limited though it might be, had been her only experience with the art of kissing. She felt unfaithful to the fiancé who had jilted her to have enjoyed Cole's kiss so much. Well, no, now, that seemed a bit complicated and not at all what she meant. Perhaps she wasn't sure what she meant, but one thing she knew: The only reason the kiss had stimulated her in the least was that Cole resembled Cass so strongly. That was the only reason why her mouth still tingled and she grew slightly breathless when she thought about last night. She knew she was being a fool. Cole Claxton had probably kissed a hundred women.

Wynne rolled onto her side and glared in the direction of his camp. She couldn't see him, couldn't see that devilishly handsome face. But in her mind she could see those penetrating blue eyes, that thick curly hair that a woman would long to push her fingers through.

Oh yes, Cole Claxton was steal-your-breath handsome—Wynne groaned aloud with frustration—but he was also cruel, unrefined, uncivilized, and a big bully with little regard for a woman's gentle nature.

Yet considering her own eagerness to be captured by his younger brother, and considering the way the two men resembled each other, it was little wonder that she was only one of a number of women intrigued by Cole.

Still, she wasn't about to make the same mistake twice. She wanted Cole Claxton out of her life. She was good and tired of his following her day after day, taunting her, laughing at her lack of experience in the wild. And she intended to do something about it, starting right now.

She crawled out of her bedroll, talking to herself as she folded the blankets and tried to smooth some of the wrinkles out of her dress. She was going to lose that scoundrel if it was the last thing she did. She was more than capable of taking care of herself, regardless of what he thought.

Once she had her mind made up, it took very little time to wash her face and hands, change into a fresh dress, and break camp. In a few minutes Wynne was urging the mule out of the grove of trees as the sun rose over the Missouri hilltops.

"Giddyap, you ornery critter!" she commanded in a hushed tone, giving the animal a smart kick in the ribs. For once the mule complied with her wishes and set off in the bone-jarring trot that rattled her teeth and jerked her neck about painfully. She smiled, thinking how surprised Cole Claxton would be when he woke up this morning. That would teach him to grab a decent woman and kiss her. He wouldn't be so impulsive the next time.

Cole leaned against a spreading oak, whose base was shielded by a thick undergrowth of wild grapevines, and watched the mule lope away with its ungainly rider. He shook his head.

Now what was she up to?

She'd carefully smoothed her hair and perched that silly hat back on top of her head. Why she insisted upon wearing that hat and her Sunday dress he'd never understand.

He pushed away from the tree trunk and strode toward his own camp. What he ought to do was turn around and go home. He was tired of sleeping on the ground and having to hunt for every meal. He'd lived like that for the past four years, and he was sick of it. He'd looked forward to getting home after a four-year absence, and here he was riding around the countryside keeping an eye on an addlebrained female who was probably going to get them both killed.

Going home was such a persuasive thought that it almost brought him pain, but then another equally disturbing idea worked its way back into his mind. For a brief moment Cole let himself think about how good it felt kissing Wynne last night. Even having been on the trail for days, she still smelled feminine—nice, like the lilac bushes that grew wild across the countryside. And her hair. The copper strands had felt like that piece of material he'd bought Ma for Christmas one year. The tinker had had a bolt of it in the back of his wagon. Silk, he'd called it, and it was real pretty. Wynne's hair had lain across his bare arm like rich, elegant silk, and it made a man long to run his fingers through it.

Cole irritably cinched his bedroll onto the back of his horse and stared in the direction she had taken. He was tired—tired of responsibility, tired of duty. Just once he wished there was a simple answer to a problem. But he'd looked after Beau and Cass since the day Pa died, and he guessed he wouldn't be stopping now.

Not when Wynne Elliot was running around the country-side, threatening to blow his brother's brains out.

It was truly a glorious morning. Songbirds chattered in the trees, and the sound of an occasional woodpecker held Wynne's attention as the mule trotted along.

She turned her face up to the sky and took a deep breath, smiling happily. It felt marvelous to be free of the specter of Cole Claxton following her within hailing distance.

She urged the mule in a more northerly direction, concentrating on making her trail harder to follow. By the time Mr. Know-It-All woke up, she'd be only a memory.

Wynne prayed she could keep her sense of direction and not become hopelessly lost. The blacksmith had said to steer north, and that's what she had been doing.

She had to laugh when she thought about how incensed Cole would be when he realized how easily she had ridden out of his life. It only served him right, she thought smugly. It was high time he was made aware he wasn't dealing with a complete imbecile. Mr. Cole Claxton was dealing with Wynne Elliot, a courageous woman who had survived the deaths of her parents, who had held a plantation together—if only for a little while—and who could take care of herself on the trail and do just fine without a man's help.

Her delighted laughter rang out over the hillsides. He might not believe she was capable of anything other than making a fool of herself, but Mr. Claxton would know differently soon enough. Oh, would he ever!

By midafternoon the sun was a blistering red ball, the heat so oppressive that Wynne could hardly breathe. The mule had slowed until it barely ambled along, picking its way over a narrow trail of overgrown prickly briars and thicket. Vines trailed across the path, brushing her face and catching her hair. She had abandoned the main road hours ago to guarantee her getaway but was still careful to travel northward.

Wynne periodically reached up to swipe halfheartedly at the moisture beading her flushed features. She would give anything she still owned for a drink of cool water, but in her haste to break camp, she had forgotten to fill the canteens.

Ordinarily water shouldn't have been that hard to come by, but with the recent lack of rain, most of the streams and gullies she had crossed had been bone dry.

She really should stop and throw this blasted corset away before she fainted from the heat. She wasn't sure what was caus-ing the most agony: the pantaloons, the corset, the layers of petticoats, or the lack of water, but she wasn't about to part with any of the three items of apparel. A lady should maintain propriety even in the wilderness. At least she remembered that much of Miss Marelda's teaching. She dabbed daintily at her cheeks and throat.

If and when she ran into Cass, she wanted to look her best, although she had to admit her dress was sadly lacking in style. Of course, she had two other dresses packed away in the valise, but they were not nearly as nice as the one she was wearing. It was foolish to dress so nicely every day on the remote chance she might actually encounter Cass, but her pride prevented her from traveling in comfort.

Her hand absently reached up to readjust her hat, and a thin layer of dust trickled off the brim and caused her to sneeze. When he saw how beautiful she looked, Cass would be absolutely sick that he had walked out on her. She wanted him to hold that thought, just before he became absolutely dead.

A few hours of daylight remained when Wynne finally had to admit she couldn't go another mile. She halted the mule on a hill overlooking a deep valley. A growing sense of despair threatened to sap what little fortitude remained. She was tired, hot, sticky, and convinced by now that she had no idea where she was or if she was even going in the right direction.

Gnats flew around her face and stuck to her bare skin. The sun had burned her face and cheeks in spite of the hat, and the tops of her hands were blistered. The tip of her nose itched and was peeling, and she didn't want to guess what it looked like. It was impossible to go on, yet she didn't know what else to do.

The combination of heat and lack of food and water made her head swim. It was all she could do to hold herself upright in the saddle, and she still had to make camp and try to find something to eat before darkness fell.

For a moment she almost wished the pompous idiot were still following her. She turned in the saddle and peered almost longingly behind her. He wasn't there, of course. She had been too thorough in her escape. By now he was probably on his way back to River Run, where he would have a wonderfully clean bed to sleep in and a huge plateful of Willa's chicken and dumplings to gorge on. The thought of all those rich dumplings swimming in golden gravy with plump pieces of tender chicken made Wynne feel faint.

She straightened her shoulders and forced herself to think. This was no time to start feeling sorry for herself. She had a goal, and she was going to reach it no matter what.

She had two matches and plenty of bullets left. Surely to goodness she would be able to kill one small rabbit for her supper. She was getting better at hitting the targets she chose.

Wynne nudged the recalcitrant mule with her heels, holding on tightly as she urged it down a steep incline. Rocks tumbled over the mountainside and hit the walls of the shale canyon, but she refused to look down. She was dizzy enough. It was all she could do to hold on because the dumb mule kept trying to brush her off on the scrub brush that grew close to the narrow path. Vines and limbs reached out and snatched at her clothes and hair. At one point the mule nearly succeeded in knocking her off against a jutting oak covered with strange-looking vines. Right after she shot Cass, if she had a bullet left, she was going to use it on this mule. Anything this cantankerous and contrary didn't deserve to live.

Wynne decided to plan her next steps as a means of keep-

ing her wits about her. She would camp at the bottom of the
valley tonight. With luck there would be water available. She
closed her eyes and prayed that would be the case. Then she
would try to find something to eat, a rabbit or a squirrel, but
most likely just berries again. Her mouth watered at the
thought of fresh meat roasting over a fire. Maybe she'd catch
a fish with her hands—though she hadn't spotted any in the
shallow streams.

It seemed to take forever for the mule to make its slow
descent, but the path finally widened and leveled off.

The air was a bit cooler down here. The tall limestone bluffs
gave partial shelter from the sun's burning rays. She pushed at
the thick mass of hair on her neck and vowed to find something
to tie it away from her face before she started out again in the
morning, even if it meant ripping a piece of cloth from her petticoat. She brushed at the leaves that had settled and caught in
the material of her dress.

By now she had removed the hat—her one concession to
ease her agony—and tied it on the saddle horn. She could always
put it back on should she run into Cass unexpectedly, and it was
sheer heaven to let the faint breeze blow freely through the
thick mass of her hair.

Suddenly a new aroma filled the air. Her nose lifted slightly
at the unmistakable smell of fatback sizzling over an open fire.

Cole! Had he followed her? But jubilation quickly turned to
smoldering resentment. How *dare* the man continue to follow
her when she had made it perfectly clear she didn't want his
company?

Still, the aroma of his dinner tempered her anger somewhat
as she urged the mule into a faster gait. Perhaps he would be

kind enough to share his meal with her tonight, although that might be pushing optimism to the very limit.

In her eagerness for food she let the mule break through the clearing with the grace of a runaway stage. She quickly yanked the animal to a halt as six revolvers came out of their holsters and centered directly on her.

Wynne's eyes widened and she stared openmouthed at the tattered, dirty men standing around the open fire. Realization slowly dawned. She had not smelled Cole's fatback cooking. Somehow she had blundered into a camp filled with frightening-looking men. She didn't think they were the outlaws from the stage robbery, but they looked like they were cut from the same bolt of cloth.

"Oh, dear." She yanked the mule's head around and kicked his flanks. While she knew escape was futile, she had to at least try and correct this newest blunder.

The mule hadn't taken three strides before she was hauled off the animal's back and roughly flung to the ground. In another part of her mind, Wynne was aware that the sleeve of her dress was ripped from the bodice. She kicked and screamed, trying to scratch the eyes of the man holding her down, but to no avail. Recognizing defeat, she went limp, staring up at the bearded face of her captor.

"Well, well, boys, look what we got here," her assailant crowed. His thin mouth twisted into a smile as a lusty gleam lit his eyes.

A thread of real fear raced down Wynne's spine. She remembered the way Cole had warned her of renegades who prowled these hills. By sheer bad luck, she had just ridden into their camp like a ninny. *Addlebrained.* That was the proper word for her.

The bully hauled her over his shoulder and carried her, kicking and twisting, to where the others stood around the campfire, drinking coffee. He dropped her unceremoniously at their feet, and she hit the ground with a thump. The odor of his unwashed body was so strong it made her stomach roil, and she had to swallow hard to fight the growing nausea that threatened to overtake her.

For the first time in her life, Wynne lost her voice as a cold, paralyzing fear froze her vocal chords. The men surrounding her were a terrifying sight to a lone woman. Besides the one standing over her, three others stood around the fire, and another sat on a large rock. He caught her attention momentarily. It looked as if he was reading a book! He didn't appear to be the slightest bit interested in what was happening, and his apathy chilled her.

A sixth man stood a little way from the group, almost hidden in the shadows at the edge of the small clearing. Apparently he was on watch while the others ate their supper.

Wynne swallowed hard and sat up a little straighter, determined to look death straight in the eye. Even while she willed her pounding heart to quiet, her mind automatically formed impressions. None of the men looked to be more than twenty-five. They were filthy and unkempt, with long hair and untrimmed beards, their clothes worn and dirty. They stared at her with callous observation that made her feel like a thing rather than a woman. She was afraid to guess what they might be thinking.

One of the men called out, "Right pretty-looking girl, Sonny. Invite her to supper!" He stepped over to examine Wynne more closely. Her breath caught when he reached a grimy hand out and touched her head. He grasped a lock of her hair, absently sliding the shiny mass through his fingers, all the while staring into her terrified eyes.

"Real pretty," he repeated. Something in his voice compelled Wynne to study him more closely. He looked young, terribly young.

"Please," she finally managed, "let me go—"

"Ah, Jesse, you think they're all pretty." One of the men chortled, and the others broke out into a new round of laughter. But the young man holding a lock of Wynne's hair seemed unruffled by their friendly kidding.

"That may be rightly so, but this one's *real* pretty." He seemed to be speaking more to her than to the men, and his voice was soft and soothing.

"Now look, Jesse, I got her first," Sonny said.

"Maybe so, but I'm not sure I'm going to let you keep her," Jesse returned, his attention centered on Wynne. "Where you going in such a hurry, honey?"

"Nowhere—to Kansas City," she corrected hurriedly when his eyes narrowed.

"Kansas City? That's a mighty long way for a woman to travel alone."

"I'm not exactly alone," Wynne lied. "I—I have this man with me. He'll—he'll be riding in any moment. . . ."

The men laughed at her attempted bravado.

"I'm supposed to be making camp while he hunts our supper." She continued her bluff. "He'll be quite upset if he finds out you have detained me, gentlemen. He's big and short-tempered, and he doesn't put up with a lot of nonsense." She began to edge slowly back toward the mule.

"Ohhh me, oh my! *He* probably will be real upset if we

detain her, gentlemen," one of the men mocked in a feminine voice. The men roared again, and goose bumps brushed Wynne's arms.

The man reading the book glanced up and frowned as if the racket bothered him. He carefully placed the book on the rock, stood up, and stretched. Wynne's eyes widened in disbelief when she noted the title of the book: *Venus and Adonis* by William Shakespeare.

Jesse turned and grinned at him. "Where you off to, Frank?"

Frank and Jesse. The men's names rang a bell in Wynne's muddled mind, yet she couldn't think where she had heard them before.

"Thought I'd check the horses," Frank announced.

"Ah. Did we bother you?"

"No," he said. "Just thought I'd stretch my legs."

"Do you mind if I go with you?" Wynne piped up in a shaky voice. She had no idea if this man was as bad as—or possibly worse than—the rest of them, but anyone who read Shakespeare didn't seem so frightening.

"No, you can't go with him," Sonny exclaimed. He jerked Wynne back toward him. "You're staying right here, sugar face."

Wynne sent him a sour look. She'd sugar his face with a round of buckshot. First chance she got.

Sonny seemed amused by her dour expression. He dragged her close to the fire and shoved her down onto an old blanket. "How about some supper, honey pie? We was jest about to 'dine' when you dropped in."

"No thanks." As badly as she needed nourishment, she refused to take anything from this bunch of brigands.

"Aw, have we spoiled your appetite?" Sonny grinned. "Better eat a bite while you got the chance."

Jesse's gaze lingered on her.

Fear had eliminated her hunger, and she shook her head at Sonny's urgings to eat. She stared into the fire, trying to bite back her fear. If only she had been content to leave well enough alone. She'd brought this on herself. Cole was stubborn, but she knew she could trust him. Now she was in deep trouble with no way out that she could see.

"Better eat, woman," Sonny urged. "Chow's hot."

Wynne shivered and looked away. Sonny shrugged and filled his plate. She turned her back to the men and plucked ineffectually at the torn threads of her sleeve. What was going to happen to her now? She blinked away the tears that hovered very near the surface. These men would probably take crying as a sign of weakness. She knew almost instinctively that if she let them see her fear, it would only bring out the worst in them.

Her gun was in the saddlebags on the mule, and the one they had called Frank had led the animal away a few minutes earlier. There was no way they would allow her to go hunt for it.

It hurt her pride even more when Cole's numerous warnings about the likelihood of such an occurrence bounced loudly in her head. Why hadn't she listened to him? Why had she undertaken such a ridiculous venture in the first place? This time she couldn't hold back the tears.

It was getting dark when the men had finally eaten their fill. Some stretched out on the ground to let their meal settle, while others sat and drank coffee. They had eaten like swine, belching and smacking, eating with their fingers since there were no utensils.

Wynne found herself comparing the motley group before her with the way Cole and Beau had looked the first time she met them. Actually there was no comparison. The Claxton brothers had been dirty, but not bone-deep nasty like these men.

Cole's image kept running through her mind, and she suddenly, desperately wished she hadn't been so foolish. Even if he did annoy her, and she got on his nerves something powerful, and she had to take food from him at gunpoint, she knew he would have protected her from this, no matter how much he disliked her.

A rumble of thunder broke into her thoughts. She glanced up and saw dark storm clouds rolling overhead. The thought of rain held no elation for her now. A flood of raindrops would never be able to wash away the pain and degradation she was about to experience.

The realization of what was going to happen made her bury her face in her hands and weep in silent despair.

CHAPTER 12

Well, now the fat was in the fire. Cole kept a tight grip on his horse's reins as he crept closer to the camp. If Wynne Elliot didn't get them both murdered, he'd be a monkey's uncle. And it was going to rain like pouring water on a flat rock in about three seconds. That fool woman could come up with more ways to cause trouble. Of all the ruffians out here she had to pick the James gang to fall in with.

The summer storm rolled in, heralded by a cannon roll of thunder and flares of intermittent lightning. Wind picked up, lashing the treetops. Showers of red sparks spiraled from the campfire and skipped across the parched earth.

Cole hoped the storm would distract the outlaws. He recognized a few faces—Frank and Jesse James, Sonny Morgan—desperados, every last one of them, most happy when they were causing trouble. Frank and Jesse might have had reasons during the war for their rebellion, but the war was over and they had no call to prey on unsuspecting females.

"Looks like it's a bad'un," one of the men shouted above the roar of wind.

Cole watched as Jesse scanned the ever-darkening sky. Greenish-looking clouds boiled and churned and puffed out periodic gusts of wind that stripped leaves and sent tufts of dried grass rolling over the hollow. Cyclone weather. He wouldn't have been surprised to see a funnel dip down at any time. No wonder Jesse was nervous.

Cole kept his head down, hoping the approaching weather would distract the outlaws. He crept closer, moving as silently as possible. The roar of the wind helped mask the sound of his movements. Now all he had to do was wait for the ideal moment to make his presence known—not that he was looking forward to the encounter, but one thing he knew for certain: Someone would walk away with Wynne Elliot, and he planned to be the one.

Wynne's hair whipped wildly in the fury of the wind. Cole watched as she struggled to bat fire off the hem of her dress. Men shouted and raced about, trying to quiet the animals spooked by thunder and lightning.

Chaos reigned and the wind blew gale force. Suddenly Wynne bolted for freedom, running straight at him. His jaw dropped. Did she know he was here?

Sonny lunged after her, long arms flailing. He caught her around the waist.

Wynne screamed and fought like a wild thing, scratching and kicking as Sonny dragged her back to the camp. His laughter rose above the screeching wind.

Cole tightened his grip on his rifle. He didn't want to kill Sonny, but it looked like he might have to.

The outlaw dropped Wynne on the ground and stood over

her. "No need to run, sweetie. Ol' Sonny'll take care of you!"
Laughter rang out from the others, and Sonny lifted his face to
the sky. "Whooeee! Got us a fighter here, boys!"

A woman with spirit, Cole thought. Just what he'd thought he
wanted. Beau would have a heyday with this one.

Sonny reached down and yanked Wynne to her feet.

"You slime!" She sank her teeth into the outlaw's meaty
forearm, but he only laughed harder, shaking her until her head
whipped back and forth like a broken doll.

Cole tensed; his anger burned brighter. He shot a glance in
the direction of the others and decided he'd have to make his
move.

Wynne spat in Sonny's face, and he slapped her, hard.

Cole took a deep breath and stepped into the clearing holding the barrel of his Springfield rifle leveled squarely at Sonny's
chest. "Let go of her, Morgan."

Cole's arrival was met with a startled silence. Sonny stood
slack-jawed with surprise. Cole's eyes swept the men, making
certain the six he'd seen from where he had been hiding were
well within the range of his rifle. Wynne couldn't have picked a
worse group to annoy. Frank and Jesse James and some of the
others had ridden with a splinter group of Quantrill's Raiders
during the war. Sonny Morgan was plain mean, with a reputation as long as your arm. Lawmen everywhere were looking for
this bunch, and Wynne had found them without trying; think
what she could do if she put her mind to it. He silently shook
his head. The thought was enough to make a grown man weep.

Wynne sank her teeth into Morgan's hand. Pain crossed his
rugged features but he held tight. "Claxton? What are you doing
here? This ain't none of your business."

The men had begun to move in closer but then stopped when Cole motioned for them to throw down their guns. They reluctantly unbuckled their belts and let them drop to the ground.

Cole spared a glance in Wynne's direction, sending a clear message that she had foolishly gotten them into this sticky situation, and she was going to hear about it if they made it out alive. "Are you all right?" he asked curtly.

She nodded. "They—I didn't know they were here."

"Obviously."

She flushed, and he figured she'd gotten his message that this was all her fault and it would be a miracle if they got out of this mess in one piece.

He turned his attention back to Sonny. "Okay, Morgan. Let her go, and we'll ride out without any trouble."

"Ah, Claxton, what's it to you?" Sonny argued, pulling Wynne possessively to his chest. "I found the little spitfire, so I figure that makes her mine."

Cole's gaze never wavered. He raised the barrel a fraction higher. "Sorry. This one's mine."

Sonny was slow, but he got the point. His smile wilted. "How come? Never knowed you to argue 'bout a woman."

"Perhaps this little lady is different." Jesse made the observation in a casual tone. He tipped his head in a mock salute to the man holding the gun on him.

Cole waited. He'd met up with Jesse during the war and they had taken each other's measure. Neither one of them would want to go up against the other.

Jesse's grin didn't reach his eyes but he echoed Cole's thoughts. "You don't want to go up against Captain Cole, Sonny.

He's fair when it comes to a fight, but he doesn't make empty threats. I believe it might be best to hand over the woman, particularly when he's got a rifle and we don't."

Sonny sent Cole a resentful look. "She your woman?"

That was a tricky question, one Cole didn't care to answer. He shrugged noncommittally. "Let's just say I'm looking after her interests at the moment." His finger rested on the trigger. "Hand her over real gentle-like, Morgan, and we'll be on our way."

Sonny glanced expectantly at Jesse, who nodded his silent agreement. After weighing the situation for a few moments longer, Sonny shoved Wynne roughly away from him. "Take her. She weren't nothing but a peck of trouble anyways."

"You noticed that?" Cole drawled.

Wynne shot him a look that should have struck him dead in his tracks, but she edged closer to him, like she was afraid he'd go off without her. He guessed she'd rather be with him than against him in this situation.

He slipped his arm around her waist and started backing slowly out of the camp. "Good to see you again, Jesse," he said pleasantly. "You and Frank still reading Shakespeare?"

"Nice to see you, Claxton." Jesse still wore a slight grin, but there was that air of danger about him that spoke louder than the smile. "Still reading Shakespeare."

"Frank doing all right?"

"I'm fine, Cole," the man standing on the right side answered quietly. "Good to see you again."

Cole nodded briefly and continued to retreat in measured steps. He could feel Wynne trembling against his thin shirt, and he squeezed her waist in quiet assurance.

"Looks like we're going to get a good rain," Cole continued conversationally. The tension in the air was so thick you could have cut it with a bowie knife, but he kept his voice moderate, as if they were enjoying a Saturday-night social.

"Sure could use it," Jesse agreed.

Rain peppered down. Cole reached behind him for the mare and then helped Wynne into the saddle. He swung up behind her, still keeping the gun leveled at the men who watched his every movement.

"Take care now," he said politely.

Jesse nodded. "You do the same."

The storm struck with hurricane force. Cole reined the mare in a half circle and set home the spurs. Thunder rocked the hollow. A blinding glare of lightning was followed by a deafening cannonlike blast. The scent of sulfur cut the air. A huge oak to the right of the camp split down the middle. Cole clutched Wynne against him, thanking God for the cover of the storm as they rode straight into the heart of the deluge.

"My mule!" Wynne shouted above the pounding rain.

"What about it?" Cole yelled as he urged the horse over the uneven trail. He doubted the men would follow, not in this downpour, but he wanted to make sure there was plenty of distance covered in the shortest possible time.

"We forgot it!"

Well, that did it. Like he hadn't been busy enough trying to save her neck; she expected him to cart along her mule too? Let Sonny have the mule! Come to think of it, you could say it was an even trade. Sonny got an old white mule and he got Wynne Elliot. He figured maybe Sonny got the better deal.

"You want to go get it?" he asked.

"No! But now I won't have anything to ride or wear. And my gun! What about my gun?" she yelled. "And I'm about to drown. Can't you slow down a little?"

"Pipe down!" he yelled back. "I'm a little out of sorts with you, lady!"

"Me?"

"You! That was a crazy trick you pulled this morning, and you're lucky I stuck around to save your hide!"

"Why, of all the nerve! I didn't need your *help* in the least!"

"No? It sure looked to me like you did!"

"I didn't!" She twisted around, trying to look at him.

Cole tried to ignore her. He'd risked his neck to save her, and she didn't appreciate a thing he'd done. For two cents he'd take her back and make Sonny Morgan a gift of her. No. He couldn't do that. A conscience was a terrible handicap. Being a decent, God-fearing man had its disadvantages sometimes.

"I was about to make a run for it when you showed up!"

"I saw how well you made the break," he snapped.

"How long were you standing there, Cole Claxton?"

He'd been there almost from the first moment she'd wandered into the James camp, but he'd decided to teach her a lesson. As long as she wasn't in immediate danger he thought he'd let her sweat. From now on she'd listen to what he had to say. "Long enough to see you were in over your head." His arm tightened around her waist.

"Stop!" she screeched, nearly busting his eardrums.

He hauled back on the reins and the horse slowed. "What's the matter now?"

"You're going back the same way we came," she said.

"Oh, for—just be quiet, will you!" Cole nudged the mare in

the flanks. He wanted to get out of this jungle and back on solid ground. Little rivulets of water had begun to flow down the hillsides. The trail was slick with wet leaves and mud. Wind-driven rain lashed the ground and struck his unprotected shoulders with needlelike force. And this addlebrained woman wanted to argue. How much was one man supposed to put up with without taking matters into his own hands?

"We've already covered this ground," Wynne yelled. "Now we'll have to double back, and that will take more time!"

Really, Cole thought. *Well, how about that?* He didn't care how much time it took her. If he could delay her by an hour, he'd jump at the chance.

The horse lumbered up the hump of the slope and out into a clearing. A flash of lightning exposed the road, and Cole breathed a sigh of relief. He'd been afraid the mare would lose her footing on the steep trail.

The horse raced through the stormy night into the teeth of the worsening storm. Deafening claps of thunder shook the earth, and lightning cut ragged paths across the sky. They'd be lucky if a fire bolt didn't strike them. It was beginning to dawn on Cole that the person who was in the biggest danger of getting killed could be him.

The rain slacked enough to improve visibility. Cole figured they had lost any pursuers who might have tried to follow. He had a hunch Jesse and his boys would have had their hands full taking care of their own affairs in this downpour. He reined the mare to a trot. Storm clouds rolled in the distance. Sullen rumbles of thunder still rattled the silence, but the rain had slowed to a fine mist.

He squinted, trying to see through the gathering darkness.

Had to find shelter. Both were soaked to the skin. The full load of his grievances hit him again. Aggravating woman. He could have been killed back there, and did she care? Not a bit. What he should do was set her down in the middle of the road and let her walk to Kansas City. That's what he should do. She'd been nothing but a thorn in his side from the moment he'd met her. Wouldn't listen to a word he said—constantly goading him, not to mention her unmitigated gall.

He wasn't going to forget that she took his rabbit at gunpoint either. Nor would he forget the reason for this ill-conceived trip across Missouri.

Even if she did smell like lilacs.

They rode in silence now. Wynne slumped against him, exhausted. For the first time since he'd met her she'd been quiet for at least ten minutes. A record, he believed. His anger cooled and he remembered how helpless she had been back in camp. He knew exactly what would have happened to her at the hands of that bunch of outlaws. He was thankful he'd managed to get there before things got out of hand.

I hope she's learned something valuable from this experience, Lord. I might not be around the next time. . . . Things had changed since the war and roads weren't safe anymore. Given time, he guessed things would settle down, but feelings still ran deep. A woman traveling alone sent the wrong message to the wrong men.

He tightened his hold on the reins, aware that he liked the way she felt nestled against him. They fit right—like two pieces of a puzzle. He mentally groaned. How was he going to ride all the way to Kansas City with her on the same horse and keep his distance? He had to keep reminding himself of her intentions to shoot Cass. Blood ran deeper than—what? this feeling he suddenly had for her?

Now that he thought of it, she might shoot Cass. Baby brother's luck was bound to run out sometime. Be a pity if he survived the war only to be shot by a vengeful woman.

Cole looked down at the curve of her cheek, felt the softness of her hair brushing his face. He sighed.

He should have gone back and gotten the mule.

Wynne realized he was watching her. She leaned back against him, relishing the strength of the arms that held her. There was something solid and comforting about Cole Claxton. She thought of the men at the campsite. Rough, dirty, violent. She knew in her bones Cole would never mistreat a woman. Look at the way he had followed her to make sure she was safe after she'd tried to run away from him.

Why was she so hateful to this man? He'd risked his life to save her. And instead of being grateful she'd vowed that she didn't need him, which wasn't true at all. She'd been awfully glad to see him standing there, six feet tall, all brawn and muscle, with that Springfield rifle leveled at Sonny's chest. Wynne shivered as she remembered the glint in those icy blue eyes as he had challenged the men. She couldn't remember when she had ever been so glad to see anyone.

The outlaws hadn't argued with him either. She was beginning to suspect there was more to Cole Claxton than she had realized. He didn't like her. Had told her so to her face. Didn't want to be anywhere near her, but still he had come to her rescue. She'd fought him and resented him, but in spite of it all, she knew he was a good man. Funny, because of Cass she had vowed never to trust another man. Now Cass's brother, because of his actions today, had taught her to trust again.

The horse plodded on, and weariness overtook Wynne. She sagged against Cole, grateful for his chest to cushion her back. Odd how utterly safe she felt when he was there. From the moment he had showed up on her trail, she had felt more at ease, less alone. Oh, she had fought with him, even stolen his food and tried to hate him for not helping her, but even when he camped some distance from her, she felt comforted just to know he was close by. There was something reliable about Cole Claxton—and wonderful and exciting and breathtaking.

She could feel the strength of him at her back, the warmth of his breath against her cheek. Strong arms held her close against him. Unbidden, the memory of his kiss, of his mouth touching hers, pushed its way to the forefront of her mind.

Her cheeks heated when she realized where her thoughts had led her. This was risky territory. True, Cole had helped her today, but he had no interest in her. That kiss was just something that happened. It didn't mean anything to him. It didn't mean anything to her, either. It was only because he reminded her so much of Cass that she let herself even think about such things. He was only following her to keep her from hurting his brother.

Cole's mannerisms reminded her of Cass quite often, but the brothers were as different in nature as corn and sweet rolls, she found herself thinking a few moments later. Cole had a certain maturity about him that Cass had yet to acquire. She thought Cole was the more dependable of the two. Certainly Lilly depended on him.

And she had also come to the conclusion that their looks weren't *all* that much alike. Now that she had been around Cole more, she saw that he was the handsomer of the two brothers. His hair was thicker, curlier, and coarser than Cass's. And their eyes—both were blue, but Cole's had a deeper, more vibrant hue. Cole was taller and heavier, while Cass had the body of a young man yet to fully mature.

It suddenly occurred to her that if she had met Cole first, she might never have given Cass a second thought. Now her mule was gone. So were her clothes and her gun. She was completely at Cole Claxton's mercy; she should be frantic, but strangely, she wasn't.

If Cole had been decent enough to save her from a fate worse than death with those horrible men, then he would surely see that she was taken care of, at least for tonight. Tomorrow she could start worrying again.

Having a man around might not be all that bad, she thought as she grew drowsier. If a woman was lucky enough to find the right man. She was beginning to suspect that she had made an error in judgment with Cass. Surely all men weren't liars and deceivers.

Wynne sighed. Perhaps she would reconsider going into a convent when this was all over. It was entirely possible she would find a man someday who would love her and respect her the way Beau did Betsy.

For the first time she noticed that her resentment of Cass was actually beginning to be more trouble than it was worth.

Try as she might, she couldn't seem to summon that terrible, gut-wrenching agony she had experienced toward him only a few days ago. Not even a hint of the bitterness she'd clung to so desperately the past few months. What had happened to change her?

She thought of something else. No matter what happened it seemed to work out for the best. The stage had been robbed, but Beau and Cole had shown up to help. She'd found Cass's family and discovered that they were nice people. She'd run away, but Cole had followed her. She'd been hungry and he fed her. Now he had risked his life to save her.

It was almost as if God had sent him. She examined that idea more closely. It was hard to imagine Cole Claxton as a God-sent protector, but perhaps she hadn't been abandoned after all. Could it be that God wasn't angry with her?

In my Word I've said, Thou shalt not kill.

The words echoed to the beat of the horse's hooves. Words she didn't want to acknowledge. A chilly rivulet from her wet hair trickled down her nose. She surely had a lot to think about.

Wynne stirred and sat up straighter, then almost immediately sagged back into Cole's arms. Such a nice place to be . . .

"You've gone without eating again today, haven't you?" His stern voice broke into her thoughts.

"How did you know?"

"I've followed you all day."

The admission should have upset her, but it didn't. "I'm glad you did."

"Glad? You were chewing me out a few minutes ago."

"That was a few minutes ago. I'm thanking you now—so don't make me mad again." They rode in silence for a while before Wynne spoke again. "Why did you follow me? You could easily have ridden away and been rid of me."

"I wanted you to learn a lesson."

"You would." She sighed. "But I'll admit I probably have learned a lesson. From now on I'll listen more closely to what you say."

"I'll have to see that to believe it. Want a drink of water?"

She'd been without that precious commodity all day. The rain had come too fast, too hard to do more than get her wet. All that water and nothing to drink. She swallowed against the dryness of her throat. "Please."

Cole leaned sideways to unsnap his canteen and handed it to her. "Don't drink too fast," he warned.

She drank long and greedily until he pulled the container away from her. "That's enough for now. You'll make yourself sick."

She submitted to his authority, leaning back against his chest as she gazed up into the sky. Low clouds raced across the horizon, and in the distance you could still see traces of lightning, but the storm in all its fury had moved on.

"Who were those horrible men?" she asked when Cole replaced the lid on the canteen.

"Frank and Jesse James, plus a few men they ride with."

She shuddered. "Are those the men Lilly and Beau and Betsy were talking about at dinner the other night?"

"They're the ones."

"They're disgusting—except the one called Frank. He seemed more . . . civil than the others." She remembered the book he had been reading. Sonny Morgan probably never read a book in his life.

"They'd just as soon shoot you as look at you—Frank included."

Wynne turned to look at him. "How do you know those men?"

"The James boys have been around for a while. They're Missouri born. As for the others, you meet all kinds in a war. A woman is looking for trouble if she's running around the countryside without a man's protection."

She could have argued, but the past few hours had made her realize that he was right. This was the second time he had saved her. He and Beau had arrived just in time at the stagecoach. God and Cole Claxton had kept her safe both times.

Wynne settled more comfortably in his arms. He smelled nice. Like rain and soap and pine needles. And he believed in God. Lilly Claxton had raised her sons right. "Where are we going to camp tonight?"

"We passed what looked like a deserted cabin earlier this afternoon. I thought we might hole up there for the night." His eyes scanned the sky briefly. "My guess is it'll rain again before morning."

"I don't recall seeing any such lodging." She hoped he was wrong and the storm had blown itself out. A handful of stars twinkled overhead, but this was Missouri. One of the men on the stage had talked about the way the weather here could change in hours.

Cole shifted in the saddle. "Couple of miles more. We'll be there soon."

The horse plodded down the rain-soaked trail. The air was cool now and smelled of damp earth and moist vegetation.

Wynne dozed, roused, and nodded off again. She was so tired she couldn't think straight any longer.

Finally they rode into a clearing. Cole suggested she stay on the horse while he checked to see if the dwelling was occupied. In a few moments he was back with good news: it was empty.

When he lifted her off the horse, it occurred to her that a temporary truce now held between them. *Thank You, God. Please give me the wisdom to amend my earlier behavior.* She was indebted to Cole now. Owed him her very life.

Guilt beset her. Would God forgive her if she carried out her mission? He loved His children, and Wynne was His child . . . and she was acting like a child. Peeved. Spoiled. Self-centered. Besides, if Cole knew God, it was entirely possible Cass did too— which made Cass God's child. And God probably loved Cass as much as He loved her. Wynne sighed. Life had gotten awfully complicated since last night.

Cole carried the saddle into the small lean-to. "Let's see what we have here."

Wynne followed him inside and looked around at what would be their home for the night. The cabin was barely adequate shelter. There were a few stray pieces of furniture strewn about the dirty room. Dust and cobwebs conquered corners and rafters, and the sound of rats scurrying for cover when they'd entered was a bit disconcerting.

Yet the cabin looked like a castle to Wynne. At least it would be a roof over her head tonight, and that was more than she had been used to the past several days.

Cole knelt in front of the hearth and began to build a fire to dry them out and cook their supper. Some other weary traveler must have used the cabin before them because the wood box was filled with dry wood. Wynne huddled close to the fireplace, her teeth chattering, wondering if she would ever be warm again. Her rain-wet dress clung to her. Her hair was soaked and stringing around her face. Her shoes, which were coming apart, pinched her toes where the leather had begun to dry.

A flame shot from the kindling, licking at the dry wood. Cole straightened. "I've got the valise you left in the road on the way to River Run. I'll step outside while you change out of those wet clothes."

The rainstorm had cooled the air until it was almost chilly. She glanced about and located an old blanket lying on a bed in the corner of the room. It wasn't clean, but it was better than catching her death of cold from wearing wet clothing. Her nose was already tickling with a sneeze.

A few minutes later she had peeled off her wet dress, keeping her pantaloons and chemise on for modesty's sake. She draped the blanket around her shoulders, covering herself from head to toe, suddenly glad Cole Claxton was a God-fearing man. She'd never been in a situation like this before, and she felt extremely vulnerable.

By now the fire was going and the room was cozy. She busied herself hanging her dress over the back of a chair so it would dry.

Cole returned with her bag and left again while Wynne quickly dressed. Imagine him carrying it all the way from River Run. If she hadn't been so contrary with him, he'd probably have given it to her much sooner. On second thought, it was a good thing he hadn't, or this one would be back in the campsite with her mule.

Cole brought in his saddlebags, and within minutes she smelled salt bacon frying and coffee boiling.

"Well, looks like we'll eat tonight," she said, smiling.

Rain had started to fall again. Wynne could hear it on the roof as they settled around the fire. Looked like another front had moved in.

The day had been long and arduous, and Wynne realized she was exhausted. Had it only been this morning she had tried to run away from Cole? Why had she done anything so foolish? It wasn't the first time her impulsive nature had gotten her into trouble and probably wouldn't be the last. She thought about the way she had bolted from Moss Oak, determined to find Cass and wreak her vengeance on him. Had that been another leap-before-she-looked moment? Seemed like time and the recent events had sort of changed her outlook.

They ate their supper in silence, wrapped in blankets before the roaring fire. Wynne glanced in Cole's direction, but he seemed deep in thought, so she let him be. Nothing she had learned from Miss Marelda Fielding had equipped her for this awkward moment.

She cleared her throat. "Penny for your thoughts."

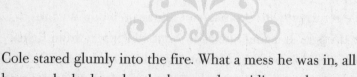

Cole stared glumly into the fire. What a mess he was in, all because he had to play the hero and go riding to the rescue. Now he was obligated to this woman; now he was responsible for her safety. How could he find himself in such a trap? If he followed his inclination, he would ride off for home in the morning, and she could come along or stay. But he knew that he wouldn't, because men like him didn't leave a woman alone in the wilderness, helpless, prey to every no-account renegade that came along. He could never live with himself if he did that.

He glanced at Wynne out of the corner of his eye, aware she was waiting for an answer. Penny for his thoughts. She wouldn't like them. The light of the flames painted her skin with a rosy glow. Her eyes were shadowed, but he knew them the way you knew a favorite, well-read book. Knew when they laughed, when they sparked with anger, or when they were thoughtful and pensive, like now.

He had never met a woman who could annoy him so quickly yet make him forget all about anger when she leveled those strange-colored green eyes on him. She was feisty, unreasonable, bullheaded, and had the fortitude of six women. Yet she was one of the most beautiful creations he had ever met.

He'd read somewhere that the eyes held the essence of the heart. If that was so, he had looked deep into the heart of Wynne Elliot.

And he didn't like her! Why did he keep forgetting that?

She reached up to brush a damp lock from her face and his eyes traced the line of her throat. *Lord, I need help here. I never asked for this situation, but it's been handed to me. Don't let me face any kind of temptation You and me together can't handle.*

He got to his feet, reaching for the coffeepot. "I believe the rain's stopped. Think I'll go check the mare."

He shut the door behind him, relieved to be out of there. The thought crossed his mind that right now would be a good time for Sonny Morgan to get even if he happened to be passing by. He'd left his guns inside, hanging over the back of a chair. That's what happened when a man let a woman invade his thoughts—made him crazy. Good way to get them both shot.

He sucked in a breath of fresh air, waiting for his racing pulse to slow. When he felt he'd given himself enough time to clear his thoughts, he went back inside. She turned to face him with a hesitant smile. He figured their being here like this was hard on her too. Not as bad as it was for him though.

Women didn't have the same impulses as men had.

Wynne lowered her eyes. Her hands smoothed her skirt. "Still raining?"

He sat down in front of the fire. "It's about over." He picked up the poker and stirred the fire. "You'll want to go to bed."

She looked startled and he backed up. "You're tired—right?"

"Oh . . . yes, I am."

He shifted uncomfortably. Now, wasn't that just like her? Most of the time she chattered like she'd been vaccinated with a phonograph needle, but she hadn't said a dozen words since they'd got here. This wasn't easy for him either. She could help him out here.

"You take the bed," he said. "I'll bunk on the front porch."

Relief flooded her eyes. An emotion he had never associated with Wynne Elliot. He reached out to touch her hand, and her expression stilled. "It's all right. You're safe. Nothing's going to bother you now."

Her eyes met his and he saw a new expression in their depths. Something he'd never expected to see . . . trust.

They got to their feet at the same time, standing close. She lifted her face to meet his eyes. And then it happened. Like a moth irresistibly drawn to flame, he slowly lowered his head, not intending to but unable to help himself. His lips hovered a breath away from hers; his arms went around her, pulling her close. Blood pounded in his temples when she reached up to lock her hands behind his neck.

Her eyes closed; her lips parted softly. It was the hardest thing he had ever done, but he reached up and pulled her arms down, holding her hands lightly in his. He'd asked the good Lord to help him, so it seemed only right that he do his part.

He touched her cheek with one finger. "Sleep well."

She gazed up at him, serious, eyes searching his as if looking for answers. Then she nodded and, without a word, stepped away from him.

Later, he lay on the porch, reliving the moment. He could have kissed her so easily. It would have been effortless to lose control, which would have put him pretty much on the same level with Jesse and Sonny. Something he never wanted to happen. Even during the war, he had never mistreated a woman.

Besides, a man like him didn't kiss a woman like Wynne Elliot unless he had marrying on his mind, and he sure didn't. He wasn't the marrying kind, and even if he was, Wynne Elliot wasn't his kind of woman.

The words rang a little hollow even to Cole.

CHAPTER 13

Wynne opened her eyes and blinked at the unfamiliar surroundings. The cabin looked even worse in daylight. Cobwebs hung in every corner. The floor was filthy, the furniture shabby and broken. But last night it had been a haven.

A watery sun streamed through the broken windows, signaling that the storm had moved on. She sat up and swung her legs over the edge of the bed, wondering if Cole was still asleep. Her bare feet touched the rough, splintery floorboards. She stood up and tiptoed to the front door, opening it as quietly as possible. Her brave rescuer was snoring louder than the last trump.

He looked different in sleep. The tired lines around his eyes and mouth had softened, making him appear much younger. It was hard to believe this was the same man who could make her so angry without even trying. She had to admit he was the handsomest thing she'd ever seen. Nothing back home could compare with Cole Claxton. True, he was as cantankerous as a bear with a sore paw, but she had a feeling the right woman

could tame him. Not that she was looking for the job. She had better things to do.

The kiss two days ago had been so soft, gentle. Cass had kissed her a few times, but he hadn't stirred her the way Cole did. She absently scratched her arm. That blanket must have been slept on by a mangy goat or something even worse. Even after the thorough soaking she had received from the storm, she needed a good scrubbing. In fact, this entire cabin needed a good cleaning, but she didn't plan to be here long enough to play housekeeper.

Wynne sighed. One had to be honest, and to be perfectly honest she wished Cole Claxton would kiss her again. And she was humiliated to even think such a thing. Her gaze traveled back to the sleeping form rolled so tightly in a bedroll.

It was even more painful when she thought about the fact that he was a Claxton. Maybe if Cass had not broken her heart and trampled on her pride she would have felt differently. She might even, in time, have fallen in love again.

That new and disturbing thought brought her meanderings to an abrupt halt. No, that was ridiculous. She couldn't be falling in love with Cass's brother. Until last night she hadn't even liked the man. You would think, after the misery she'd been through the past few months, she'd have learned her lesson about men. Yet, strangely, it seemed she hadn't.

She scratched her arm harder, and it felt heavenly. A large, irritated area spread long pinkish fingers almost up to her elbow. Wynne frowned as she studied the tiny, watery blisters with growing concern. What in the blue blazes was that? Fleas? Flea bites?

Whatever it was, it was annoying and painful. She thor-

oughly scratched the area but her clawing fingers brought little relief. It felt good when she scratched, but as soon as she stopped it was like fire burning her skin. She'd never experienced anything like it before.

Cole stirred as she watched him, scratching his chest beneath the blanket. He mumbled something unintelligible. Wynne bent over to peer at him and saw the same watery blisters erupting in patches on his arms. Whatever she had, it must be contagious.

She switched her attention from his arm and chest to his face and encountered a pair of arresting blue eyes now open and staring up at her. "What are you doing?"

"Looking at your arms." She bit her lip in vexation, wishing she could take back the words and give a more proper answer.

He grinned, a completely male reaction.

She shook her head impatiently. This was no time for humor. Whatever was wrong, he had it too.

Cole drew back, squinting at the arm she suddenly shoved in his face. "What is it?" she demanded.

"I don't know—flea bites?"

"Maybe—but you have them all over your arms too."

Cole glanced at his own arms, and his eyes widened in disbelief. He reached out and grasped her arm, peering at it more closely. "I don't *believe* this."

"What? What is it?" she asked, looking half afraid.

"It can't be!" He sat straight up in the bedroll. He'd had all kinds of luck since meeting this woman, all of it bad, and this was the worst of the lot. He exhaled in disgust. "It looks like poison ivy!"

"Oh, is that all?" She released a sigh that sounded like pure

relief. "The way you acted I was afraid you were going to tell me it was some horrible plague."

Cole was busily inspecting his chest for further signs of the outbreak. "What do you mean, is that all? I'm sensitive to this stuff."

"Then you should have stayed clear of it."

"I do stay clear of it! I have since I had a particularly bad case of it when I was a kid. I must have got it chasing after you."

"Me! Why does it always have to be me who causes the trouble?" Wynne jumped to her feet and glared down at him. "Just what makes you so sure I led you through poison ivy, and who asked you to come chasing after me anyway?"

"Because I'll ride five miles out of my way to avoid getting the stuff on me," Cole snapped. "Can you say you've been as careful, Miss Elliot?"

"How would I know? I don't know what poison ivy looks like."

"Obviously not." With bleak resignation he indicated her arms, which were puffing up by the moment. "You must have rolled in it somewhere!" And there'd been enough juice on her clothes to infect him. He'd ridden through the rain with her clutched against his chest and in return she gave him what looked like a rousing case of poison ivy. That's what he got for trying to be a gentleman. If he had it to do over, he'd have let her walk.

Wynne's temper flared. "There is no reason to be so snippy. I suppose you could be right. I *did* wade through a lot of thickets and briars, and I *did* fall off the mule a few times. There were some strange-looking vines on that old oak tree the mule brushed against. I guess if you were following me, you probably

went through some of the same vegetation, but I'm so tired of always doing the wrong thing."

Suddenly, to Cole's horror, she burst into tears.

He rolled hastily to his feet. He'd rather face the James gang any day than to have to deal with a squalling woman. "Don't cry. It's not the end of the world."

"But I'm—I'm for-e-ev-er doin-g su-ch stu-pi-d th-in-gs," she sobbed. "Now I've caused you to get poison ivy."

"Come on now, stop getting yourself all upset." He fumbled in his back pocket for his handkerchief, intending to hand it to her if he could get her to stop bawling long enough to take it. There were very few things that could bring him to heel, but a woman's tears were one of them. He'd do anything, short of grabbing her by the shoulders and shaking some sense into her head, to make her stop. But he was afraid in her agitated state he might make her even madder. Not that he was afraid of her— but she could be unpredictable. At least she didn't have a gun in her hand this time.

He shifted uneasily. All the blubbering and sniveling was making him uncomfortable.

She snatched the cloth out of his hand and buried her face in it, sobbing harder.

He let her cry it out, casting uneasy glances in her direction. All that squawking and bellowing was going to make her sick, but he didn't know how to put a stop to it without bringing on more of the same.

When the squall finally abated, Wynne lifted red-rimmed eyes to meet his.

Cole sagged with visible relief. "Feel better?"

"N-o," she said, and hiccupped.

"You'd better hurry and get it all out of your system," he said, trying to be nice so she wouldn't turn on the tears again. "We have work to do."

She viewed him with open skepticism as she blew her nose. "What work?"

"We have to find a whole lot of jewelweed. As fast as possible."

"Jewelweed?" She peered up at him as if he had lost his mind. Well, the same thing had occurred to him several times in the past few days. "What for? I wouldn't know a jewelweed plant if it came up and spit in my face!"

"We make poultices out of the weeds and hope they'll keep the poison ivy from spreading." He paused, not wanting to set her off again. It wasn't easy to smile like an idiot. "Mind you, I said *hope* that it won't spread any further."

"But it could?"

He shrugged, absently scratching. "With my luck? It'll spread like wildfire. By night we'll both be miserable. You don't know the meaning of trouble until this stuff spreads."

The woman was a menace—no longer any doubt about it. He'd come through the war without a single bandage. He'd led his men into battle day after day, watching them fall around him in droves, yet he'd managed to escape unharmed. But now, after becoming a one-man rescue mission for the most infuriating female that had ever been born, he was faced with a threat he feared even more than death. *Poison ivy.* The words struck dread in his heart.

When he was a kid, he had been flat on his back in bed with the dreaded ailment for more than a week. After that, his mother made sure he was dosed heavily each spring with sulfur, molasses, and a pinch of saltpeter. He wasn't sure it had helped, but as bad as it had tasted, it surely had cured something. At any rate it hadn't killed him.

He'd come to recognize the little three-leaved vine from a mile away and to avoid it. Wynne wouldn't have noticed the plant, and since the juice had probably been all over her clothing; she might have a worse case than he did.

Too late to worry about it now. If he hadn't been so intent on keeping up with her, he'd have paid more attention to where he was going. *Let there be a mess of jewelweed growing somewhere nearby, Lord.* The plant was usually found in the vicinity of poison ivy, as if God wanted to provide an antidote.

His gaze drifted back to Wynne, who was trying to pin up her mass of hair. How could someone so aggravating be so beautiful? Women were a mystery to him. In his opinion, God never intended for them to be understood. They were put on the earth to irritate men. Look at what Eve had done to Adam in the Garden of Eden. Adam had been enjoying life, going about his business, naming the animals. Then God had created woman and the trouble started. And she had been causing trouble ever since.

Cole figured he could rest his case.

Take Wynne, with her hair straggling down like that, dress dirty, shoes coming apart. She was still easily the loveliest woman he'd ever seen. Even someone as pretty as Betsy couldn't hold a light to Wynne. It seemed odd to him that God would make such a soft, pretty woman and give her a disposition that would sour milk. A man wouldn't have a day's peace with a woman like that sharing his home.

A woman of spirit . . . He dismissed the thought, instead recalling how soft her lips had felt beneath his. Warm, inviting. Inexperienced. Not that he was an expert, but he could tell she hadn't been kissed many times. Probably Cass had—He stopped right there. It made him uncomfortable to think of Cass holding Wynne in his arms, or anyone else holding her for that matter. He had been ready to shoot Sonny last night, and the world would be a better place if he had. Sonny Morgan was a menace to society, including himself.

He sighed, relieved Wynne had quit crying, but the pensive look on her face bothered him. What was she thinking up this time?

Cole gathered up his bedroll. "You start breakfast. I'll be back shortly."

"There now. Are you feeling any better, Bertie?"

"It's getting bearable." Bertram G. Mallory rolled to his side as Fancy gently tried to help him into a more comfortable position. "Agghhh . . ." A low groan escaped him. "The ache runs straight up my spine."

"Doc said if you needed any more laudanum, he would send you over some."

"Have I taken the whole bottle already?"

"Almost." Fancy picked up the brown glass container sitting on the table among all the wooden animals he had carved these past few weeks. A regular Noah's Ark. His carving was getting better; he could almost tell the last one he'd worked on was a horse. He wondered if Fancy would want to keep them to remember him by when he left.

Fancy plumped his pillows, fussing over him in a most pleasing way. Bertram G. Mallory hadn't had many women fuss over him. It was a real nice experience.

"I brought dinner, Bertie. Hope you're good and hungry tonight."

He sniffed the air, eyeing the tray covered with a red-checkered cloth she had set on the table. "What'd you bring me?"

"Stew and corn bread."

Bertram grinned. "Stew's my favorite, and you know it. Wouldn't happen to be a piece of blueberry pie on that tray, would there?"

Fancy grinned back. "There just might be."

"You're going to spoil me, Fancy."

"I want to, Bertie."

Bertram humbly knew that he was about the best thing that had ever happened to her. In the time he'd been delayed in Springfield, the "soiled dove" had fallen deeply in love with him. She'd said that he was the kindest, gentlest man she had ever met and that she wanted to cry when she thought about how empty her life would be when he left town. He thought he might shed a few private tears too. Fancy was about the sweetest woman he'd ever met. He'd take her with him if he wasn't on this mission that seemed doomed from the start. But he'd come back for her. Just see if he didn't.

He knew the fact that he was looking for a woman worried Fancy. At times when he'd talked about it he'd sounded desperate, and at other times he'd been frustrated when he talked about his leg healing so he could go on with his trip. He couldn't stop until he found Miss Wynne Elliot and did what he had to do. He wished he *could* talk it over with Fancy and ease her fears, but ethics demanded he keep quiet.

Fancy had told him she couldn't imagine him being on a spiteful mission. He was too kind to be an evil man, and he appreciated her vote of confidence. Yet every time she tried to question him on why he was looking for this Wynne Elliot, he'd had to clam up. His mission was of a personal nature; he had to find the woman. Period.

He knew he spoke in riddles. Fancy didn't know what he meant, but she said she was sure it was important for Bertie to complete his mission. Bertie. That's what she called him. He liked the name, and it made him feel good the way she was willing to trust him.

His mission would be over and done with if he hadn't stopped to help Elmo Wilson fix a wheel that had come off his buggy Sunday morning.

He'd been leaving for River Run when he'd come across Elmo and his wife, Sadie, sitting in the middle of the road, hot and sweating in their Sunday best. He could tell Sadie was about to expire, so he got off his horse and offered to help. Elmo had instructed Bertram to lift the left side of the buggy up easy-like so he could slip the wheel back in place. Wouldn't take a minute and they all could be on their way.

Well, what was a man to do? Bertram had agreed the task was simple enough for a strong man like himself, so he had proceeded to heft the left side of the carriage, when all of a sudden his back went out. He got so mad words poured out of his mouth he didn't even know he knew. Didn't even care if

Sadie was listening, because his back hurt so bad he thought he was going to be sick right there in the middle of the road. And throwing his back out was going to delay him. Again.

Sadie had almost jumped right out of her skin because his salty language scared her so badly, but the pain grabbed him around his middle something fierce. Even worse than the time he fell off the train and more ghastly than when he broke his ankle. He simply couldn't help letting off a little steam.

And what with his leg being fresh out of the splint just that morning, the jolt had set the fracture aching like all get-out. Seemed like this assignment had brought him nothing but pain and frustration.

He looked at the pretty face bending over him, concern in her beautiful eyes. Well, there was some good in everything, he guessed. If he hadn't been trying to find Wynne Elliot, he would never have met Fancy.

Elmo and Sadie had brought him back to Springfield and taken him to the doctor's office. Then they'd thoughtfully sent someone to inform Fancy about the accident, since the two of them had gotten awfully close lately. He guessed the whole town knew and gossiped about his friendship with Fancy, but they'd better not say anything to him. He'd not stand still for anyone bad-mouthing a sweet little thing like her.

Fancy smoothed his pillow and sat down on the bed beside him. "Poor Bertie. You're having a terrible run of problems lately."

Bertram thought that was an understatement if he'd ever heard one.

Fancy went on talking in soft tones; her voice sounded as sweet as a spring breeze. "However, Bertie, sweetheart, I'm just elated to have you around for a while longer."

Bertram caught her hand in the middle of all her fussing and brought it to his lips. "You're mighty good to me."

"Aw, I'm not, Bertie. You deserve so much more than somebody like me caring for you." Fancy dropped her eyes, looking shy when his grip tightened on her hand. He knew she'd known a lot of men in her time, but somehow this quiet, almost naive woman could make him feel like a schoolboy again. He had a notion that Fancy wanted out of the kind of life she lived. People didn't always get a choice in this world. If things had been better, he didn't believe she'd have ever gone into saloon work. There wasn't much else for a woman to do to support herself if she didn't have menfolk to take care of her. Fancy was as much a prisoner of her world as he was of his. Soon as he could find the Elliot woman and do what he had to do, he was going to come get Fancy, and they'd go somewhere else and make a world all their own.

"I don't ever want to hear you say such a thing," he said. "Why, you're the best-hearted woman I've ever known, Fancy."

Bertram meant it. Other people might judge her harshly, but he didn't. He saw beyond the saloon-girl paint and glitter. He saw the lonely, sometimes frightened woman she really was. The woman who wanted a different life than the one in which she was trapped. Bertram understood, and he loved her.

"Thank you, Bertie. It's not true about me being nice—you know what I do. But I surely do appreciate you thinking so." She tenderly smoothed thinning hair away from his forehead.

"You *are* nice," he whispered, "and as soon as I finish what I'm sworn to do, I'm going to come back and get you, Fancy. Then I'm going to marry you and take you home with me."

He knew Fancy thought that when he left she would never

see him again. No one had ever cared enough about Fancy Biggers to come back for her, but Bertram would be back. He loved sitting beside her talking, or holding her in his arms while they lay on an old blanket and looked up at the sky. He'd make up silly stories about people who would travel out there among the stars someday, and she would laugh and declare that he was getting addlebrained.

No, she never would let herself believe that she would someday marry Bertram G. Mallory, but she was in for a surprise. God willing, he'd complete his duty and he'd be back for her. They'd get married, have three or four children, and the two of them would grow old together.

Bertram kissed the palm of her hand and winked at her. "Now don't start doubting me. You wait and see. One of these days you're going to be Mrs. Bertram Mallory or I'll eat my hat."

She wanted to believe—he could see hope reflected in her eyes. He wanted to say, *Believe, Fancy!* "We're going to live in a big house sitting on top of a hill—"

"With a big white fence around it," she said, playing the game.

He smiled. "And lots of flowers and a big vegetable garden—"

"And kids—"she grasped his hand tighter— "at least six kids, Bertie . . . maybe more."

Bertram laughed. "However many you want, Fancy. A dozen—maybe more."

"Oh, Bertie." Fancy couldn't hold back tears. "I love you with all my heart."

He gently patted her hand. "As soon as I get my business taken care of, we'll start our new life. I'm even going to change professions when this is all over. The one I have now is too harrowing. My body can't take all these injuries."

"Oh, Bertie."

"I'll take care of you, Fancy. From this moment on, you don't have to worry about another thing." He meant it too. She was the best thing to happen to him in a long while.

She rested her head on his pillow and sighed. Tears slipped silently from the corners of her eyes, and he used his fingertip to blot them. "About you going to River Run . . ."

"Yes?"

"I know you're looking for someone, but maybe that person won't be there anymore. After all, you've been here so long. You said this Wynne Elliot was supposed to be visiting there."

Bertram frowned. "I've thought about that."

"What if this woman's left by now?"

Bertram sighed, a long, weary sound. His hand absently stroked the top of her head. "Then I'll have to keep searching until I find her."

"I wish you'd tell me why it's so all-fired important for you to find her."

"Because Bertram G. Mallory is a man of his word," he stated.

And that was that. He would not stop nor say another thing until he stood face-to-face with Wynne Elliot.

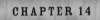

CHAPTER 14

One month. It was hard to believe they had been gone for almost a month and still weren't more than twenty miles out of River Run. For the past two and a half weeks they had been holed up here, and Cole had cabin fever.

He lay on the old bed in the cabin and stared at a wasp circling the ceiling. His face was still a mass of puffy red welts, he itched all over, and his body was covered with crusted, oozing sores. The places that were healing had formed new skin, but he still had a lot of rash that was just starting to blister. He knew not to scratch, but sometimes he couldn't help it.

He could hear Wynne humming happily as she worked around the cabin. Oh, she *could* hum, he thought resentfully and gritted his teeth to keep from clawing at places already raw from his fingernails. Her case of poison ivy had turned out to be mild, while his had raged out of control.

And if that wasn't enough, the horse had pulled up lame. He figured riding that steep trail in the dark had contributed to the injury. At any rate they had to wait until the animal's leg healed.

Good thing, because while he could have traveled, it wouldn't have been pleasant. He thought he'd had trouble with poison ivy before, but this outbreak was the worst he'd ever had.

He was puzzled by Wynne's behavior. He'd thought she surely would have stolen his horse and gone in search of Cass, but surprisingly she had stuck around to care for him. She wouldn't have gotten far on a lame horse, but as impulsive as she was, he figured she'd have tried. Instead, she'd slept on a pallet she had fixed on the porch, without complaining. Every day she fed him, brought water for him to bathe, and made new poultices to apply to his swollen body.

In the long night hours, while she slept undisturbed, Cole tossed and turned, plotting ways to get even with his little brother for putting him through this nightmare. Cass had a lot of explaining to do.

Wynne noticed Cole was awake and crossed the room to check on him. "Good morning. How are you feeling?"

"Rotten."

"Oh, you always say that. Surely you're feeling somewhat better today." She was getting so used to his complaints they no longer bothered her. She tried to examine the progress of his rash, but he brushed her hand away.

"I'm all right."

"Fine. I was only trying to help." She went back to arranging wild daisies in the empty glass jar she'd found in the refuse dump behind the cabin.

While Cole slept during the heat of the day, she'd taken to searching the area, looking for edible wild roots and berries for their supper. Up until now she'd been successful, but all she had come across today had been the lovely flowers. She'd brought them back to the cabin in the hopes of cheering up Grumpy, but it looked as if her efforts had been wasted.

She knew their forced delay had been hard on Cole, so she didn't begrudge his being a bit touchy. If she'd been as sick as he was she would have acted the same way—well, maybe not exactly the same way, but close. The unexpected turn of events hadn't upset her in the least.

Cole was worried about the horse too. That injured leg didn't seem to be healing as fast as it should. The mare needed the enforced stay. Wynne led her around the open space in front of the cabin every day, but her left hock was still swollen and sore.

Actually Wynne welcomed the short reprieve. It was wonderful to sleep with a roof over her head every night and be able to walk down to the pond and bathe every morning. At times she even found herself forgetting why she was here in the first place. There were hours when she no longer cared whether she ever found Cass. It was hard to hold on to the blazing anger and humiliation she had felt when he'd left her standing at the church waiting for a bridegroom who never arrived.

The bitterness and anger were slowly leaving her, and suddenly she found herself . . . well, almost happy once again. Even thinking about Cass failed to dampen her spirits like it once had. She was drawing closer to God again too. She'd taken to praying while walking in the woods or lying on her front-porch bed. Seemed like the more she thought about God, the less she hated Cass. And the less she hated Cass, the more she wondered what she'd ever been thinking to have been so determined to kill him.

"What would you like for dinner tonight?" she asked.

"Since when is there a choice?"

"There isn't, actually. I tried to catch a fish out of the pond this morning, but I'm not fast enough with my hands."

He grunted and closed his eyes.

She searched her mind for some topic of conversation to keep him interested. As long as they were cooped up here together, they might as well try to get along. He was probably extremely uncomfortable, so obviously it was her duty to keep him entertained.

"When I was a small girl, Papa used to take me fishing. We had this large pond that was close to the house, and it was stocked with all sorts of interesting-looking fish." She continued to arrange the flowers as she chatted. "You know, fish are really fascinating. Have you ever noticed that?"

Cole grunted but didn't open his eyes.

"Some of them are truly magnificent, with nice, plump bodies and charming characteristics. And then there are those poor things that have nasty dispositions and are just plain ugly— big, bloaty-looking eyes and horrendously fat lips."

She glanced at him and thought he looked a little strange, sort of green. "It's a shame folks don't eat the mean ones and leave the cute ones alone." She glanced back to check on him. "Don't you agree?"

One blue eye opened, showing pained tolerance. "With what?"

"That the ugly fish should be eaten first."

"I've never given it a moment's thought."

It suddenly occurred to her he might be trying to rest. "Am I bothering you?"

"No."

"Well, as I was saying—"

"What about supper?" he interrupted.

"Oh." Her thoughts returned to the earlier discussion. "Well, I could always make stew again."

He sighed. "Anything but berries."

"Cole! You really should be grateful for what the Lord has provided. At least we haven't gone hungry."

"I am grateful. I'd just like a change in the menu."

"Well, I couldn't find any berries today, so you're in luck." She hoped God wouldn't be hard on him for his complaining. Surely the Almighty could see he was a sick man. Although to be honest, he didn't sound much better when he wasn't sick.

Some people just didn't have a gift for being grateful.

She called that luck? He called it God being merciful. He was sick of berries. She couldn't hit the broad side of a barn with a gun, so they would have to eat that unappetizing root stew until he could get back on his feet and kill fresh meat.

It didn't matter. He'd had very little appetite lately, and it hadn't been helped by the nauseating messes she came up with. He wondered what she put in that stew. Dig the wrong kind of root and you could have just bought yourself a one-way ticket to the pearly gates. Was she smart enough to know poisonous plants from the good ones?

Wynne stuck a daisy into the jar, cocking her head to examine the effect. "If you would lend me your gun, I could go and kill a rabbit for our dinner."

He wanted to laugh, knowing she was irritated because he had hidden his gun from her and she couldn't find it. He rolled to his side, and a new round of itching hit him. "I'm not letting you have my gun."

She turned to face him, holding a flower in her hand. "That's not *fair*. You're sick, and I'm the only one able to provide our food."

"If I give you the gun, either you'll run away and leave me stuck here without a horse or a way to protect myself, or you'll shoot yourself and I'll have to get up and bury you. I don't feel well enough to tackle that yet."

She rested her hands on her hips. "I'm hungry, Cole. Now give me the gun. I won't run away. If I had wanted to do that, I would have left days ago."

"I said no."

She shrugged. "Then I'll just have to think of another way to kill our supper, because I'm not going to bed hungry again tonight."

"Good luck."

A slamming door signaled that the slaughter was about to begin. He figured any game in their immediate vicinity could probably plan on living to a ripe old age.

Cole stared at the ceiling. He should get up and move around more. Spending so much time lying around was getting to him. He'd be so stiff that he couldn't move if he didn't get more exercise. He watched dust motes drift aimlessly in a vagrant ray of sunshine. This enforced time of doing nothing had given him time to think.

He'd never really thanked God enough for keeping him safe during the war—not only him, but Beau too, and hopefully Cass. He credited Ma's prayers for that. Oh, he'd prayed too, every day, but praying in an emergency was different from spending time with God in a slow, leisurely way, not much on your mind but just talking and listening to Him. Cole had learned to enjoy the listening. Seemed like he'd never had time before. The war had taken a lot from him, but he knew nothing would ever take away the joy of his salvation.

For the next couple of hours he dozed off and on. The cabin became an oven, and he woke up once drenched in sweat and itching all over again.

It was late afternoon when he heard a terrible ruckus erupt in the front yard. The sound of feathered wings flailing in the air and terrified squawks, mixed with Wynne's screams, shattered the stillness.

Cole shook his head to clear his mind. The fracas got louder and more intense. He eased off the bed and fumbled for the gun he had hidden under a loose floorboard. The fight outside raged unchecked as he rose to his knees. There was no telling what the woman had gotten into this time, but it sounded as if the Battle of Vicksburg were being fought again on the doorstep.

About the time he reached the door, Wynne burst through, a triumphant grin on her flushed face. Her soiled dress was hanging in tatters, and her hair was matted with twigs and chicken feathers. She held the proof of her earlier words dangling limply from her hands. "Look what I have, Mr. Claxton!"

Cole stared blankly at what looked like a chicken, minus its head, dripping blood on the cabin floor. "Where did you get that?"

"I ran it down," she exclaimed. "And then I swung it around and around until its head popped off! I've watched the servants at Moss Oak do that. Getting the head off wasn't as easy as it looked, but I managed."

His lips twitched. "I see you did. It must have been quite a battle. Sorry I missed it."

Her cheeks pinkened. "It was wandering around in the woods, and I ran until I finally caught it, and then I brought it back here. Isn't that marvelous?"

"Well, yes, I'd call it that." And miraculous—and a gift from God. He didn't have to eat either roots *or* berries tonight.

"I don't need your gun anymore, sir," she informed him, then grinned impishly as she swirled the chicken in a wide circle like a drawstring purse. "I think I've finally got the hang of it!"

Cole groaned and sank weakly into a chair. *What will this woman do next, Lord?* Now he'd have to hunt down the farmer who owned the chicken and pay the man. Chicken thieves weren't taken lightly in these parts, and if she had been thinking, she'd have realized it was stealing.

But she acted then thought.

Seven more days passed before the horse's leg showed real signs of improvement. During their extended stay, Wynne had settled into the cabin as if it were to be their permanent house. The room looked a lot different now than it had when they came.

Cole looked around, noticing the changes. It looked . . . homey. Wynne had ripped off the lower half of her petticoat and made several cleaning cloths. The cabin was spotless now, the old floor scrubbed clean, and fresh flowers sitting on the table every day.

She'd managed to stretch the chicken over an entire week and then miraculously went out and ran down another one. She'd even discovered an old root cellar in the back of the house and found a leftover bushel of apples and two jars of honey. Somehow she managed to turn the fruit and sweetening into a tasty dessert.

Cole watched her move about the cabin and noticed that not all of Miss Fielding's teachings had gone astray. There was a certain beauty and elegance about Wynne that he had failed to notice earlier. She went about her work with the grace and refinement of the most regal Southern woman, even when she was down on her hands and knees, scrubbing the rough wooden floor with a scrap of petticoat.

Instead of the clumsy, addlebrained girl he'd first encountered, Wynne was proving every day that she was indeed the genteel lady her papa had raised her to be.

At night they lay in the dark—he in the bed she had insisted on his taking and she on the front porch—and talked through the open window, surrounded by hoot owls and cicadas. Wynne told stories of growing up on a large cotton plantation, while Cole regaled her with tales about the war. They had grown so comfortable with each other that one night she even told him about Cass and how they had met and fallen in love.

When she started weeping, Cole had lain in the darkness, hurting as her bitterness and grief spilled over. After the tempest had passed, they talked long into the night. Cole now believed that his brother was partly responsible for her unhappiness, although he couldn't understand how it could be. The boy hadn't been raised to act like that.

He told her all about Cass and how he had been as a child. With each word he could sense more of the rancor slowly draining away from her. Cole told her he was the strong one, Beau the optimist, and Cass the dreamer of the Claxton family. Three men with the same parents and background, but each one different.

Then one morning he took Wynne outside the cabin and gave her a lesson in shooting.

"Why are you doing this now?" she asked, her eyes questioning his motives.

He couldn't blame her, considering the way he'd refused to let her touch his gun. "If anything unforeseen happens, you'll be able to take care of yourself."

Alarm filled her eyes. "But nothing's going to happen to you," she protested.

"Nothing's going to happen to me," he assured her. "But you need to know how to take care of yourself." He couldn't shake the image of Sonny manhandling her. If he could help it, no one would ever touch her that way again.

They were sitting in the yard, and she asked the question he had been dreading. "Aren't you afraid that I'll use this new knowledge to harm Cass?"

He didn't allow his gaze to waver. "I know you'll do what you have to do, Wynne." It was the closest he could come to saying he understood why she was doing what she was, but he hoped it was enough.

"Thank you. I appreciate your faith in me."

He nodded briefly and returned his attention to the lesson.

Wynne proved to be a fast learner. After only a few tries she hit the target, a scrap of paper he had nailed to the trunk of a large oak. He'd found some old bottles at the refuse dump behind the cabin and considered using them for targets, but decided against leaving a mess of shattered glass for someone else to clean up.

He watched as Wynne took careful aim, grinning as she frowned in concentration. She tackled everything with total abandon. The first time she had pulled the trigger she hadn't held the gun butt close against her shoulder. The resulting kick had made her yelp, but she hadn't quit. He was beginning to suspect that word wasn't in her vocabulary.

He found himself enjoying the way she stood, head slightly bent to sight down the rifle barrel. The wind teased loose strands of that bonfire-bright hair into unruly tendrils that curled and clung in a very enticing way. Standing at the side like this he had a good view of her womanly shape too. Small and slight, she would be a mighty sweet armful.

She pulled the trigger, and a tiny piece of paper fell from the target. "I hit it," she crowed, swinging around to face him. "Did you see that?"

He ducked, throwing up an arm for protection, although he couldn't say what protection he thought it would be against a bullet. "Point that thing somewhere else!" Why in the name of good common sense had he put a gun in the hands of this hare-brained female?

"Oh, sorry." She moved the gun barrel a scant four inches from his head. "Did you see me hit it?"

"I saw it," he gritted from between clenched teeth. "Watch where you point the barrel, and never point it at anything you don't plan to shoot. Can't you remember anything I told you about gun safety?"

"Of course I remember," she sputtered. "Why do you always talk to me like I'm lacking somewhat?"

"You're lacking a whole lot." And he was about to list a few of the ways. They should have had her fighting on their side in the war. She'd have wiped out a whole battalion of Johnny Rebs without batting an eye.

"I happen to be a woman—," she began.

"Yeah, I noticed. You're not lacking in that area."

"Oh." She flushed. "Oh, well . . ."

He grinned, enjoying her discomfiture. It wasn't often he bested her. Victory was sweet.

She flounced around, pointed the gun at the tree, and without taking time to aim, fired. The recoil knocked her flat. He couldn't help it. He laughed. She glared at him, temper blazing in her eyes.

Too late he remembered she had the gun. "Sorry about that. Are you hurt?"

She got to her feet, brushing off the back of her skirt, the barrel of the gun swinging in erratic circles. "Much you'd care if I was. You are the most despicable, infuriating man I have ever met."

"Yes, ma'am. I apologize; I surely do, but that thing has a hair trigger, and I'd be a lot more comfortable if you would point it in a different direction—preferably one that I don't happen to be occupying."

She glanced at the gun in her hands. "Oh yes? You think I'd shoot you after you saved my life? Is that the sort of poor, disloyal creature you think I am?"

"No, ma'am, not on purpose, but you do seem sort of accident prone."

Wynne bit her lip, tears beading her eyelashes. She hurled the rifle on the ground and Cole winced. That was *his* gun.

"Hey, where are you going?" he demanded when she took off down the trail, arms swinging, stepping out smartly as if she knew exactly where she was heading.

When she didn't answer, he ran after her, puffing to catch up. He was out of shape, which came as no surprise. Time spent lying in bed recovering from a roaring case of poison ivy and living on roots and berries hadn't done much to develop his muscle tone.

He grabbed her arm, swinging her around to face him. "Hey. What's wrong? Don't run off like this. It isn't safe. You know that."

She turned her face away, but not before he saw tears streaming down her cheeks. He pulled her into his arms and smoothed her hair back from her flushed forehead. The silken strands clung to his fingers, as if binding him to her. Her eyes, blurred with tears, blinked up at him.

"Honey, I'm sorry. I didn't mean to upset you. It's just that I don't think too well with a gun pointed at me, and while you probably didn't intend to shoot me, you sure looked mad enough to try. You can't blame me for being a little shook."

"You laughed at me."

"I did, and I certainly won't do it again."

He tried to keep his mind off the way she felt in his arms.

Almighty God had created something wonderful when He made a woman so soft and so cuddly and who smelled so good. He caught a glimpse of the fire still burning in her eyes. Almighty God had a sense of humor too. His greatest creation had a temper that could ignite a forest fire.

"Ah, come on, honey. Don't be mad. What would you have done if that old gun had knocked me flat? Wouldn't you have laughed just a little?"

She started to grin then clamped her lips shut in a hard line.

"Just knocked me backwards, bruising my dignity something fierce. You know you'd have thought that was funny," he said.

A twinkle started in the depths of her eyes, and then a chuckle erupted, followed by a full-blown laugh. They clung to each other, laughing like idiots, tears rolling down their cheeks.

His knees felt weak. The scent of lilacs filled his nostrils. Their eyes locked, and he could see the wonder in hers. He lowered his head as her lips parted to receive his kiss. She met him halfway, standing on tiptoe to clasp her hands around his neck. His senses reeled. If he didn't get a grip on his emotions, this situation could get out of hand in a hurry.

He lifted his head and looked down at her lashes, lying like shadows on her cheeks. The days spent out-of-doors had tanned her complexion to a soft gold. Her lips were as sweet and as red as wild strawberries. He wanted to push her away, get on his horse, and ride off, but even as the thought crossed his mind, he knew it was a lie. What he really wanted was to stand here like this, warmed by the glow in her eyes.

Cole knew he was playing with fire and that the mistake

would follow him the rest of his life. He didn't want her in his heart—but she was already there. Somewhere between here and River Run he'd fallen in love with this woman, and he no longer had the will to ignore it. Yet he had no idea how he would deal with the knowledge either. How could he have fallen in love with a woman who had vowed to kill his brother?

He sighed, letting his arms drop. *I didn't want this, Lord. What am I going to do? Why did You let me fall in love with the one woman I can't have? Why couldn't I have found her first?*

Wynne stared up at him, a question in her eyes.

"We'd better get back to the cabin. It's not smart running around here unarmed." Which it wasn't, and he should have known better. He was glad to see the clearing in front of the cabin was empty, the rifle still lying where she had flung it. All that target practice would have been audible for miles around. They'd be lucky if every gang and wannabe bad guy in the county didn't pay them a visit.

That night he lay in bed, listening to the sounds of tree frogs and katydids in the grass and trees outside the cabin. A stray shaft of moonlight tied him to Wynne, who slept on her porch pallet. Tomorrow he was taking her back home with him. The horse had been walking better, barely limping. They could have left a couple of days ago if he'd been willing to walk, but he hadn't wanted this time to end. He didn't think Wynne was as determined to catch up with Cass as she had been. Maybe a few days spent with Ma and Betsy would bring her to her senses. He didn't know what he would do if she refused to go.

The moon was going down behind the cabin when he finally fell asleep.

The following morning Cole was sitting at the table when Wynne finally awoke.

"Hello." She smiled, waltzing into the cabin as pretty as a sunrise.

"Hello."

"Why didn't you wake me?"

He shrugged noncommittally. "There was no need."

Wynne stretched lazily. "Did you sleep well?"

"Yes."

She grinned. "I did too. Your rash looks almost gone this morning."

He shoved back from the table and began pulling on his boots.

"Where are you going?" she asked.

"Home."

"Home? River Run?" She turned to stare at him.

"That's right." The boots were on, and he straightened to face her.

"But what about me?"

"I think you would be wise to come with me," he said.

"But why?"

He felt his expression lose some of its earlier harshness, but he dreaded the coming fight. "Give it up, Wynne. Come back to River Run with me. There's no telling where Cass is—he may even be back home by now. It would be crazy for you to keep looking for him. You don't have a horse or a gun."

"You could stay with me," she pleaded. "When I find Cass, you can be there to warn him about me." She was talking desperately, he knew, any feeble excuse to keep him with her, but he couldn't stay. Not now.

"I can't do that." He turned away from the pleading in her eyes for fear he would give in; he couldn't do that either.

"Why?" Her fingers grasped the sleeve of his shirt and turned him back around to face her. "Why *not*, Cole? Hasn't our time here—together—meant anything to you?"

Meant anything to him? It had changed his life. "I'm leaving in thirty minutes. If you want to go with me, then I promise to see that you get back to Savannah safely. If you don't want to come—" he looked away from her—"then I guess you're on your own."

He knew the words were cut-and-dried, unemotional, and final. Sometimes life wasn't easy, but if he gave in now that would make them both fools.

Tears gathered in her eyes and her hand came up to cover her mouth. He could see the hurt in her eyes from the lie he'd perpetuated: that the past few weeks had meant nothing to him.

"Well?" Cole ignored her tears and got up and reached for his hat.

"All right," she said lifelessly. She kept her face averted.

"You'll come back with me?"

"Yes. I don't guess I have much choice."

He nodded and walked to the door. "I'll saddle the horse."

CHAPTER 15

So they started home. Cole knew he was doing the right thing, but he already missed the companionship he'd shared with Wynne at the cabin. Granted, he'd been sick most of the time, but the time they'd spent together would be an experience he would always remember. He guessed marriage wouldn't be so bad after all.

With the right woman.

Wynne rode sheltered in his arms, but they spoke only when necessary. She seemed weary, and most of the fire had gone out of her. He didn't feel like talking much himself.

An hour before dusk, they stopped to camp. Wynne prepared the meal while he brought wood and water and took care of the horse. They worked well together, sharing the tasks in silence. There was a barrier between them. A barrier he had erected and couldn't tear down. At least not yet. If ever.

At night they lay across the campfire from each other, not speaking. The silence was deeper than anything he had ever imagined. He watched the flames playing over her bedroll, and it was as if a great gulf lay between them. As much as he wanted to deny it, she'd had some sort of relationship with his brother. Until he learned the truth from Cass, he wasn't free to express his love to Wynne. He was alone in his own private world without the right to ask her to share it with him.

Whatever had been between Wynne and his brother was over for her—he was certain of that—but he hadn't heard Cass's side of the story or how he felt. He'd been like a father to both of his brothers. He couldn't take Wynne from Cass any more than he would try to take Betsy from Beau.

Cass was a charmer, no doubt about it. What if, when they met again, he used that charm on Wynne? Could he stand aside and let his brother have the woman he loved? Cole sighed. Life didn't use to be this complicated. He always figured once you fell in love you spent your time having a lot of romantic thoughts. Well, he had the thoughts all right, but he couldn't act upon them. If the good Lord had ever created a more exasperating woman, Cole had yet to meet her.

Morning dawned after another sleepless night. He carefully avoided the hurt in Wynne's eyes. It was hard speaking of things that weren't important and pretending the past few weeks had never happened. He knew she didn't understand the change in him, and he didn't have the words to explain. All he could do was take care of her and keep his distance. There were matters they needed to talk about, but he was waiting for the right time.

He talked to God often, asking for guidance. Trouble was, God wasn't doing much talking back. The past few days Cole had felt like he was stumbling through the fog, trying to find his way. Maybe that was what the preachers meant when they talked about living by faith. He'd always thought if you trusted in God the path would be clear—lit by constant sunlight. At the cabin, when he talked to God, Cole had felt like he was walking in that sunlight, but out here on the trail it was different. Colder even in the hot sun. Maybe it was supposed to be that way. Sometimes you walked in the light and sometimes you walked in deep shade, but either way God was there. If you could see where you were walking all the time, he guessed you wouldn't need faith. And right now faith was all he had to hold on to.

He rode behind Wynne, repeatedly challenging his sanity at the way he had let himself fall in love with this woman. Even if she were to give up the foolish idea of killing his brother, she would always bear a deep resentment toward Cass.

The family would be divided, something he found intolerable. How could he choose between the woman he loved and his family? His prayers were disjointed dialogues with God, alternating between raging disappointment and abject apology on his part. So far God wasn't contributing much to the discussion.

The Claxton family had stood together through thick and thin. It was inconceivable that an outsider, wearing a crazy little bird hat, could waltz into his life and come between him and family, yet the thought of putting Wynne on the stagecoach back to Savannah tore him apart. Right now he couldn't imagine what his life would be like without her.

Toward evening of the second day they stopped to water the horse. Wynne knelt beside the stream and splashed a handful of cool liquid against her grimy face. Trail dust was thick and ground into her dress. Her hair straggled from the few remaining hairpins, and weariness etched her features. He thought she had never looked more beautiful.

Cole watched as she closed her eyes and trickled water over her neck. She had been no trouble at all lately, doing her share of the work and never complaining. She'd been submissive and unusually quiet, not at all like the fireball he'd found standing in the middle of the road one day, waving a gun at him. The change only served to deepen his anguish.

Wynne shaded her eyes and watched a rider approach. The stranger paused across the stream, dismounted, then led his horse to the water. Maneuvering down on his knees with stiff, careful movements, he bent to cup his hands and drink. It appeared he was wearing some sort of brace on his back. He had no waist motion, and bending seemed an effort. She watched as he quenched his thirst.

"Someone you know?" Cole asked.

She frowned. "I think I've seen him before."

Cole's brow lifted sourly. "Oh?"

She watched a while longer, her face pensive.

"Let's move on." Cole waded the horse out of the stream and waited while Wynne took another long drink, then rose and joined him.

Their eyes met as she waited for him to help her up. He reached out as if he meant to touch her face, then let his hand drop back to his side.

She gazed up at him expectantly. "What's the matter?"

"You have water on your nose."

"Oh." She reached up and wiped away the droplet, then smiled at him. "There. Is that better?"

Cole nodded, keeping his eyes averted, and quickly lifted her into the saddle.

She was incredibly close, near enough for him to see into

the depths of her green eyes. "I wish you wouldn't look at me that way," he said.

"And I wish you didn't look the way you do." Both tones were tempered with something close to affection. She watched him closely.

He gathered up the reins and turned away.

"Aren't you going to ride?" she asked when he walked the horse down the rutted lane.

"No, ma'am. I'm walking."

She stared at the stubborn set of his shoulders. Something was bothering him. Well, good. She was bothered too. Their time together at the cabin had opened her eyes. She had never loved Cass. Not with the strong, sweet emotion she felt for Cole. She wanted to tell him how she felt, but she knew he wouldn't want to hear.

The time spent at the cabin had taught her something: She could never have killed Cass. That had been hurt and anger talking. She didn't believe God would have let her pull the trigger. She had sinned: lied, stolen, and determined in her heart to commit murder. God wouldn't let those sins go unpunished, and she feared her punishment would be more than she could bear. She'd learned what it was to love, but Cole could never be hers because the man she had planned to kill was his brother.

They made camp early. Wynne appreciated the thoughtful gesture. Both knew this would be their last night on the trail. Cole shot a rabbit, and she roasted the meat on a spit.

She glanced up to see him watching her, a look of sadness and regret in his expression. "What?"

"Nothing."

"There must be something. You've been watching me like that since we left the cabin."

"I was just thinking how pretty you are."

She stared at him before erupting into a laugh. "You can't be serious. Look at me. I've worn this dress for weeks, my hair is hanging half down my back, and I'm covered in trail grime. I know how I look. Try again."

He shook his head. "You beat anything, you know that? Try to give you a compliment and you throw it back. Is that any way to attract a man?"

Wynne jumped up, hands on hips, eyes flaming. "What makes you think I want to 'attract a man,' as you put it? Have I made any effort to *attract* you?"

"No, ma'am, you sure haven't," he said. He'd had women set their cap for him, and he knew the tricks. This one had mostly tried to kill him or get him killed. Maybe that was why he *was* attracted to her. The change of pace had thrown him. A man sort of expected a woman to be all wide-eyed and admiring. Cute and cuddly. This one looked at him like he was out of his mind. And probably he was. What else could explain the way he felt? His pulse raced like a sixteen-year-old's in the throes of puppy love, and this old dog had better rein in his imagination before he found himself walking down an aisle.

Wynne was peeved. Did that man *really* think she was attracted to him? Well, she was, but that didn't mean she had to put up with his behavior. From the moment they had left the cabin he had been acting funny. Like when they had seen that other rider at the stream. He'd seemed disturbed that she might know the man, and at first she had thought he was jealous, but then he froze her out until she felt like an outsider again.

"I didn't ask you to follow me," she said.

"Don't start that again." He pointed a finger at her. "You know why I followed you. I had family obligations."

"Well, you carried them out. I'm not after your brother anymore." She knew she was picking a fight with him, but she didn't care. At least if he was angry at her he was talking, and he'd done precious little of that since leaving the cabin.

Cole stared into the campfire, eyebrows knitted tightly together. "If Jeff Davis had given you a gun and put you on the front lines, the war would have been over in a week. The troops would have been so whipped down no one would have had enough gumption to fight."

She glared at him, unable to trust her ears. "I can't believe you said that. What have I done that makes you think I'm such a hooligan?"

She thought he was going to choke. "What *haven't* you done would be more like it. Think back a little. I believe you stole my rabbit."

Her jaw dropped in amazement. "That was weeks ago. I can't believe you're still upset about that. Are you the type to carry a grudge?"

He glared at her. "Who's the man back at the stream? The one you were so interested in."

She laughed. "You're jealous."

"I am not. I am, however, responsible for getting you back safely. So I'm asking you again, who is he?"

He *was* jealous. She was delighted! "I don't know who he is, but I've seen him somewhere—maybe on the first part of my journey—except then he had a splint on his leg. This time he seemed to have something wrong with his back." She grinned. "Very handsome man, don't you think?"

She laughed at the expression on his face, as if he had just bitten into a sour pickle. Cole might act like he was indifferent, but she had a feeling he was more aware of her than he let on.

Let me have him, Lord, and I'll never ask for anything else again.

"If you ask me, he looked kind of puny," Cole said.

"I didn't ask you." She resisted the urge to stick her tongue out at him. She flipped the stick away from the fire and removed the rabbit. "Supper's ready."

The following morning, Cole released an audible sigh of relief when the Claxton farm came into view. Wynne's close proximity the past two days had his nerves humming like telegraph lines. She had gone from saying nothing to picking on him. He could hear the teasing in her voice, and she seemed to be laughing at him most of the time. He couldn't turn her over to Ma and Betsy to see if they could do anything with her fast enough. In his opinion, which she hadn't asked for, no one could do anything with Wynne Elliot when she made up her mind to oppose him, which seemed to be about 100 percent of the time.

The courtyard was busy when he lifted Wynne off the mare. Tables and chairs had been set up in the cherry grove, and there was a general air of festivity.

"What's going on?" he wondered out loud.

"Looks like your mother's having a party."

Willa waved from the clothesline, her large body dipping up and down rhythmically as she retrieved the wet pieces one by one and pinned them into place.

Cole waved back, taking in all the commotion, then watched as Wynne started toward the house, her steps gradually slowing. Considering how she had sneaked out after Ma and Betsy had been so good to her, he figured she was having a case of guilt.

His heart contracted. She looked so shabby. He wanted to pick her up, dust her off, and protect her from curious eyes. But he couldn't do that. Wynne, like everyone else, would have to take the consequences of her behavior, and Ma and Betsy had a right to an explanation. He hoped Wynne didn't reveal her real reason for leaving. Ma probably wouldn't take kindly to hearing the woman she'd taken under her roof planned to shoot her baby boy.

Betsy came out of the house, her face lighting when she spotted the newcomers. She grabbed Wynne and hugged her exuberantly. "I do declare, you're a sight for sore eyes. Where in the *world* did you disappear to?"

"I had to leave suddenly." Wynne glanced at Cole, her face as red as the blossom on the rambler growing over the fence at the side of the house.

Cole watched, fascinated by the way women acted. Men would have shaken hands and that would have been the end of it. Women, now, they hugged, cried, got embarrassed, talked, and made noise. A lot of noise.

Lilly poked her head out the door, then flew across the porch, her feet barely touching the steps. "Wynne, darling, how good to see you back! And Cole! I do declare, this is a happy day!"

After a tight hug Lilly held Wynne's thin shoulders and surveyed her disreputable condition. "Oh, dear, I suppose this means your trip has been unsuccessful. You didn't find your friend?"

Wynne looked down. "No, I wasn't able to find him."

"I'm so sorry."

"It's all right. I've changed my mind about trying to locate him." She lifted her eyes to meet Lilly's. "I'll be going back to Savannah instead."

"Well . . ." Lilly heaved a sigh and glanced in Cole's direction. "I suppose that would be for the best, but I was hoping you would stay for a while."

Cole approached the group of chattering females, figuring it was time to make his presence known.

"Land sakes alive! Finish your business in Kansas City at last?" Lilly hugged her oldest son, peering hopefully around him. "I don't guess you ran into your brother anywhere along the way?"

"No, Ma, but I heard Cass made it through the war."

"You did!" Lilly clapped her hands together. "Well, praise the Lord! I just knew he would. Surely he'll be riding in any day now."

Cole grinned and shrugged. "I suppose anything's possible."

"Why, of course it's possible," she said. "He'll be home

anytime—you wait and see." She turned back to Wynne. "How did you get here, dear? I only heard one rider."

Cole slipped an arm around Wynne's waist. "I ran into Miss Elliot a ways back on the road. Her, uh, animal bolted and ran away, so I gave her a ride."

"Your horse ran away?" Lilly's face instantly filled with concern. Her eyes ran over the bedraggled young woman standing forlornly beside Betsy. "Why, I thought you left on the stage."

"No—no, I decided to buy other means of transportation."

Cole grinned at Wynne and she kept her eyes on Lilly. He noticed she didn't mention the mule. She couldn't without telling the rest of the story. He didn't think she would want Ma and Betsy to hear the extent of her adventures.

"Great day! I'm glad I didn't know that." Lilly sighed. "I'd have worried myself to death. I hope you weren't hurt when the horse threw you, dear."

Wynne smiled. "Not a scratch." She brushed grime from her dirty dress, looking embarrassed. "But of course all my clothes went with it. Now I don't have a thing to wear."

Betsy rushed to allay her worries. "Don't you worry a bit. We'll get you into a hot tub of water, and after you're bathed, you can borrow some of my things. I'm a little larger, but I have a yellow calico that will look wonderful on you!"

"Thank you, Betsy. I would appreciate it." She glanced at Cole then looked away. Betsy draped a protective arm around her shoulders and led her toward the porch. His future sister-in-law was still chattering like a blue jay as the two women disappeared into the house.

Lilly followed at a slower pace, her arm wrapped around her son's waist. "You think she's really all right, dear?"

Cole's eyes pursued Wynne until he could no longer see her. "She's okay, Ma."

"She's sure a lucky little thing. Imagine, you coming along at the right moment to save her." Lilly glanced up, meeting his eyes. Cole felt a slow burn creep up his collar. Ma was smart; she'd give him the benefit of the doubt, but she knew coincidences were rare. He recognized that gleam in her eyes. She was matchmaking. She wanted her boys married to good, decent, God-fearing women. Well, she didn't know it, but he'd marry Wynne Elliot in a heartbeat if Cass hadn't proposed first.

"I suppose," he said. "Where's Beau?"

"Mending fences. He'll be along after a while to eat his dinner. How'd your business go in Kansas City?"

"Fine." His eyes took in the cherry orchard once more. "What's going on?"

"Oh, Beau and Betsy were getting all astir to announce their engagement. We decided we'd have an informal party—let friends and neighbors know that the wedding was still on."

"You were going to have an engagement party without me and Cass?" Cole said with mock astonishment. He knew Lilly would never consider such an event without having her entire family present.

"Why, no, dear, the party isn't an official engagement announcement—more like a Saturday-night shindig. Beau and Betsy's actual wedding announcement won't be until later in the fall."

Cole squeezed his mother's shoulder. "I'm just teasing you, Ma. I know you wouldn't do that."

She reached up and tugged the wiry growth that lay dark and thick across his face. "I look at you and I see your daddy.

My firstborn, and you're Sam Claxton all over again. It makes me want to shout for joy that the good Lord has left a small part of him on this earth to give me such comfort."

Cole grinned down at her. "Don't go all sentimental on me."

She playfully slapped his shoulder. "You think I don't know you and your tomfoolery by now? You get on into the house and tell Willa to fetch you some bathwater. There's going to be a party tonight." Her eyes sparkled with anticipation. "There's going to be singing and dancing the likes of which you haven't seen or heard for four long years!"

CHAPTER 16

Around four o'clock, buggies started arriving. Buckboards and
surreys filled the Claxton courtyard. After four long years of war,
folks were ready to celebrate. The melodious tones of fiddles
and guitars filled the air, and the sound of laughter floated over
the hillsides as the party got into full swing.

Wynne listened to the sounds of merriment floating through
the open window while she finished dressing. She studied her
reflection in the mirror and wondered if she'd ever feel the
same. She had changed so much since leaving home. She looked
the same on the outside, until she looked herself in the eyes. An
older, wiser woman looked back at her. She had arranged her
newly washed and dried hair in a mass of curls on top of her
head and dusted a smidgeon of Betsy's face powder to conceal
the freckles. Long days in the sun had damaged her skin. Tilly
would be upset, and Miss Marelda would say she should have
been more careful.

Wynne didn't care about her skin; it was her heart that had
irreparable damage.

Tonight was intended for celebration; she didn't begrudge the silly shenanigans going on below, but her smile slowly faded when reality closed in on her. She only wished that she and Cole could be a part of the lightheartedness.

What a wondrous delight it would be if they could overcome the differences that lay between them. She wished he would swing her up in his arms and haul her off to the barn to steal a kiss. But Cole would never do that. He never teased her or showed his feelings, except for the brief moments when he let his guard down. And he would most assuredly never haul her off to the barn in front of everyone. Lilly would never stand for that sort of tomfoolery.

And she shouldn't be thinking of such things. Miss Marelda Fielding would be disappointed in her. According to her, ladies never thought about what she called "baser traits" until after marriage. Well, you could be fairly certain that Miss Marelda had never spent weeks alone with a man in an isolated cabin—all perfectly innocent. Cole had been nothing but a gentleman.

Her own thinking had been altered, though. She'd spent a lot of thought on the way she felt when Cole held her—particularly on the way she felt when he kissed her. She could tell Miss Marelda a thing or two about kissing and thinking that would make her eyes pop.

Wynne smoothed the skirt of the yellow calico. She would miss Betsy when she left. Good friends were hard to come by, and Betsy was a good friend. God had granted Beau someone special, and by the look in his eyes when he held his fiancée, he recognized the gift. The two would have a good life together. She was happy for them, but she couldn't shake the envy.

The two women had talked long into the afternoon. Betsy

had encouraged her to stay in River Run, but Wynne would not be convinced. She planned to leave on tomorrow's stage, and her decision was final. There was absolutely no reason for her to remain where she was not welcome.

Cole's aloof behavior during the ride home proved to her that he would make no effort to change her mind. She had teased and goaded him, trying to get a rise, but he had remained steadfastly detached. If he cared about her, he would have said something—anything—to keep her from leaving, and he hadn't. On the contrary, he'd offered to pay for the stagecoach ticket.

She rested her case.

When she'd informed him of her decision an hour ago, he'd met her announcement with the same indifference he had shown when they first met. He'd merely asked that she be ready by first light, and he'd take her into town and *buy* a ticket, if that was what she wanted.

So tomorrow morning she would be on her way back to Savannah with a broken heart, but at least it would be a fresh break. She would do her best to revive Moss Oak and turn it into a paying plantation again, but her heart and thoughts would always be back here in Missouri.

It would have been better if she had never set off on this wild chase for revenge, but God had taught her a lesson, one she should have known all along. Sin brings shame to the name of Christ, and her heart had been full of sin when she met Cole. Sin robbed her of God's blessings, and most of all, sin only complicated life, not enhanced it.

She leaned her arms on the windowsill, watching the people below. *I knew all along it was wrong to want to kill anyone, Lord. And I know that thinking those thoughts was a sin. I know I couldn't have gone through with it, and I'm glad I was never put to the test. Wherever Cass is, give him a safe trip back home to Lilly. She's so worried. And please, God, when I leave tomorrow, don't let me cry until I get out of town.*

Betsy's knock on the door interrupted her prayer. "You ready to go down now?"

"As ready as I'll ever be."

They walked down the stairway together and were greeted by whistles of male admiration. Beau waited at the foot of the stairs to claim his Betsy, while Wynne was surrounded by friendly, smiling men anxious to catch her attention. But there was only one man's reaction she wanted, and he was nowhere to be seen.

It was late evening before Cole joined the festivities in the cherry orchard. Wynne's heart threatened to stop when she saw him pause to speak to Betsy's sister, Priscilla June. He looked utterly striking: clean shaven, wearing a jacket and dress pants. Wynne was certain that her love for him was written so clearly on her face that everyone would know her secret.

She wasn't the only one who had spotted his entrance. A crowd of women had gathered, vying for his attention, but Priscilla had already staked her claim. She cooed and fussed over Cole until Wynne wanted to march over and snatch her bald-headed.

Cole glanced up from saying something to Priscilla, and their eyes met; suddenly for Wynne, every other person at the party disappeared.

She struggled to hide her emotions but knew she failed miserably. She could only stare back at him with her heart in her eyes and pray he wouldn't look away.

The blue of his eyes darkened as they gently ran the length of the yellow calico. She knew the dress fit her nicely—and was her color. Betsy had given her a locket, and the gold sparkled at her neckline. Her hair was arranged in the latest style. Funny how knowing you looked good gave you more confidence. She lifted her chin, smiling slightly.

Waiting.

For a moment they stood transcended in time. It was as if the world held no one else but them. And then he smiled at her, a slow, easy smile that told her he had not forgotten what they had shared.

She smiled back, enough to let him know that she understood and shared his remembrances. They would be all she had to cling to after tomorrow. No matter what the future held for her, the days spent with Cole at the cabin would be a golden treasure to be kept forever.

The magic was broken when Priscilla took his arm. Wynne moved through the crowd, biting back welling tears. Cole would marry Priscilla June. Or he would if Miss Pris got her way. No matter. She wouldn't be here to see it. Let him do whatever he wanted. She didn't care.

The night blurred. She danced and laughed and tried to forget that after tomorrow she would never see Cole Claxton again.

Around midnight she gave up all pretenses and slipped quietly around the corner of the house to go to her room.

Cole's voice stopped her when she reached Lilly's flower garden. "Turning in so early?"

Her footsteps faltered. Closing her eyes, she took a deep breath. She didn't have the strength to stand another encounter with him tonight. "I'm a little tired."

"I can imagine. It was a long trip, and you have another one facing you tomorrow."

"That's right." Wynne could only see a darker shape where he blended into the shadows of the shrubbery, but his cologne drifted to her. Soft. Musky. "If you'll excuse me?" She gathered her light shawl around her shoulders and started to walk on.

"What's your hurry, Miss Elliot?" he asked in an easy tone.

Her steps faltered again. *Walk on. Walk on!* "I told you. I'm very tired."

He stepped out of the shadows and joined her. Her breath caught and held as she gazed up at him. The rays of the silvery moonlight played across his face, and she longed to have him take her in his arms and tell her that he loved her, that it didn't matter what she had been about to do to his brother. The only thing that really mattered was that she was in love with him now, and it would be sheer insanity to throw away that rare, wondrous miracle simply because of her past foolhardiness.

He could do worse in a bride, Wynne told herself. She could make him proud. She would use all the skills Miss Marelda had taught her until one day he would look at her as a lady, not some bumbling nincompoop!

But how did she tell him without making a complete fool of herself? He'd made it clear that he didn't return her feelings. He would only laugh and tell her she obviously didn't know what man she loved. First Cass, now him.

She could never bear that.

She turned and started on, but his hand reached out and blocked her. "Don't go in yet." His earlier arrogance was gone. Instead, his tone held a soft, almost urgent plea. Her breath caught when he swung her roughly around and into his arms.

She melted like snow on a warm day. The world stood still. This was what she'd wanted, what she'd longed for all evening. His mouth lowered to kiss her.

She could only guess where the embrace would have ended if Beau hadn't interrupted. "Wynne? Are you out there?"

Cole caught her back possessively. "Don't answer." His mouth captured hers again with fierceness that shook her to the core.

Beau's voice persisted. He came closer to where they stood sheltered in the shadows of a lilac bush. "Wynne?"

"I have to answer," she whispered between broken kisses. "In a few minutes he'll see us, Cole."

He must have realized the truth of her words, because he slowly released her. A moment later she stepped quietly out of the shadows. "Yes, Beau?"

"Oh, there you are." He came forward with a large grin on his face. "There's someone here looking for you."

"Me?" Wynne asked with surprise.

Beau shrugged. "Yeah. Some fella came riding in a while ago. Said he would have been here earlier, but his horse threw a shoe. Oh, hey, Cole. Didn't see you standing back there." His grin widened.

"Who's looking for her?"

"Don't know. Some man who says it's real important that he talk to Wynne."

"She's not talking to any man tonight," Cole said flatly. "Tell him to come back tomorrow morning and call on her proper."

"Good heavens, Cole. He's not *calling on* me," Wynne protested, thrilled to hear jealously seeping into his voice. She couldn't imagine who her visitor could be. She didn't know anyone in River Run. "Where is the man, Beau?"

"He's waiting in the parlor. Ma made him sit down and drink something cool. He looked a mite peaked when he got here."

Wynne glanced at Cole. "It wouldn't hurt for me to see what he wants, would it?" She couldn't bear the curiosity until morning.

Cole shrugged, looking cross. "I don't like it, but go ahead. Talk to the man."

She smiled and turned to leave when Beau spoke up again. "Aren't you going to go with her?"

"I don't tell her who she can talk to," Cole said curtly, but Wynne was pleased to see that he followed at a distance. After all, she didn't know who was waiting out there. It might even be Sonny Morgan coming to press his claim to her. She felt better to know Cole would be close by.

When Wynne entered the parlor, the young man waiting for her smiled in spite of his obvious discomfort. She could see the back brace he wore was hot and bothering him something fierce. He looked frazzled, as if it was the end of a long and particularly tedious day.

When Wynne approached, his face immediately went slack with astonishment. For a moment the two stared at one another. Then she broke into a smile and moved across the room to take his hand. "Well, hello again." He was the same young man she had seen twice before. Once sitting on a porch, whittling, when she had ridden through Springfield, and again when she and Cole had stopped to water their horse.

"*You're* Wynne Elliot!" His voice cracked, sounding as though he was in the throes of puberty.

She smiled expectantly. "Yes."

A protruding Adam's apple bobbed up and down as he tried

to regain his composure. "Miss Elliot . . . I had no idea that was you . . ." His voice trailed off.

Wynne continued to smile at the pale young man, wondering what in heaven's name he wanted with her. If Cole thought she was addlebrained, he should meet this man. He seemed to have trouble putting his thoughts together.

He wiped his hand nervously on the side of his trousers then politely extended it to her. "Bertram G. Mallory, ma'am."

"Mr. Mallory." Wynne tipped her head and accepted his hand, the way Miss Marelda had taught her. Perhaps this was another one of the lawyers from her father's estate, though he certainly didn't look like a lawyer. Matter of fact, he looked like a saddle tramp, but you couldn't always tell.

"Oh, ma'am, you don't know how nice it is to finally meet you!"

"Why, thank you." She smiled again. "I believe you wanted to speak to me?"

"Oh, yes, ma'am. I still can't realize you're standing in front of me. I'm with Pinkerton's National Detective Agency—you've heard of us, haven't you?"

Wynne nodded. She had read about Allan Pinkerton from Glasgow, Scotland, in a paper one time. He now lived in Chicago and had made a name for himself by recovering a large sum of money for the Adams Express Company. The paper had said he was also credited with foiling a plot to murder President Abraham Lincoln.

"Well, ma'am, I was hired by Mr. Claxton to return this to you." He began to search through his pockets, extracting his billfold, a comb, a pocketknife, and his gun, all of which he promptly handed to her. "Excuse me, ma'am, could you hold these for a moment?"

"Yes, certainly." Wynne took the items and he continued his search. "You said Mr. Claxton sent you?"

"Yeah . . . yeah . . . now, wait . . . I know it's here somewhere." His face suddenly brightened. "Yes! Here it is!" He quickly slapped a leather pouch into her hand and immediately smiled as if a ton of weight had just been lifted off his shoulders.

"Cass . . . Claxton?" she asked. Her smile faded.

"Yes, ma'am. It's the money you lent him."

Wynne's hand clasped the pouch and the wallet and the comb and the gun. Her eyes narrowed in anger. If this was someone's idea of a joke, it wasn't funny. "The money I *lent* him? What are you talking about?"

"It's all there, ma'am. Every cent of it—with interest. Cass gave it to me to give back to you the day you two were supposed to be married." Bertram peered back at her from eyes that were bloodshot and ringed with road grime, but they were good, honest eyes. "I've tried real hard to find you, ma'am. I surely have. I had been in bed with a bad case of the miseries the day Mr. Claxton came to my door, so I couldn't bring the money over then. I got up early the next morning and went to your house, but you were already gone back to Miss Fielding's school, so I went looking for you there, but I missed you again."

He sighed hopelessly. "From then on every time I got close to you, either you disappeared again or I had another one of those . . . accidents."

Wynne smiled sympathetically. "I noticed you had been injured."

Bertram sighed. "Just thinking about my ordeals makes my ribs, my legs, and my back start to pain all over again. I've not had an easy time, ma'am, and I'd appreciate it if you told Mr. Claxton so—on account of me being so late in finding you."

He drew a cleansing breath. "Then I heard you were on your way to River Run, so I figured I'd try to catch you before you got to Mr. Claxton's folks. He told me he came from River Run originally, and he'd been visiting kinfolk in Savannah. I was afraid you'd arrive ahead of me and be under the impression Mr. Claxton swindled you out of your money, which would be a tragic misunderstanding, because Mr. Claxton has the highest ethics. I'm afraid it was I who dropped the ball." Bertram hung his head sheepishly. "Sure sorry I didn't make it in time. I know you must be thinking all sorts of bad things about Mr. Claxton—and, ma'am? About his intentions to marry you? I am to inform you that he loved you, but he developed a case of what is known as cold feet. I believe he decided it would be unfair to you to continue with nuptials—and he didn't have the heart to tell you. He told me he knew he was making the mistake of his life, but his conscience prevented him from marrying."

While Bertram rattled on, Wynne battled through a range of emotions: disbelief, jubilation, incredulity, exultation. If what Mr. Mallory was saying was true, then these horrendous past few months had been for nothing! She had been running around vowing revenge on a man who was guilty of nothing more serious than marriage aversion. Cass hadn't wanted to *hurt* her even more by going through with an ill-advised wedding, which actually made a lot of sense.

Wynne's knees turned to water, and she stared at Bertram's gun, still in her hand. What if she had been able to find Cass? She would never have actually killed him—she couldn't. No, never. In a way Cass's rejection had been a blessing. She knew now that what she had felt for him was not love, not when she compared her feelings for Cole. Her smile faded. And what was *he* going to say, other than "I told you so," when he learned that his brother had made provisions to return the money all along? She had been too busy seeking revenge to stop long enough for Mr. Mallory to find her.

She breathed a long, deep sigh. It was all very confusing.

"Ma'am?" Bertram looked like he wasn't quite sure how she was taking the news.

She glanced up. "Yes?"

"Are you . . . all right?"

"Oh yes. Better than all right, Mr. Mallory." Or at least she would be as soon as she was able to digest the shocking news. "I can't thank you enough for finally locating me. You've made me a happy woman."

"Oh, that's all right, ma'am." Bertram gathered up his wallet and comb from her safekeeping. "Mr. Claxton paid me handsomely; I'm only doing my job."

"Nevertheless, I am grateful. You have a great dedication to duty, Mr. Mallory."

"Thank you, ma'am; I try."

She thought he looked rather sad. Perhaps his back was hurting him.

Outside someone let out a loud war whoop as the sound of approaching hoofbeats thundered into the yard. A crescendo of voices rang out. "Cass! Cass is coming!"

Bertram stepped to the window and lifted the curtain. "Oh my, looks like Mr. Claxton could have delivered the money a whole lot easier. Uh, maybe there's a back door? If so, I'll excuse myself and be on my way. I have my own wedding to attend in Springfield."

Wynne suddenly came back to life, the shock of the past few moments finally wearing off. "Good heavens! Cass is home!"

An hour ago those words would have meant very little, but now all she could feel was extreme joy. Cole and Beau would have their brother back, and Lilly's youngest son would have returned home safely.

Letting out a squeal that would have shocked Miss Marelda right down to her prissy old corset, Wynne bolted toward the front door. She wanted to be one of the first to greet him. Cass was home, and he wasn't the scoundrel she had thought him to be at all! She had to tell him she forgave him and make peace. Then maybe she and Cole . . .

She skidded to a stop halfway across the parlor and whirled around to rush back and give Bertram a large, energetic hug. "Ooooh, thank you, Mr. Mallory; thank you ever so much!" She spun around and raced out the wide parlor door at full speed.

"Ma'am, my gun—"

Wynne heard him, but his words barely registered. Cass was home.

Cole was on his way to check on Wynne when she buzzed by him like an angry hornet, flailing a gun in the air, nearly bowling him over in her hasty exit.

"Hey, where's the fire?"

He reached out to slow her passage, but she shrugged his hand away and yelled over her shoulder, "Can't stop now! Cass is home!"

A man Cole vaguely remembered seeing before ran past him, calling in a panicked voice, "Ma'am, my gun!"

The smile on Cole's face drained when the meaning of Wynne's words sank in. And she had been waving a gun. He tore off after her.

"Wynne, wait!" he shouted.

Wynne burst through the crowd on the porch and down the steps, racing toward the rider who had just entered the courtyard.

Bertram was making progress in his dash to intercept her when Cole rushed by like a streak of lightning. Mallory slowed and grabbed a nearby table for support.

"Sorry, fella." Cole hurriedly steadied the swaying form. Bertram straightened up and readjusted his hat, and Cole started running again. "Wynne!" he shouted. "Don't do it!"

He had the impression that everyone had stopped what they were doing and frozen in position, like a child's game where no one could move except on command. He knew he and Wynne were making a spectacle of themselves and that he was going to have to come up with a full explanation to Ma for acting like this when guests were present, but he had to stop Wynne before she made the biggest mistake of her life.

"Wynne! No! I won't let you do it!"

A dog ran between his feet, slowing him. He took a flying leap and tackled her as Cass reined his horse to a skidding halt.

Cole knew Cass was sitting openmouthed on his horse, watching his older brother knock Wynne Elliot off her feet. He had to be wondering what was going on. Well, join the party. So was half of the county. Cole had always been conscious of his position as the head of the family, but now he had just driven a woman to the ground in front of practically everyone he knew. His reputation was shot.

Over to the side, the stranger had managed to get one foot in the stirrup, but his horse was antsy with all the racket going on. The man couldn't mount, nor could he get his foot loose.

Cole knew someone should go to the stranger's rescue, but he had his hands full right now. Evidently his landing on her had not only surprised Wynne, it made her mad. Extremely mad.

"Get *off* me!" she screeched, kicking and elbowing him. "What in the world is the matter with you?"

"Don't do it!" Cole tried to still her flailing limbs, fighting to gain control of the gun. His heavy body pinned her to the ground. He grasped her wrists tightly and pinned them above her head. "Don't . . . Wynne."

"Don't *what?* What are you babbling about?"

"Don't shoot him—please."

"Shoot him? What are you talking about?"

Cole's eyes locked with hers and he pried the gun from her hand. He saw realization dawn in her eyes. She looked down at the handgun he now held out of her reach.

"Oh, darling! I wasn't going to shoot him!" she exclaimed. "I was going to thank him for being so honest and nice. . . ." Her words trailed off when his eyes narrowed with disbelief.

Cole felt anger swell his chest to the bursting point. He knew from the expression on Wynne's face that he was scaring her.

"*Thank* him!" he exploded.

He had nearly killed himself these past few weeks trying to prevent his brother from being ambushed by her, and now she was going to *thank* him for being so nice! What was wrong with this woman? Was it asking too much for her to act sane? He never knew where he was with her, and that was a real handicap to a man who was used to being in charge.

"Well, yes . . ." Wynne slowly got to her feet, dusting off the yellow calico. "You see, that man who wanted to see me in the parlor . . ."

Cole listened with amazement to her explanation until the sound of running horses caught their attention.

With a boil of dust and a loud "Ho! Ho, there!" a buckboard driven by a rather flamboyant young woman swung crazily into the yard. She bounded down in a flash of red satin and rushed to the stranger's rescue.

"Fancy!" the man blurted, dancing on one foot to keep up with the horse.

"Oh, Bertie, darling, let me help you." She grabbed the reins of the horse and managed to still the animal while Bertram jerked his bound foot free from the stirrup.

"What are you doing here?" he asked.

Cole watched as the woman reached out and reverently touched the man's cheek. "I thought you might need me, Bertie, and I wasn't taking any chances. You, Bertram G. Mallory, are a rare man, and you are *mine.*"

"Aw, Fancy, I do need you." Bertram grinned humbly. "For the rest of my life."

Cole shook his head, thunderstruck. Now that was a woman who knew how to treat a man. He hoped Wynne was paying attention. She could stand a lesson in men versus women—and come to think of it, he probably could stand one too. He was glad to be home and glad Cass was all right, but he had some business of his own to take care of.

By now Cass had leaped off the horse, and Lilly had him in a tearful embrace. Cole wasn't going to worry about him anymore. He gave his full attention to Wynne Elliot and her continuing explanation, most of which he had missed in all of the commotion.

"—and so you see, darling, I don't *hate* Cass anymore," Wynne was saying. "He didn't steal my money or my heart. I just thought he did."

"You . . . *thought* you were in love with him."

She nodded. "But I'm not."

He heaved a relieved sigh. "Then you've finally got all this avenging nonsense out of your head?"

Wynne nodded, gazing up at him.

Cole cocked his head and looked back at her. "Any idea of what man you might love?"

She nodded.

"Well?"

"I'm not saying until you say what you're supposed to say."

"What if I say it and you don't agree?"

"That's what we'll have to find out, isn't it?"

She had him beat. He was in love with her and she knew it. Clearing his throat, he said softly, "I don't know how good I'll be at saying it. . . ." Cole had never told any woman he loved her.

"Just say it," she begged, her hands framing his face.

"I love you," he admitted. "I think I loved you the day I met you. I know you might have reason to doubt those words coming from a Claxton, but I mean them, Wynne." He pulled her closer, his mouth only inches away from hers. "You *know* I mean them."

She gazed up at him with those beautiful eyes, looking lovelier and more kissable than any woman ought to look. "You really do?"

Cole suddenly felt playful. "Are you strong as a bull moose, healthy as a horse? Can you wrestle an Indian brave, cut a rick of wood without raising a sweat, and still be soft and fresh as lilacs?" He already knew the answer; he'd known it for weeks.

She smiled at him sweetly. "I can be anything you want me to be."

He pulled her closer. "I really love you, lady." They kissed, oblivious to the stares.

She drew back only momentarily. "Well, there is Moss Oak . . . I don't know . . ." The teasing light in her eyes said she was joining in the fun.

"We'll live at Moss Oak, or we'll live in Missouri, but wherever we are, we'll be together. I believe God has brought us together, Wynne, and I want you beside me every day of my life."

She turned serious. "You honestly believe that?"

"I do, and I think we've fought Him long enough, don't you? Do you want a double wedding or one of our own?"

She didn't hesitate for a moment. "Which will be the quickest?"

He grinned. She blushed.

"Our own, then. Next Sunday. I'm an impatient man, lady. What's so funny?" he asked when her grin widened.

"I thought you didn't know the meaning of romance, but I'm learning you're a romantic at heart."

Cole bent to kiss her a second time. "Well now, you've got a lot to learn about me, lady."

"Ummm," Wynne whispered. "I can hardly wait."

He had a feeling life with this woman would never be dull.

He just prayed he'd be up to the challenge.

Dear Reader,

I am so thrilled to start a new Tyndale House series, Men of the Saddle. I've always loved the Old West and the values and faith of its people.

If *The Peacemaker* rings a bell with you, it is because this story is a new version of an earlier title that I wrote during my ABA years. I sold my first book in the ABA market in 1982. I published over fifty romance novels during the following years but always with the longing to express my Christian values and beliefs. Eventually God answered my prayers and opened a door for me in the Christian market. What a thrill it is to now write stories that reflect my personal faith and convictions.

God is so good that He has now allowed me to rewrite this story—one of my favorites—and tell it the way He intended. Two other books in this series will also be revisions of earlier books and will continue the story of the Claxton men. The fourth book in the series will be new material, depicting a brand-new rough-and-ready cowboy of the Old West!

Thank you so much for your response to the Brides of the West series. I read and enjoyed each one of your letters, and I thank God for such wonderful, insightful readers. God faithfully puts each book in the hands of the reader who seems to need it most at that time. I pray Men of the Saddle will serve, glorify, and uplift Him. I am indeed grateful to serve my Lord and Savior though my writing.

Until we meet again,

Lori Copeland is a prolific writer, best known as the author of more than fifty romance novels published for the ABA market, where she received numerous awards. Now she devotes herself to writing inspirational romances. One of the first writers for HeartQuest, the inspirational romance line from Tyndale House Publishers, Lori is the author of the popular best-selling Brides of the West series.

Lori masterfully uses the romance genre with humor to share biblical truths about love, relationships, family, and the vitality of a personal relationship with Christ. Brides of the West, Morning Shade Mysteries, and Heavenly Daze are some of Lori's most popular series. Her novel *Stranded in Paradise* is a Women of Faith fiction title.

Lori has been honored with numerous awards throughout her career. She has received the *Romantic Times* Lifetime Achievement Award, the *Romantic Times* Reviewers' Choice Award, the *Affaire de Coeur* Silver and Gold Awards, and has been named a Waldenbooks Best Seller. In 2000, Lori was inducted into the Springfield, Missouri, Writers Hall of Fame.

Lori resides with her husband in Missouri. They have three grown sons and five grandchildren.

She welcomes letters written to her in care of Tyndale House Author Relations, P.O. Box 80, Wheaton, IL 60189-0080.

Turn the page for
an exciting preview of
Lori Copeland's next book,

MEN *of the* SADDLE

The Drifter

ISBN 0-8423-8689-0

Available spring 2005 at a bookstore near you.

The Drifter

Charity stopped kneading bread and cocked her ear toward the open window. The dogs were setting up a howl on the front step, and in the distance she could hear what sounded like animals in some sort of fight.

She wiped flour from her hands and hurried to the mantel. *Pesky coyotes,* she thought irritably, reaching for the rifle. They'd probably attacked a stray dog or calf. The noise increased as she stepped out of the soddy and started toward the stream.

She'd be forever grateful to Ferrand for choosing this particular piece of land. In this part of Kansas, a shortage of rain, coupled with high winds and low humidity, sometimes left a pioneer at a serious disadvantage. But the Burk home was built near an underground spring that provided a stream of cool, clear water year-round.

Her footsteps quickened when a shrill squeal rent the air. Good heavens! Something had attacked a horse! Her feet faltered as she entered the clearing, her eyes taking in the appalling sight. A large timber wolf was ripping a man apart as his horse danced about him in terror.

Charity hefted the rifle to her shoulder and took careful aim. A loud crack sliced the air, and the wolf toppled off the man. The gunfire spooked the horse. The animal bolted into the thicket and Charity waded into the stream, flinching when she edged past the fallen wolf. The gaping bullet hole in the center of its chest assured her that her aim had been true. Her husband had taught her how to be a deadly accurate shot. She'd learned her lesson well.

She knelt beside the wounded man and cautiously rolled him on his side in the shallow water, cringing when he moaned in agony. He was so bloody she could barely make out the severity of his wounds, but she knew he was near death.

"Shhhh . . . lie still. I'm going to help you," she soothed, though she was afraid he could neither see nor hear her. His eyes were swollen shut from the lacerations on his face. As she watched, he slumped into unconsciousness.

She hesitated, not sure whether to hitch Myrtle and Nell to drag him out of the water. He was a tall man, but pitifully thin. Though she was small and slight, she was a lot stronger than when she'd first come to Kansas. She decided she wouldn't need the oxen to move him.

It took several tries to get him out of the water. He wasn't as light as he looked. She tugged and heaved inch by inch, pausing periodically to murmur soothing words of encouragement when he groaned in pain. Though she handled him carefully his injuries were so great she was sure he suffered unspeakable pain.

Once she had hauled him onto the bank, she hurriedly tore off a small portion of her petticoat and set to work cleaning his wounds. He fought when her hands touched torn flesh.

"Please, you must let me help you!" she urged.

She was accustomed to patching wounds on her stock, but she grew faint looking at this man's injuries. In her whole life she'd never seen such mutilation of a human body. But she shook off her queasiness and looked after his needs.

Her hands worked; she studied him, recoiling not only at his injuries but at his general condition; he was so unkempt, so dirty, so . . . slovenly. She wasn't used to that. Ferrand had always kept himself clean and neat. No doubt this man was a drifter, or perhaps one of those drovers. He certainly hadn't had a bath in months—maybe even years—and he was in need of a shave and haircut.

She peeled away the torn shirt and washed the blood from the mat of dark blond hair that lay thick across his broad chest. She could count his ribs. Obviously, he hadn't had a square meal in a long time. With more meat on his bones he'd be a very large man . . . powerful . . . strong . . .

Strong enough to build a barn and set fence and work behind a team of oxen all day . . . Her hands momentarily stilled.

A man. Here was a man—barely alive perhaps, but a man all the same. He could be the answer to her problems. Her hands flew feverishly about their work. She had to save him! Not that she wouldn't have tried her best anyway, but now, no matter what it took, she'd see to it that this man survived!

As far as men went, he wasn't much . . . disgusting, actually, but she reminded herself she wasn't in a position to be picky. She'd nurse him back to health, and once she got him on his feet, she'd trick him into marrying her. No, she amended, she wouldn't trick him . . . she'd ask him first, and if that didn't work, *then* she'd trick him.

But what if he has a wife? an inner voice demanded.

Don't bother me with technicalities, she thought irritably. *I'll cross that bridge when I get to it.*

Her hands worked faster, a new sense of confidence filling her now. He *would* live. She knew he would. The good Lord wouldn't give her such a gift and then turn around and snatch it back, would He?

The man moaned and Charity lifted his head and placed it possessively in her lap.

He was a gift from God.

She was certain of that now. Who else would so unselfishly drop this complete stranger at her door?

Charity gazed down at her unexpected gift and smiled in radiant relief. She closed her eyes and lifted her face heavenward.

She would be able to claim her land after all.

In her most reverent tone, she humbly asked for the Lord's help in making this man strong and healthy again, at least strong enough to drive a good, sturdy fence post.

She closed her petition with heartfelt sincerity. "He's a little ... well, rough looking, Father, but I'm not complaining." She bit her lower lip and studied the ragged, dirty, bloody man lying in her lap. With a little soap and water, he'd be tolerable. She shrugged, and a grin spread across her face. "I suppose if this is the best you have to offer, Lord, then I am surely beholden to you."

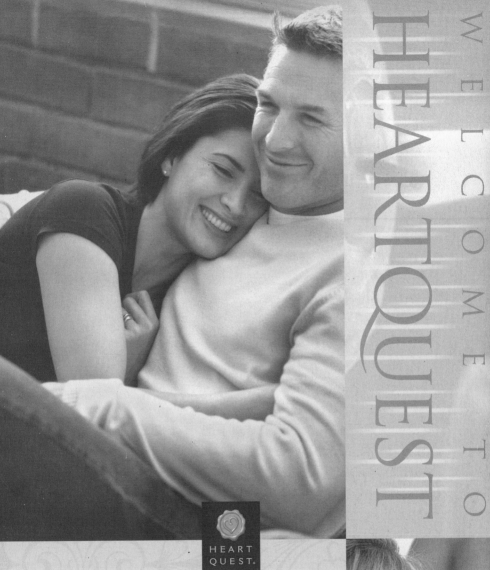

WELCOME TO HEARTQUEST

HEART
QUEST.

Visit

www.heartquest.com

and get the inside scoop.

You'll find first chapters,

newsletters, contests,

author interviews, and more!

BOOKS BY BEST-SELLING AUTHOR
LORI COPELAND

TYNDALE
FICTION

HEART
QUEST.

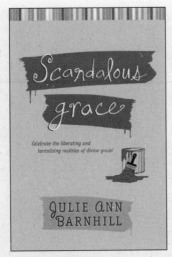

ISBN 0-8423-8297-6

If you like Lori Copeland, you'll **love** Julie Barnhill!

Join America's favorite *guurlfriend*, Julie Anne Barnhill, as she takes you on the wild and wonderful roller coaster ride that is God's *Scandalous Grace*!

Scandalous Grace is the *zing* of encouragement every woman needs to transform her thoughts about herself . . . and change her relationships, for good. With gutsy honesty and stories that'll have you "laughing so hard you snort," Julie reveals how you can live, day by day, in the knowledge of God's unconditional love in the midst of "loose ends."